PRAISE FOR
If You Can't Stand the Heat

— x — x — x —

"Allen's characterizations of restaurant workers and the inter-play between the front and back of the house at Markham's res-taurant is spot-on." —*Austin Chronicle*

"[A] red-hot saucy debut … Readers will want to see more of this laid-back Austin-style snoop." —*Publishers Weekly*

"Ideal for fans of culinary mysteries." —*Booklist*

PRAISE FOR
Stick a Fork In It

— x — x — x —

"An entertaining mystery … *Stick a Fork In It* demonstrates Robin Allen's knowledge and skill as she masters her craft and enter-tains her readers." —*Texas Books In Review*

for the Darling of Heaven

ROBIN ALLEN

Out of the
FRYING PAN

POPPY
MARKHAM
CULINARY
COP

MIDNIGHT INK
WOODBURY, MINNESOTA

MIDNIGHT
INK

FIRST EDITION
First Printing, 2013

Cover design by Kevin R. Brown
Cover illustration by Desmond Montague
Cover image: iStockphoto.com/bortonia

Midnight Ink, an imprint of Llewellyn Worldwide Ltd.

Library of Congress Cataloging-in-Publication Data
Allen, Robin, 1964–
  Out of the frying pan/Robin Allen.—First Edition.
      p. cm.—(Poppy Markham: Culinary Cop; #3)
  ISBN 978-0-7387-2796-7
1. Women in the food industry—Fiction. 2. Murder—Investigation—Fiction.
3. Restaurants—Fiction. 4. Austin (Tex.)—Fiction. I. Title.
PS3601.L4354O98 2013
813'.6—dc23
                                                                2013007517
                        Midnight Ink
                    Llewellyn Worldwide Ltd.
                    2143 Wooddale Drive
                    Woodbury, MN 55125-2989
                    www.midnightinkbooks.com

Printed in the United States of Awmerica

ONE

"Why do we have to walk through all this mud?" Nina asked. "No one told me there would be mud."

"It's a tour of a *farm*," I said. "They have to water their crops. Water mixed with dirt makes mud."

"Thank you for that recipe, Poppy. I'll ask Ursula to include it in her next cookbook."

My stepmother is amazing. Not only can she play a damsel in distress like the best stage actresses—even though she's much too surgically enhanced to fool anyone with eyesight that she's a damsel, and the distress was of her own making—she can parlay anything into a reason to bring up her daughter's cookbook.

"The invitation suggested you dress for the outdoors," I said.

"I wore slacks," she said, briefly releasing her ruby-jeweled fingers from my arm to swat at a fly, "which are filthy. And my heels are sinking into the floor."

"On a farm, it's called the ground." I flicked something brown off the sleeve of her cream silk pantsuit. "And that's called a leaf."

My father's wife and I were among a hundred or so other guests on a guided tour of Good Earth Preserves, a Community Supported Agriculture (CSA) farm on the far east side of Austin. The late-afternoon tour was part of an annual fundraising event for the Friends of the Farm, which Nina and I both are, but for different reasons. I'm a vegan who believes in supporting local farmers to keep me in good supply of organic produce. Nina is a name-dropping socialite who accepts any invitation that allows her to wear semi-precious stones and haute couture in public.

After we saw the various crops and animals where our food came from, we would dine on that food with one-hundred ninety-eight other Friends at an elaborate dinner called Feast in the Field. As I do every year, I had been looking forward to this dinner for months—savoring a gourmet meal prepared by an award-winning local chef, drinking exquisite wine I could never justify buying on my public health inspector's salary, connecting with old friends, and engaging in conversations about a food's merits rather than recording its demerits on a score sheet. This annual dinner under the sky on a Sunday evening in October hokily harmonizes my soul with nature and so fills me with peace and goodwill that I like to prolong the experience by taking the next day off work. And did I mention the nice wines?

The dinner coincides with the announcement of the new president of the Friends of the Farm. Most years, most guests show up just in time for drinks and appetizers, but this year, the order of events had been changed to announce the president after the tour instead of after dinner. Probably to end the campaigning as soon as possible. This year's contest between incumbent Randy Dove, owner of Weird Austin Spirits, a liquor supply company, and challenger Dana White, chef/co-owner of two of Austin's landmark restaurants, Vis-à-Vis and the White Wolff Inn, would raise a barbarian's eyebrows.

Randy fired the first shot across the bow with several barely anonymous calls to the health department, claiming everything from dirt under Dana's fingernails to her restaurants using illegal suppliers. When justice didn't drop the hammer swiftly enough, he contacted the media and made assertions that Dana's restaurants used conventionally grown ingredients in their 100% organic menu offerings. An accusation like that is difficult to prove, but unnecessary to. The rumor was enough to put a couple of dings in Dana's reputation and leave a few lines blank in her reservation books.

Dana is what you would call high-strung and she goes through cooks faster than Elizabeth Taylor went through engagement rings, so it surprised no one that she retaliated with higher levels of ugliness. She stopped ordering thousands of dollars' worth of wine and liquor from Weird Austin Spirits, then convinced several other restaurants to do the same.

Most food establishments are not Friends of the Farm, but they are members of the Austin Bar and Restaurant Alliance. It holds monthly meetings and has its own grapevine, which meant that Randy's anti-restaurant antics became bigger than the little Friends election, and when it came time to take sides, ABRA members took Dana's. Randy's business already wasn't doing well and the loss of so many accounts forced him to file for Chapter 11 bankruptcy protection.

Tonight, all of that would end. Finally.

"What's that smell?" Nina demanded as we stopped in front of the chicken coop.

"On a farm, it's called money."

Perry Vaughn, the hippie owner-farmer conducting the tour, began to climb an eight-foot rolling metal staircase of the type college marching bands use on the football field during halftime. In a recent *Good News of the Preserves* newsletter, Perry informed his CSA subscribers that it had been donated by a former band leader of the

Nebraska Cornhuskers, which had taken Perry's policy of full disclosure to members too far. Most of the Friends had graduated from the University of Texas at Austin, and even though Nebraska left the Big 12 Conference in 2011, a Cornhusker will always be a Longhorn's lifelong and mortal enemy, football-wise. It caused a minor gripefest among the farm's subscribers, which Perry attempted to smooth over with a free jar of pumpkin preserves in the next delivery.

Perry grinned down at us and I felt a little whirly remembering my fear of heights, which had been renewed and magnified recently when someone holding a gun tried to encourage me to jump off a catwalk.

After bragging on his well-fed free-range hens, Perry invited us to enter the chicken coop and harvest an egg we were told would later be boiled, deviled, and served with the rest of the appetizers prepared by Dana White, who was in the farm's kitchen at the moment because she was also the guest chef for the evening.

For CSA subscribers, gathering your own eggs is part of the experience, so a lot of the Friends were comfortable walking among chickens and roosters. Nina, however, had never seen eggs in their natural habitat. "I'm not going in *there*," she squawked. "What if I get bitten by a chicken?"

"These chickens have been trained not to bite," I said, "but if you want a deviled egg, I'll get one for you."

"Get one for your father, too," she said. "Without yolks. We're watching our cholesterol."

Perry's wife, Megan, stood at the entrance to the coop holding a large well-used wicker basket. I picked up twin cappuccino-colored eggs from the closest nest, then gently placed them in the basket with the others. "You've got the glam job, today," I said.

"Great, Poppy!" she said, her mind somewhere else. "Really, really great."

Now that she brought it up, she didn't look great or even just okay. The fuzzy hank of shoulder-length auburn hair shot with gray looked like she had braided it a few days ago, and the dark circles under her eyes indicated a lack of either sleep or vitamins. She appeared more worn out than she usually did, and a little troubled. I suppose I would be agitated, too, if I had two hundred city slickers traipsing through my farm, not paying attention to what they were about to step on or in.

"Where's the rest of your crew tonight?" I asked. She and Perry run the farm with their two grown sons, Brandon and Cory, along with Megan's brother, Ian McDougal; his wife, Tanya; and their son Kevin. Years ago, when Austin really was weird and didn't need a PR campaign to keep it that way, my parents were one of the first supporters of the farm, and my family's restaurant is still one of their best customers. When my cousin Daisy and I were teenagers, our families spent a lot of time at the farm, and we practically grew up with the boys.

"Tanya's down with a humidity headache, and Ian's on the back ten mending a fence that some of our cows got through. He'll be up later."

"Humidity headache?"

"That's what she calls them."

"And the boys?"

"They're around somewhere, helping Ian or Perry. Do you mind?" She handed me the basket of eggs, then put her hands on her lower back and arched into a stretch. Anyone else would have looked catlike and sexy, but Megan looked like what she was—an overworked farmer. She took the basket from me and accepted another deposit of eggs from a Friend.

At a signal from Megan, Perry called out from the platform of the staircase, "Gather 'round, everyone. Gather 'round." Then he laughed. "Gather. Eggs. Get it?"

Some did, some didn't.

"I'm sure you're all curious about fertilizer," Perry said, then began a detailed and poetic soliloquy on the topic of organic bovine excrement. He explained how the farm's unusable vegetables were composted and then mixed with manure from their cows to create fertilizer for their crops. "It's a perfect, sustainable cycle!" he concluded, searching the crowd for faces as excited as his about manure. He found a few female ones, but I knew they were smiling at something else. With his hay-colored hair, hazel eyes, and dimpled chin, the farmer is a hottie.

"As you know," Perry continued, "we wanted to buy a mobile irrigation system this summer, but the Friends weren't able to come up with their part of it. We lost quite a few crops to the recent drought." We nodded, remembering the skimpy boxes of vegetables the past few months. "But we're hoping to have it installed this spring."

Perry held up his hand and counted with his fingers. "We've seen the mechanics of planting, organic pest control, harvesting, and fertilizing." He hitched his thumb to the left. "Now let's mosey on over to the washing shed, and I'll show you how produce is prepared for your weekly deliveries." School children often made field trips to the farm, and I bet we were getting the same spiel from Perry and in the same nature-is-a-miracle way.

We waited for our host to descend the stairs, then everyone rumbled across plywood planks that had been jigsawed into walkways over the mud and followed him to a large, rectangular, three-walled shed situated between the kitchen and the office.

Against the far wall, Perry's sons, Brandon and Cory, waited for us in front of a long countertop with colorful bushels of onions, peppers, and broccoli arranged near the deep sinks. The boys—well, not boys; they're in their early thirties—resembled their father, with dark blond hair and dark eyes, both wiry and tan from working every day in the sun. They wore white T-shirts with an image of the earth on the front, and *Good Earth Preserves—Honest food from honest folks!* printed underneath.

The demonstration was delayed, however, because all of Dana's cooks began fleeing the kitchen as if it were on fire.

TWO

THE KITCHEN WASN'T ON fire, but Dana was, and she had been stoked to a roar that we could hear from where we were outside. "You're a one-trick pony, a hack, and a drunk! You couldn't cook your way out of a *papillote*!"

"I've been sober six years!" a man yelled with equal heat.

I tapped one of the escaped cooks on the arm. "Who is she talking to?"

"Some guy named Bjorn," she whispered. "He came in asking Chef for a job."

That would be Bjorn Fleming. He and Tanya McDougal occupy the farm's kitchen when testy guest chefs don't have temporary custody. He had a pretty cushy job at the farm. Why did he want to leave?

"How can I say this so you'll understand?" Dana said with forced calm. "I do not now nor will I ever need you."

"That's the wrong answer," Bjorn said evenly.

"Out of my kitchen, Bjorn."

"*My* implies ownership, which you don't have."

When any professional chef is at the helm of any kitchen anywhere, that kitchen is the chef's kitchen. Bjorn knows that. Being literal is an effective way to be difficult.

Bjorn stepped through the open doorway and stopped when he saw all of us staring at him. With his white-blond hair and eyelashes, skin the color of biscuit dough, and attitude the color of scorched milk, he would be perfectly cast as the victim of schoolyard bullies in a British drama. He looked over at Brandon and Cory, then pushed through us gawkers without a word.

Several people offered their take on what Dana and Bjorn had tangled over. "Are they dating?" "Did you hear her fire him like that?" "No, he said he drank six beers."

If you work in the restaurant industry and don't want anyone to spread rumors about you, take a drive up to Niagara Falls—the Canadian side—and whisper your conversation as you tumble over the falls in a barrel.

"Sorry about that, folks," Perry said. "Let's get back to the tour."

He nodded at his sons and they began bathing vegetables. Bathing? Before I raised my hand to ask, a Friend shouted, "I want dirt on my food!"

"I do, too," Perry said, "but we're now offering pre-washed vegetables for those subscribers who want to use their produce as soon as they get home."

More like for those subscribers who are used to shopping for groceries in a pristine, air-conditioned environment like Whole Foods, and have no idea that carrots spend their formative weeks underground with dirt as their blankies and earthworms as babysitters.

"For an extra ten dollars per box," Perry added.

CSA operations work on a subscription basis. Members purchase a weekly or bi-weekly subscription to whatever a farm sells—meat, eggs, cheese, milk, honey, fruits, vegetables—and either pick up their bounty at the farm or at a central location in the city. Or, like Nina, they shield themselves from nature and hire a delivery company to bring it to their doorstep.

After closing the full boxes and bowing dramatically at our applause and playful cheers of "Bravo!" and "Encore!" the guys removed their gloves and placed both boxes on a slatted wooden pallet on the dirt floor.

"And now," Perry said, waving an index card, "I have in my hand the name of the new president of the Friends of the Farm."

Our immediate attention and complete silence seemed to frighten Perry and he blurted, "It's Dana!"

I slid my eyes over to Randy Dove. He looked like he had been told he had a month to live.

The president's job is mostly a professional networking position, which is why so many restaurant suppliers want it, and Randy's visibility among restaurant owners, managers, and chefs had helped grow his fledgling liquor supply company. But every so often, a restaurant owner or manager runs for office, especially if they're opening a new restaurant or trolling for investors.

Losing the presidency would smack down Randy's ego, of course, but on top of the bankruptcy, it could also clobber his finances.

Several people patted him on the shoulder, murmuring condolences, which he ignored. I assumed he would leave, but he crossed his arms over his chest and stared into the future.

Dana White sprinted out of the kitchen, her face full of vindication and victory. She looked good for a woman in her mid-fifties who'd had two mild, but widely reported, heart attacks in the past three years and still put in a chef's day's work. And she came off rather girlish with her petite frame, blue eyes, and short dark hair.

She held a spatula in one hand and a glass measuring cup in the other filled with what looked like ice water. It's not unusual for cooks to drink from unusual containers. All food service employees are supposed to drink from cups with lids and straws while preparing food, but they often try to get away with drinking from a measuring cup or pickle jar.

If you didn't know Perry, you might assume from his big grin and enthusiastic embrace of Dana that he was especially excited that she had won the election, but Perry acts excited about everything. I've seen him welcome unannounced visits by FDA, USDA, and county health inspectors to the farm with the same smile and excitement as he does a new calf to the herd.

"Thank you, Perry," Dana said, then she faced her constituents and brought the spatula to her mouth as if it were a microphone. Polite laughter all around. "Ladies and gentlemen, friends and Friends, I hope you all have enjoyed your tour of this beautiful farm. And isn't it nice to know that the new vegetable washing process uses organic techniques, too?" Her voice ended on a high note, giving her words the emptiness of a true politician's.

I heard grumbles and mumbles from Dana's detractors. "She stole this election." "Doesn't she have a restaurant to run into the ground?" "She looks like a Cornhusker."

Dana sipped from the measuring cup, then continued, "As you all know, I'm a James Beard Award winner, a Texas Ex, and a longtime member of ABRA . . . " She waited while the applause from her supporters rose and fell, then raised the spatula into the air and said, "And I am now your president!"

More applause, more grumbles. "She's not my president." "Randy was robbed." "I'm so hungry, I could eat a Cornhusker."

Dana thanked a few people by name, including her husband and business partner, Herb Wolff, whom she said was managing their restaurants that night and couldn't make the dinner. Then she said, "I'm going to make a very special announcement after dinner, so don't eat and run." She looked at Perry, who smiled and winked at her. "Now let me get back to work so I can finish deviling your eggs," she said.

The egg hunt at the chicken coop earlier was just for show. Pre-gathered eggs had been boiled, cooled, sliced, and deviled that morning, or even the day before. That's what I would have done. Actually, I would have skipped such a labor-intensive, time-consuming appetizer altogether, but one of the promises of Feast in the Field is that all main ingredients, except the meat, come from the farm. It's kind of an Iron Chef challenge for the guest chef preparing the dinner because they never know which crops will thrive and which will fail. I remember a dinner a few years ago comprised of nothing but eggs, eggplant, tomatoes, and winter squash.

"Okay, folks," Perry said, waving another index card, "according to the schedule, it's time for aprerit-…aperti-…drinks and appetizers in the Field."

———

The bar and dining areas were set off from the washing shed, kitchen, and farm's office by a chest-high hedgerow wall that enclosed the Field. Guests came and went through an ivy-covered archway as wide as a vegetable-oil powered microbus is long. The Field is available for rent, which is how they can justify keeping it permanently fallow, and they have hosted a lot of weddings in the Field, reunions in the Field, and once, a birth in the Field.

I had lost track of my stepmother during the demonstration, and I estimated a ninety-six percent chance that she had skipped the demo and made an early appearance at the bar. The other four percent chance was that she had skipped the demo and gone to the bathroom to refresh her hair and makeup before she made an appearance at the bar. My reprieve wouldn't last long. Nina would find me soon enough to complain that her champagne cocktail wasn't fizzy enough or to ask where she could see the pigs in their blankets.

The only reason I was babysitting Nina was because my father, Mitch—who hasn't done much of anything lately except hire one of my old boyfriends to manage our family's restaurant, Markham's Grille & Cocktails, and schedule appointments with his heart doctor around golf games at his country club—told me he wanted to attend the dinner, too. Except he didn't say exactly that, and I had been so thrilled at the prospect of spending time with him that I hadn't paid attention to his semantics.

What he said was that he wanted *me* to attend the dinner with *him*, which is different from *him* attending the dinner with *me*. ("I'll buy a table," Mitch said after I accepted. "We'll make it a family affair.") By agreeing to that sneaky word arrangement, I had also agreed to spend the evening with Nina; Nina's daughter, Ursula York, which makes her my stepsister, who is the locally famous chef at Markham's and was once falsely accused of killing the world-famous chef, Évariste Bontecou; Ursula's much younger sous chef and secret paramour, Trevor Shaw, whom I like and don't mind hanging out with; my cousin and best girlfriend, Daisy Forrest, and her husband, Erik, ditto on the hanging out part; and Markham's general manager, Drew Cooper.

But because Mitch was still golfing with his attorneys; and Ursula, Trevor, and Drew were at Markham's finishing up with Sunday brunch; and Daisy and Erik had lingered in the corn field to enjoy some rare kidless time together; and Nina had misread Tour of the Farm as Pour of the Farm and thought she had come early for a wine tasting, it was left to me to keep her upright and leaf-free as she hobbled and griped about humidity, bugs, and scents that are not found in day spas, department stores, or hair salons.

The bar was on the left side of the Field, near a stretch of mature pecan trees strung with tiny white lights that would look romantic later after sunset, but looked like tree spores in the sunshine. Randy Dove stood behind a long cloth-draped table lined with several clear plastic highball cups of red and white wine, and a galvanized metal tub filled with ice and cans of soda and Lone Star and Shiner Bock beer that people could serve themselves. At previous dinners, he had poured tastings of two-hundred dollar wines, which was what I was looking forward to tonight.

So I waited while Randy spoke with the sales rep he had brought with him, a tall, dumpy guy with curly blond hair and brown eyes, dressed like his boss in khaki dress shorts and a maroon polo shirt. I thought I recognized him, but he seemed to belong in another context and I couldn't think of his name. Randy bent down to open an ice chest and pulled out a bottle of champagne then handed it to the guy. "Take this to Dana with my congratulations and compliments," he said.

"Come on, Randy," the guy said uneasily. "Not tonight."

Randy handed him a champagne flute. "Yes, tonight."

I thought Randy had made a nice peace offering by congratulating Dana so extravagantly. Perhaps I had misread his reaction to the announcement earlier and he felt relieved of the presidential burden.

When the rep left, Randy asked for my order by raising his dark eyebrows at me. "A glass of Meritage, please."

"I have the best," he said, uncorking a bottle of something with lots of scrollwork on the label. He first splashed some into his almost-empty glass, then poured a few glugs into a plastic cup and handed it to me. Had he owned a restaurant, I would have assumed his generosity to be a scratch of my back in hopes that I would go easy on the next health inspection. But Weird Austin Spirits does not prepare food, so they do not get surprise inspected by the health department, so he had no reason to bribe me. The gesture would have been pointless anyway. Every food service professional in the city knows that my fingernails are too sharp to scratch anyone's back.

I'm a Special Projects Inspector with the Austin/Travis County Health Department. As a SPI, I don't have an assigned division, and my schedule and duties fluctuate depending on what I'm working on. After growing up in the family restaurant working as a bus girl, waitress, manager, and cook, I'm used to working odd hours, and I perform a lot of late-night surprise inspections, overnight stakeouts, and other time-critical investigations.

"Sorry about the election," I said.

Randy slurped what sounded like ten tablespoons of wine and swallowed hard. "Win some, lose some."

I raised my glass. "*À votre santé*," I said, then sipped my wine. The man had not lied—it was good stuff.

Randy raised his eyebrows at another customer, and I saw Daisy and Erik waving at me from our dinner table a few feet from the bar. As I walked over to them, I turned my head to look around for my father, so I didn't see Erik raise his arms to hug me until I reached them, which put my wine in spilling range—and it did. All that good, expensive Meritage seeping into the grass.

"Sorry, Poppy," Erik said. He picked up the empty cup and handed it to me. "I'll go get you a napkin."

"And more wine," Daisy called after him.

I sat next to my cousin at a round, white-clothed table marked *Markham* with a hand-lettered sign and decorated with a centerpiece of a lit white candle inside a hurricane glass surrounded by fresh rosemary sprigs.

"Where's Drew?" Daisy asked. "I thought y'all would be here together."

THREE

IN THE ORIGINAL PLAN from months ago, the eighth person at our table was supposed to be freelance food writer Jamie Sherwood, my ex-boyfriend twice removed. Jamie runs a foodie website called Amooze-Boosh (the Texas spelling of the French *amuse-bouche*, which means "mouth amuser"). His unique take on such things as recipe theft accusations, mobile food cart wars, and the results of the Friends of the Farm presidential election is why he has readers in all four corners of the world.

He also writes a monthly column called "Taste Buds" for *Deliciousness Magazine* that helps people write their own food reviews, the idea being that it would help make them better home cooks. The magazine had taken several of their columnists on tour for the summer to give workshops on such topics as reviewing meals, styling food for photographs, and writing recipes for publication. They recently added several European cities to the tour, which would keep Jamie away for another few weeks.

To help him maintain his finger as the most important one on the pulse of Austin's food world, I had fed him regular updates on hirings, firings, openings, and closings, and occasionally chased down leads and information for him when my schedule allowed. I had agreed to be his eyes, ears, and Girl Friday at the dinner.

Jamie is twice removed because we had broken up earlier in the year when I discovered that he had forgotten to be faithful to me one night. After a couple of months, I found a way to begin to forgive him, and we were in the middle of a tentative reunion when I had been gobsmacked by who he cheated with. He had so far refused to discuss things with me, saying only that he made a mistake and it will never happen again. Which is why I had so far refused to recommit to him.

In the meantime, my boyfriend before Jamie, Drew Cooper, the one Mitch hired to run Markham's—the one I had once thought I would spend the rest of my life with until he disappeared one day without a word—returned a few months ago with a really good reason for his three-year absence and a proclamation that he intended to wait for me as long as he had to. With Jamie gone and our relationship undefined, I had allowed myself to interact with Drew in ways other than as our restaurant's general manager. At first I wanted only comfort and friendship, but it soon turned into more, a sort of test drive of our compatibility after so many years apart.

And that's why Drew Cooper was our eighth at the dinner table.

"He's finishing up brunch," I said. "He'll be here later."

"Things are going well?" Daisy asked.

I nodded and sighed. "Yeah."

"You're going to have to choose pretty soon."

"Why? Why can't I date both of them?"

"Because dating two men is not a complication you can handle," she said. "And they're men. Territorial men." Sunlight ricocheted

17

through her wine as she swirled her glass. What was taking Erik so long?

"Jamie won't be in town until after Thanksgiving, so I still have some time."

"It's not like you to not know what you want," Daisy said.

"I don't want to make a mistake."

Not to put too fine a point on it, but I'm as rigorous about the people I let close to me as I am about enforcing health codes. Quadruply so for the men I date. I would rather remain single than spend time with a man I cannot see a future with. Usually it's not a problem because once I break up with someone, things stay broken. But this was different.

I could see a future with both Drew and Jamie. Different ones, for sure, so my decision rested between the life of safety and tenderness that Drew offered versus the energy and intrigue that a life with Jamie promised. Thank goodness it would be weeks before I had to make that monster decision.

Ian and Tanya's son, Kevin McDougal, stopped in front of our table holding a doily-lined silver tray with deviled eggs on one side and cucumber crudités on the other. The guest chef traditionally brings their restaurant's wait staff to these dinners, but Perry told us in a newsletter that the families and farm help would act as waiters at the dinner.

Kevin's dark red windblown hair and freckles on a pudgy white face offered the illusion of a sweet young boy, but, like his cousins Brandon and Cory, he too was in his early thirties. He may have also been the only baby ever born without sweetness. He looked past us at the other Friends and guests as Daisy took an egg and I took a cucumber topped with something that looked like tomato coulis.

"Great turnout, Kevi," I said.

"Kevin," he said, correcting my use of his nickname from a Memorial Day picnic an era ago when all us kids decided to switch our name endings. Poppy became Pop, my little brother Luke became Lukie, Daisy became Daze, Cory, Core, Brandon, Brandy and Kevin, Kevi. I rather liked that tie to the past. It reminded me of when we spent summer nights playing hide-and-seek in the barn and eating fresh cherries until our clothes were as stained as a Civil War re-enactor's. "It's a big night for us," he said.

"I haven't seen you out here the past few months," I said.

"I've been busy with my thesis. Finally got my MBA from UT." He smiled for the first time but continued to look around.

"Oh, right. I remember your mom telling me that," I said. "Did you learn anything?"

He finally turned to us. "Of course I did," he said, as if I hadn't asked it as a joke. "I have so many plans for this place."

"Congratulations, Kevin," Daisy said. "I'm sure Ian and Tanya are proud of you. I have a couple of kids and hope they—"

"I need to mingle," Kevin said.

"—don't turn out anything like you," Daisy finished as Kevin jilted us to do his mingling with Randy Dove. "He always thought he was better than us."

"An advanced degree from UT and he's still so dopey," I said. "It's so obvious that we're better than him."

Daisy laughed, then bit into her egg. "I taste horseradish in this. Shoot."

"I think it's in the coulis, too," I said. "Why shoot?"

"Erik's deviled egg recipe has horseradish."

Another feature of this dinner is the recipe contest. Anyone can submit a recipe if they're a Friend of the Farm, they're not an industry professional, and the recipe uses one of the ingredients specified by the farm, usually the bumper crop for that season. The guest chef chooses the winning recipe and prepares it for the dinner. The winner is announced by the chef during dessert, but until then, much clucking and guessing goes on as to whose recipe was chosen. For this year's contest, the ingredients were eggs and sweet potatoes.

"Again, why shoot?" I asked.

"If Erik's recipe wins, I have to teach the kids math until Christmas."

Daisy and Erik home school their fourteen-year-old daughter, Logan, and twelve-year-old son, Jacob. Daisy teaches English and sociology, and Erik covers math and science.

"Did you enter a recipe?" I asked.

"Logan did. Sweet potato pie. If it wins, Erik has to weed the garden by himself next spring."

"That's some kind of wild and crazy life y'all lead," I said.

"You don't know the half of it," Daisy said. "Erik's got Logan doing trig this year." She sipped her wine. "So tell me why half the people here can't stand Dana White."

"You noticed, huh?"

"Even Erik noticed, and he still hasn't noticed that his own daughter has started wearing makeup."

"Mama Natural is letting her daughter wear makeup?"

"Just mascara."

I told Daisy the stories I had heard about Dana firsthand, from media reports, and through gossip.

"Is it true she drinks vodka on the rocks for breakfast?" Daisy asked.

"That's a new one," I said. "Where did you hear it?"

"Some strange little guy wearing a Greek fisherman's cap."

I laughed. "That's Jerry Potter. He was a line cook in Dana's kitchen a couple of years ago. She fired him for spitting—"

"No!" Daisy said, putting her hand over my mouth. "Just … no. I don't want to hear anymore."

"—on the sidewalk."

"*Parle du diablo*," Daisy said.

I twisted around to follow her line of sight and saw Dana White coming through the archway. She and her staff had worked in the kitchen all day chopping, marinating, basting, and broiling chicken, lamb, and pork for her famous Great White Skewers. Most chefs remove their dirty apron—something that busts the illusion that their job is all food tastings and artful garnishes—before they greet the public, but Dana still wore hers. She seemed surprised when people wanted to speak with her, which told me that she was Chef Dana at the moment rather than President Dana, and she had left the kitchen on a mission.

She gave forced smiles and quick waves to people as she continued to—oh, goodness!—the bar. I hoped she wasn't going to gloat over her win. Well, maybe I wanted her to a little. Way back, Dana was a sous chef at Markham's, so my feelings for her were softer than they were for Randy. I don't remember her from that time because I was just old enough to sit in the office and draw pictures of my Siamese cat, Pandora, dining on asparagus and goldfish, but she told me she used to sneak French fries and bread pudding to my brother and me. Mitch and my late mother attended her wedding to Herb Wolff and worked with both of them to help get their restaurants established. Dana, in turn, occasionally mentored me during my reluctant reign as Markham's executive chef.

Randy leaned against a pecan tree and crossed his arms. He appeared to be whistling as he waited for her first move.

FOUR

"I KNOW WHAT YOU'RE doing, Dove!" Dana shouted.

Conversations dribbled to a trickle as everyone stared at the incoming and outgoing presidents facing off.

"Trying to keep my business afloat?" Randy said. "Report me to the authorities."

"You hired him on purpose," Dana said.

"As opposed to hiring him accidentally?"

"You know what I mean."

"I would if you made sense."

"*This* is why they elected me president," Dana said. "I don't play dirty."

"Let's ask your waiters if that's true."

"I don't know what you're up to, Dove, but my attorneys will figure it out."

"Have at it, my dear."

Dana opened her mouth to rebut, but shut it when she noticed all of the attention. "This isn't over," she said before she left.

"Who did Randy hire?" Daisy asked. "And what did he mean about her waiters? Are you withholding intel?"

"Must be an embolism in the grapevine," I said, watching Dana leave through the archway and walk a wide perimeter around Randy's sales rep returning to base.

"I wish I was spending the evening with you two blossoms," a man said. I turned to see Brandon Vaughn in front of us holding a napkin-lined tray. "This waiter business stinks." He lifted his tray to reveal pale yellow egg smears in the area of his rib cage. "The tray keeps tipping."

"Hold it away from you and be ready for the weight change when someone lifts an egg," I said. "Like this." I stood and pulled the tray a couple of inches away from his body then made eye contact and said, "Ready?" He nodded. I took an egg and the tray moved up, but stayed level. "It just takes practice," I said. I handed the egg to Daisy then took a cucumber for myself. The tray barely moved. "See? Practice."

"Thanks, Pop," Brandon said.

"Where's Core?" Daisy asked.

"He stayed behind after the demo to make up a few more boxes. Tomorrow's a CSA pickup day."

"Bran-don!" Kevin called as he strode toward us with an empty tray.

"I should have stayed behind, too," Brandon mumbled.

Kevin stopped in front of his cousin, a sneer of superiority on his flushed face. "I've already given out *four* trays of food. *Stop* playing with the girls and go *serve* people!"

"*Jawohl!*" Brandon said in his best German accent, then rolled his eyes and moved to the next table. Kevin watched him serve a couple more people, then he made for the archway.

Daisy and I giggled at Brandon's response, but also that all of us were right back where we had been as kids—Kevin trying to bossy boss everyone, and the rest of us snickering at him behind his husky back.

Erik returned with a stack of bevnaps for me and a glass of white wine for Daisy.

"No, baby, I didn't mean for me," Daisy said, holding up her half-full glass. "For Poppy. Something red."

"Oh, sorry."

"I'll get it, Erik," I said, wiping at the drying Meritage splashes from my boots with the napkins. "Set a spell with your wife."

I walked through a swarm of familiar faces I have seen mature and then wrinkle over the years, thinking about the lives and circumstances they represented—births, deaths, marriages, divorces, stints in prison, appearance-altering surgeries, substance abuse problems. These dinners feel like family reunions. And like all families, there are those weird cousins who always seem to have their internal GPS set to your coordinates and find you no matter what.

I got within a yardstick of the bar when Jerry Potter, the cook Dana fired for spitting in a Mornay sauce, blocked my way. As short and slight as a racehorse jockey, he wore wrinkled jeans and a burnt orange Longhorns T-shirt and held a can of beer in each hand. "Have you sent anyone out to General Chow's yet?" he asked, focusing bleary red eyes on me. "I left a anonymous tip."

"Regarding?"

"They're washing raw chickens with a hose and letting 'em dry on clothes hangers."

A chicken carcass fashion show. That was weird and interesting, but not a violation as long as they used plastic clothes hangers and didn't hang them above any other food. Raw chicken is lousy with salmonella bacteria. "Are you working there now?" I asked.

He burped. "I'm cooking at the Flashlight. I can see their back parking lot from my balcony."

"They're doing this *outside*?"

He nodded and sipped his beer.

"Thanks, Jerry. I'll look into it."

"You can use my place for a stakeout if you want," he said. "I'm in apartment four oh six."

"I'll let you know."

He held out a can to me. "Want one? They're free, so I got two."

"Thanks, but I'm drinking wine tonight."

I excused myself when he began ranting against Dana White's unfair treatment of cooks who had a "mild drooling disorder."

A line had formed at the bar, and I queued up behind Bjorn Fleming. He helps Tanya prepare quiches, preserves, and other goodies from the farm's ingredients to sell to CSA subscribers and at farmer's markets. The original plans for the farm hadn't included preparing food, but they had christened their private, sustainable venture with the idealistic name of Good Earth Preserves, as in preservation of the land, and so many people thought they sold fruit preserves that they started making them. Tanya couldn't keep up with demand, so they hired Bjorn a few years ago.

Curious about his argument with Dana earlier, I said, "Lots of life in the kitchen tonight, huh?"

He looked over his shoulder, then turned to face me. "That woman," he said, running his hand through white-blond hair half a shade darker than his skin. "She's as ruthless as Hitler."

I searched for a joke in his blue eyes but found only conviction. "There are a lot of ways to interpret that description," I said.

"She's always making everything into an emergency so she can order people around. I went to tell her the reach-in door sometimes doesn't click shut and she said I was ruining the deviled eggs and ordered me out of the kitchen. *My* kitchen."

"She's a chef," I said. "It's part of the job."

"I'm a chef and I don't treat people like that." He turned around to move up with the line.

"Then why did you ask her for a job?" As a rule, I don't gossip, but I do like to be on top of the truth so I know when a rumormonger has it wrong and can correct them. Dana's cook may have lied to me about the cause of their argument, but from the way Bjorn whipped his head back to me, I knew she hadn't.

"Who told you that?" he said.

Why don't people know that if you're trying to conceal guilt, you should never answer a question with a question? "One of Dana's cooks," I said.

"They're wrong," he said. "You couldn't pay me enough to work for that Nazi." Then he peeled off into the Field.

I was second in line for a drink when Kevin started worming through the crowd, encouraging us to take our seats at the tables by clapping his hands and yelling, "Dinnertime, people. Let's go." Kevin needed to follow up that MBA degree with finishing school.

We should have all settled down quickly because the tables were only fifty feet away from the bar area, which is where everyone had congregated, and these dinners have assigned seating. However, as always happens at this and most dinner parties everywhere, the guests thought they knew better than the person who made the assignments—the person with the big picture in mind, who is privy to rivalries and friendships, who thinks that a certain chef of exotic food should sit next to a new vendor of imported ingredients—and began to switch tables to sit near friends and existing business associates.

But because they did not wait until all eight people arrived at the switched-to table before they sat down, they found themselves next to competitors, former employees, vendors they swore they would never do business with as long as Texas was part of the Union, and health inspectors who consistently gave them the poor score they deserved—creating the very situations the party planner tried to avoid—which necessitated more switching and some on-the-spot arbitration.

So the last dinner plates weren't brought out until 6:30 PM.

A couple of minutes after that, Randy Dove started choking.

FIVE

The Friends' vice president, Mike Glass, shot out of his chair and threw his arms around Randy. With one quick upward drive of both fists into Randy's sternum, he Heimliched a hunk of meat out of Randy and onto the table.

After a recovery period of approximately 1.8 seconds, enough time to draw a raspy breath, Randy coughed out, "She tried to kill me! First she steals the election, and now ... " He made eye contact with several of his Friends friends, nodding them into agreement as he said, "All of you saw. She's trying to kill me!"

Mike said something to Randy that I was close enough to hear, but his words were drowned out by all the background giggles and twitters. If it were me, I would have told Randy that the outgoing president of the Friends accusing the incoming president of attempted murder cemented his reputation as a sore loser in front of clients and colleagues.

Mike's particular words, however, had an inflammatory effect on Randy. He snatched up the expelled meat and tried to hurl it over the hedge, but because a cube of lamb weighs only a couple of ounces, even with all the spices, it didn't make it past the next table, which happened to be ours.

Since we were on a farm, I'll stay with the theme and say that Nina had a cow when the roasted kebob landed on her shoulder, which took everyone's attention away from Randy. Except mine. Nina's docudramas no longer rate with me, and I wouldn't lay odds against her already planning to shop for a replacement pant suit, plus a few accessories to soothe her mental anguish. Randy glared at Mike, then stomped through the Field toward the archway. Mike dropped his shoulders and followed his leader.

"Who's that with Randy?" Erik asked.

"Mike Glass, recently former vice president and treasurer of the Friends," I said. "He's also a sales rep for Waterloo Linen."

"He looks scary," Daisy said.

"It's all for show," I said. Mike shaves his head, has an over-developed upper body, and stays perennially coconut brown with a lifelong tanning salon membership. "He moonlights as a bouncer at Casino El Camino on the weekends. He's actually kind of sweetly dumb."

"Look at me!" Nina cried. She used both French-manicured index fingers to point to herself in case we didn't know who she meant by *me*. "I am *not* staying here like this."

"Just take off your jacket," I said.

She pushed back her chair, and I looked around for any waiter serving the vegan offering, which was rumored to be green bean casserole. The carnivorous dinners had been served first.

"Take me back to Hyde Park, Poppy."

I've been cursed with Nina as my stepmother for more than three years, so I should have known that not only would she not take my suggestion to sacrifice a piece of her Outfit, she would escalate the situation to hog more attention. (Naming the tony neighborhood she lived in, however, was well-played.) Nina didn't want to go home; she wanted to be coaxed into staying.

Fortunately, coaxing isn't part of my genetic makeup. "You drove yourself," I said.

Nina made a disapproving disappointed sound that I've only ever heard come out of her and her two spoiled dogs, then snatched her purse from under her chair. Earlier, she had set it on her napkin in the grass, then took my napkin, which made me have to ask for another. Kevin still hadn't returned with a new one or the glass of wine I asked for. I had been at this event for an hour and a half and had sipped only one stinking drop of wine and eaten two miniscule slices of cucumber.

Nina stood and made for the exit, but Perry was leaving too and hurried to meet her at the archway. I don't know what he said to her, but she came back to our table without an explanation. Her silence would last long enough for her to think of something else to embroil us in, and I was already down to the dregs of my patience with her, so I leaned over to Daisy and said, "I'm going to call Mitch again."

Yes, I know I've wanted to bit and bridle anyone who uses cell phones in social situations, but I had tried to get a hold of my father since before the tour, placing the first call while I sat in my Jeep in the parking lot waiting for Nina to arrive. Since his mild heart attack a few months ago, that man has been a consistent source of worry for me. He has the reckless spirit of a young man, but the heart and body of an ancient mariner. He also has something like a four hundred golf handicap that he's trying to improve.

I went to the washing shed, which is less like a traditional shed where people store garden tools they can't get to for all the boxes of sentimental junk inside, and more like a large open area between the kitchen and office buildings, and twice as big as either. It had been unproductive space until a few years ago when Good Earth decided to make the CSA subscriber experience more comfortable. They tacked on a corrugated metal back wall and slanted roof to keep out the elements, and added counter space and a sink where farmers and interns could wash up.

I like neatness and order, straight lines and right angles, so every time I come to the farm, I'm a little uneasy surrounded by all of the unplanned development and slapdash buildings. During the tour earlier, I had lingered in front of the long, neat rows of arugula to restore mental order—and to calm myself after Nina asked whether it would be too dark later to see the cows come home.

I opened my phone, but didn't redial Mitch's number because a much more interesting conversation was happening within eavesdropping distance in the shed's storage pantry in the back right corner. I put my silent phone to one ear and backed up a few steps to get close enough to listen with the other.

"We have a farm full of people tonight," a man said. It took me a moment to realize that it was Perry because I had never heard him sound irked. "Why are you bringing this up now?"

"You *never* want to discuss it," another man said.

"We're an organic farm, son. There's nothing to discuss."

Perry has two sons, so either Brandon or Cory said, "We don't want her here."

"You've all been clear on that, but the vote is final," Perry said. "Now, let's tend to our guests."

I heard something thud on the dirt floor as I hurried away from the pantry. I stood just outside the shed and extended my arm and moved my cell phone through the air, pretending to scout for a signal while I waited for Perry and his son to emerge. I wanted to see which one he had argued with. Cory is the younger son and has always been a bit of a lamb chop, but Brandon butts heads with Perry over everything from how to water the crops to what price to charge for cauliflower at the farmers' markets.

Discovering which one of the Vaughn boys had a problem with Dana being president of the Friends wouldn't affect my life one way or another, but it gratified me to know that I wasn't the only child who wanted to discuss family business matters at the wrong moment. Even though I had traded a paycheck from Markham's for one from the Travis County Health Department two and a half years ago, I will always be part of our restaurant.

Perry came out of the pantry and smiled when he saw me. "Are you surprise inspecting private parties now?"

I shook his righteously calloused hand. "I'm just here for Dana's cooking."

"Did you hear?" he asked. "She's the new president of the Friends."

"Yes, I came early for the tour," I said. "I think she'll make a good leader."

"Me too."

"What did you say to Nina a few minutes ago to get her back to her table?"

"I told her we're making a big announcement at the end of dinner that she won't want to miss."

"What's that?"

He laughed. "You'll have to find out with everyone else." He rolled his wrist to look at his watch. "I haven't seen Mitch."

"No one has, except the golf staff at the SNOBS club." I held up my phone. "I'm fixin' to hit redial for the twenty-seventh time tonight."

"I'll leave you to it while I check on the vittles," Perry said. He has a master's degree in horticulture, so the simple farmer talk is just for show.

Mitch answered on the fifth ring. "Hi, honey."

"You were supposed to be here an hour ago," I said.

"I'll be there soon."

"Do we have a family crest? Because that should be our motto."

"Save me a glass of wine," he said. "Without the H."

"I'm not whining, Daddy. I—"

"We're almost finished," he said, then hung up.

Aside from Mitch, we were still missing three other dinner companions. I scrolled through my contacts until I got to Ursula's name at the bottom of the list, then thought better of calling her. As a professional chef, she's more precisely aware of timing than the guy who sets Greenwich Mean Time, and she knew exactly when the dinner started. Plus, I don't much like her. The main reason I quit my family's restaurant is because Mitch had forced me to share chef duties with her. After seven months of her grouchiness, unpredictability, and tantrums, I had to decide between permanently maiming her or disappointing my father. The decision was harder than it should have been.

It would be pointless to call Trevor because he's always set to Ursula Mean Time. And I knew that Drew would arrive as soon as he could.

I closed my phone and peeked into the storage pantry. Except for the shelves stocked with natural soil enhancers, small garden implements, and other supplies, it was empty. Whoever Perry argued with must have slipped out while my back was turned.

I stepped onto the wooden sidewalk and inhaled deeply, filling my lungs with the fragrances of dirt, greenery, fertilizer, and humidity, enjoying a peaceful interlude before I had to return to Nina.

And that's when the screaming started.

SIX

THE COMMOTION CAME FROM the kitchen, and by the time I sprinted inside, every cook under Dana's command was either perfecting the pitch of their screams or crying or ventilating hard, but it wasn't immediately apparent why.

No fire or fist fight in progress. All of the dinners had been served, so they hadn't run out of meals. Perhaps dessert had been ruined. But that didn't account for their hysteria or why they were staring at the floor in horror. A mouse or a snake? Which, if you can believe it, would not shut down a restaurant kitchen.

"*Do* something!" one of the females yelled to the room.

I pushed past two cooks to see Dana out cold on the floor, something white and bubbly trickling down her lower lip and chin. I thrust my phone at the yeller. "Call nine one one. Tell them to cut their sirens before they drive onto the farm." We didn't need two hundred Friends coming over to investigate the emergency and sucking up all the fresh air in the room.

I could think of no foodborne illness with a symptom of foaming at the mouth, but a million other things crossed my mind: *rabies, heart attack, poison, champagne residue, I could die trying to save her, can she be saved, why are those stupid cooks standing around like mooks, they're drinking from open containers, did Dana slip on this wet floor...*

I dropped to my knees and felt for a pulse. Nothing. I pointed to a cook with the most Tarzan-looking upper body. "You. Chest compressions. Thirty at a time with a break for me to breathe."

I wiped Dana's mouth with her apron, pinched her nose closed, and began resuscitation on the break. Between rounds of breaths, I said, "All of you dry up and tell me what happened."

"We don't know!" one of the girls cried. "She was talking to us about dessert, and we were laughing at a joke she made, then her eyes got wide and she fell."

Someone else said, "We thought it was another joke at first, but then ... "

I became aware of more people arriving behind me, asking questions that no one answered. "Is she okay?" "Will the restaurant still open?" "Is Randy still president?"

After a few minutes, I heard Perry say, "Give them room," then an efficient man in a dark blue uniform tapped my shoulder, and the EMTs took over for me and Tarzan. They hooked Dana up to a little machine that confirmed a wobbly pulse.

With all the heat, bodies, and activity in the small space, I felt compressed myself, so I stepped outside into the crepuscular evening, sweating and pumped full of my own adrenaline. My lips felt raw, and my stomach gurgled resentment at its delayed dinner.

The EMTs had crowded out Megan and Brandon, too, and they waited together in the washing shed, all fretting brows and anxious eyes. I figured them to be the latecomers asking questions.

I looked for Megan's brother, Ian McDougal, but remembered that he was mending a fence. He could have fenced an entire acre for all the time he had spent on the back ten. It was just as well he wasn't around. Ian thinks he knows everything about everything, a personal trait that's appropriate and appealing in people like Albert Einstein and Leonardo da Vinci, but it's not true about Ian and guarantees he'll make any good situation bad and any bad situation intolerable.

As the paramedics wheeled Dana away, I felt a hand pat my arm. "Nice job taking over in there," Perry said. "Dana's going to make it thanks to you."

"Sometimes my control issues are a blessing," I said. "Do you know what happened?"

"Another heart attack, I'd imagine," he said.

Megan and Brandon walked up to us. "What do we do now?" Brandon asked. "Are we going to finish the dinner?"

Perry looked at the cooks loitering in front of the kitchen door, waiting for their next order, then asked me, "What do you think?"

"No reason not to," I said. "If Dana had cut or burned herself really badly, you'd be in the same situation."

Perry smiled, apparently glad for confirmation that plans should go forward. No one at the dinner knew that Dana had collapsed, but they would find out when Perry told everyone that she wouldn't be making the after-dinner announcement she alluded to in her acceptance speech. If he told them the truth, that is. If it were me, I would spin it a little and say that Dana had to leave suddenly for an emergency appointment.

I waved toward the Field. "Y'all go do what you have to do. I'll get her crew on track."

Perry and Brandon went to the Field, Megan went to the office, and I went to the kitchen. Dana's cooks were saying, "I bet it's from all the stuff with Colin." "Did anyone tell Herb?" "Do you think we still have a job?"

"Who's Dana's sous?" I asked, trying to establish myself as knowledgeable and in charge in case they had ideas about derelicting their duties.

They looked at each other.

"Her sous chef," I said. "Second in command."

"We know what a sous is," Tarzan said.

"Good. Now, do you know *who* it is? I'll give you a hint. It's one of you."

One of the chicks, Cheri according to her embroidered white coat, said, "He quit a couple of weeks ago. Chef hasn't replaced him."

"Who wants to be Dana's sous?" I asked. Three cooks pointed to Tarzan. "You're deputized," I said to him. "Get dessert going."

The cooks knew what to do, but a team operates better with a leader, if only to take the heat if one of them had forgotten to pack the decaf or if a guest found their molars being flossed by a hair in their casserole. Two of the cooks used large knives to slice several sweet potato pies, placing dark orange triangles on white dessert plates, others emptied coffee pots into tall black service urns.

I didn't want to chance that the pie was made with real butter, which vegans don't eat, but coffee never had a face or a mother. I filled a cup, then stepped out of the kitchen and saw a better dessert: Drew Cooper, walking up from the parking lot, smartly handsome in casual black pants and an emerald green long-sleeved shirt. He smiled when he saw me and hurried his pace, the slight limp owing to his prosthetic lower-left leg hardly noticeable.

"There's my cowgirl!" Drew said when he reached me.

Instead of dressing like a jewel thief in my customary black clothes, ponytail, and natural face, I had worn a dark brown T-shirt, short denim skirt, and old brown cowboy boots. I had also stroked on a little mascara to open up my green eyes and wore my blond hair down, long and straight.

I hugged him. "I was fixin' to worry about you."

"Cats and Bats traffic," Drew said, referring to a fundraiser going on downtown. He placed his hands on my waist and leaned in for a kiss, then pulled back. "Are they serving chicken pox for dinner?"

"What?"

"Your face. It looks blistered."

I put my hand to my mouth and felt bumps. "Is it bad?"

"It's not good," he said. "What happened?"

"I'm not sure." I relayed the story of Dana passing out, emphasizing my heroics. "It's probably from the friction."

Drew made a face. "Maybe if Dana had a beard."

I felt embarrassed and self-conscious. My appearance is the last thing I concern myself with because I marinate in sweat, grease, and gunk when I work, and I work all the time. But I had made a special effort to look good for Drew. "Let me check this in the bathroom," I said, then pointed to the archway. "Daisy, Erik, and Nina are in the Field. Go left and they're at a table by the bar."

A procession of Tarzan, followed by the two chick cooks, passed by us. They carried large oval trays crammed with plated pie slices and coffee cups.

"Have you eaten dinner?" Drew asked.

"Not yet."

Drew headed down the walkway, and I ran to the bathroom behind the washing shed. My face was a horror show. Chalky white welts floated in a sea of inflamed skin around my mouth, which burned now that I laid my eyes on the damage.

After my father's heart attack, I researched them so I would recognize the warning signs if he had another one. Dana had been foaming at the mouth, which I learned can sometimes happen, but human-produced enzymes don't burn human flesh. I still couldn't think of any foodborne illness with that symptom, but there are lots of rare toxins I don't come across on a daily basis, such as tetrodotoxin that lives in the gonads, liver, intestines, and skin of poisonous pufferfish, ingestion of which results in paralysis and often death.

It seemed unlikely that Dana had consumed pufferfish gonads, so perhaps it was something more mundane, like a food allergy, although I have never had a negative reaction to any allergen, not even to cedar trees, which makes sufferers of "cedar fever" want to scratch out their own eyeballs this time of year. I've heard that you can develop allergies later in life, and I could deal with an allergy to green beans, but not to red wine. Please, not red wine. Although, since I hadn't consumed either yet, I could rule them out for now. An allergy to Nina would be ideal, which is why it would never happen.

Or it was something yet to be discovered! The Centers for Disease Control are always issuing bulletins for a single reported case of an illness. The chances of me being present at the awakening of a so-far-dormant bacteria or pathogen was exciting! As a conscientious health official, I had the duty—and great fortune—to research *in medias res*. They might even name the illness after me: *Poppycoccus markhamicola.*

I opened the cold tap and drenched a paper towel, then patted my face with it, but it had no permanent effect on the heat of the blisters. I went into a stall and sat on one of the toilets to wet-wipe the wine stains from my boots and got a look at my knees. They, too, had chalky white welts. Perhaps Dana had suffered a more severe allergic reaction to whatever this was.

I left the bathroom for the Field and made it as far as the washing shed when I saw Nina coming through the archway, her platinum-blond bob glowing like radiation. I quickly backed into the dirty, smelly safety of the storage pantry and waited for her to pass.

"Poppy?" she called. "Poppy, are you still here?"

What prompted Nina to leave a party full of people giving her attention to seek out someone who can't stand her? To give me more dietary instructions for her ugly, overindulged dogs while she and Mitch go on their second honeymoon in Venice next month? To ask if I want to contribute a recipe to Ursula's cookbook? Answer: no, because Ursula has already stolen several of my recipes for which I'm surely not going to get credit.

Maybe Nina wanted to say goodbye.

I came out of storage. "I'm still here," I said.

"What are you doing in there?" she asked.

"A chicken tried to bite me."

"I thought you said they were trained—"

"Are you leaving? I can walk you to your car."

"Goodness, no! I'm having too much *fun*. Drew Cooper arrived. He is a *delightful* man." She giggled. "Do you think he and Ursula—"

"Nina!"

"What?"

"Drew is *my*—" I stopped. I had started to say boyfriend, but that wasn't accurate. We weren't anything until I decided between him and Jamie. "Why exactly were you looking for me?" I asked.

"Your father called and said he's not coming. He doesn't like to drive in the dark, you know."

No, I did not know, but I didn't believe that excuse. "Thanks for telling me."

"You'll have to take me home," she said, tick-tocking a full glass of white wine in front of my face. Nina doesn't get drunk, but she likes to pretend to be. Making people take care of her is another form of attention.

"Ursula and Trevor will be here soon, and they can give you a ride."

"They're already here," she said, "but they drove out on Trevor's motorbike."

"Okay. Go have fun and I'll find you when I'm ready to leave." Or when I can talk Mitch into retrieving his mildly tipsy wife.

"Oh, I also wanted to remind you that Dolce and Gabbana can't have chocolate," she said.

"Then they have something in common with all the mangy mutts on the streets of Calcutta."

She made that sound again, the vocal equivalent of an eye roll, then took off, passing Brandon on her way down the plank path. He carried a large tray piled high with bundled-up tablecloths.

"Are you breaking down already?" I asked when he reached me, hoping he wasn't, but knowing he was, which meant no dinner for me. At least not sitting down at a table under the stars and using utensils.

"Yeah. The band's supposed to play in thirty minutes," he said. "I wish they'd start sooner. Everyone's drunk and talking smack. I've already had to break up a couple of food fights."

I pointed to the washing shed. "Speaking of fights, was that you arguing with your dad a little while ago?"

Brandon shook his head. "Ask Core. They've been going at it a lot lately." He lifted the tray of dirty linens. "Gotta get these into the kitchen."

"Sure," I said, then heard someone call, "Poppy!" and I looked up to see the worst thing I could possibly see.

SEVEN

Jamie Sherwood walked toward me from the parking lot, effortlessly dreamy in a pair of blue hiking shorts and long-sleeved white T-shirt, his long, dark curls like little smiles all over the place.

I'm a planner. I like to know every little detail about every little thing. When I enter a walk-in refrigerator, I like to know that I'm going to find butter and milk and lettuce, not a flock of unplucked pheasants filled with buckshot hanging from the shelves. When I attend an event, I like to give myself plenty of time to arrive and greet friends so I can stand at the front of the tour line instead of bringing up the rear because my stepmother called me every five minutes for thirty minutes to tell me that she was two minutes away and to wait for her. But I hadn't decided what to do with Jamie once he returned from his travels.

In fairness to me, though, he wasn't supposed to be back for another six weeks.

I started for him, and we met in front of the office. "What are you doing here?" I said.

"What kind of welcome is that, Poppycakes?"

"Sorry. It's just ... I thought you were in Europe until Thanksgiving."

"I missed you." He stepped closer to me and cupped his hand under my chin.

What was this? A kiss from Jamie? After our rough parting a few months ago? After only an innocuous greeting? I closed my eyes and breathed in his familiar scent, turning off my head so I could let my heart feel him, waiting for him to—

"Have you been making out with a cactus?" he asked.

I opened my eyes and turned my face out of his grasp. "It so happens I've been saving Dana White's life," I said, then briefed him on recent events. "I told Perry I'd keep things going in the kitchen."

"Where's Colin Harris?" Jamie asked.

That's where I knew Randy's sales rep from! I had only ever seen Dana's sous chef in a white chef's coat and beanie. "Dana's cooks told me he quit a couple of weeks ago," I said. "He's working for Randy Dove now."

"That milquetoast? Hawking beer and wine? I doubt that."

"I was at the bar when Randy sent him to deliver a bottle of champagne to Dana. Colin tried to get out of it, but Randy insisted."

"Randy sent champagne to Dana?"

"She's the new president of the Friends of the Farm." I took a moment to process the major revelation being deposited into my knowledge bank now that I knew who Colin was. "Wait, it wasn't the delivery that was important, but the person delivering it! Right after that, Dana came out to the Field and laid into Randy about playing dirty."

Jamie picked up the storyline right away. "If Colin quit, it was probably because Randy hired him away from Dana."

"That's what I'm thinking," I said. "Rough stuff losing a key employee to her sworn enemy."

"What else did I miss?" Jamie asked.

"Bjorn Fleming asked Dana for a job and she called him a one-trick pony and said she had no use for him. Perry's son, Cory, is upset that Dana is president. And Randy accused Dana of trying to kill him after he choked on a lamb kebab."

Oh, and I've been seeing Drew Cooper for the past few months, and he's waiting for me at our table.

Jamie is a professional, so headlines weren't enough. He wanted to know the five Ws, so I told him what I remembered. Our relationship has always had a high intellectual component, and by the time I finished my stories and answering his questions, I felt back in tune with him.

My decision between him and Drew was going to be harder than I thought.

Jamie watched the guests, cooks, and family waiters moving through the archway on their way to the bar, the bathrooms, or other conversations. "All the players are here tonight," he said. "I won't have to track them down for quotes or background."

"Except for Dana," I said. "Can you find out how she's doing? I don't know where they took her."

Before Jamie began devoting his articles and opinions to food and foodies, he worked as a newspaper reporter and still has both official and underground contacts in every crevice of the city.

"I'll make some calls."

"There's one more thing," I said.

Telling Jamie about Drew would be better than him happening upon Drew at our family dinner, but only in the way that telling a neighbor his dog had been run over by a moving van is better than him finding its limp body in the driveway.

"What's that?" Jamie asked, but he was looking past me, and his face changed to something like relief, which I didn't understand when I saw the reason.

A woman walking up from the parking lot. She wore dark blue Wrangler jeans, a red plaid shirt, and a straw cowboy hat over shoulder-length black hair. She staggered up to us in shiny red cowboy boots that were so new the toes didn't have a single scuff or wine splotch on them. She put her hand on Jamie's arm and kissed his cheek. "Sorry I'm late," she said. "My flight was late, then the cab was late picking me up, and traffic out here was *horrid*."

I waited for Jamie to explain this cupcake, but he was smiling at her, his left dimple making a rare showing. "It's the Cats and Bats," he said. "I just arrived myself."

"The what?" she asked. Her manner of enunciating each letter would scrape a linguist's nerves.

"Austin Cat Fancier's show," I said. "They let the bats fly around to keep the cats entertained."

Jamie chastised me with his eyes, then explained, "It's a cat show that also benefits bat conservation."

"All that gridlock for flying *rodents*?"

She didn't have an accent so much as an affectation, like she attended an exclusive East Coast women's college that handed out master's degrees in the Fine Art of Pretension.

I extended my hand. "I'm Poppy Markham. And you are?"

She blinked a couple of times as if the question were too hard, then said, "What is all over your face?"

"I've been making out with a cactus," I said.

She winced, then shook my fingertips. "Mindy Cotton."

"Charmed, I'm sure," I said, still waiting for Jamie to explain her. Had he acquired her while on tour in Minnesota or some other state where they think all Texas females dress like Pam Ewing on *Dallas*?

"Mindy produces the *Foodie's Taste* show," Jamie said with a disgusting amount of pride. "She's been working on a special project for the magazine and decided to film a *Foodie's Taste of Austin*."

"And you're the foodie?" I said.

"Where is the ladies' room?" Mindy asked. "I would *love* to freshen up."

I pointed at a hive of women. "Down the walkway, then make a right. It's behind the washing shed." She thanked me then walked toward the group, swinging a blingy silver purse. *Jeez.* Like Pam Ewing ever carried one of those.

"When did you become a Southern belle?" Jamie asked. "'Charmed, I'm sure.'"

"It's called being polite," I said. "How long will Miss Cotton be camping in our fair city?"

"The show films for a week, so she'll stay through next weekend."

"Where's her film crew?" I asked. "Or are her new red boots her secret super power to doing it all?"

Jamie smiled and shook his head at my jealousy. "They're arriving tomorrow. I invited her to meet me out here so I could introduce her around and we can make a game plan for filming."

"Are you going to take her to Markham's?" I asked.

"Take who to Markham's?" Drew said, coming up behind us.

Jamie gave me an angry, wounded look, then said, "Cooper."

"Sherwood," Drew replied.

Except for their six-one height, physically, Jamie is completely different from Drew. Jamie has coppery brown eyes, high cheekbones, smooth pale skin, and a muscular, but slender build. I'd had reservations about dating such a beautiful man, and they quickly sprang to life in Technicolor detail. The amount of aggressive female attention Jamie attracts, even when he's with me, would test the patience of a blind woman with dementia.

Drew has a solid physique, black hair that he keeps military short with regular trips to a barber, and a strong, honest face. He's the type of man who grows more attractive as you get to know him. I don't have to worry that random girls will keep pen manufacturers in business writing down their phone numbers on cocktail napkins.

"Mindy Cotton," I said, answering Drew's question. "She's the producer of *A Foodie's Taste*. They're filming in Austin."

"That's one of my favorite shows," Drew said to me. "Markham's would be honored."

Jamie didn't respond, and I knew he hadn't decided if helping my family's restaurant would be worth helping Drew, too.

"Is there any wine left?" I asked Drew.

He nodded. "I've had a glass of Opus One waiting for you at the table for twenty minutes."

A full glass? How did he manage that? Opus One was one of the wines Randy poured only a taste of. "Will it wait a few more minutes?" I asked.

"I'll check," he said, gallantly releasing me from the Pythagorean theorem I was caught up in.

After Drew left, Jamie said, "I hear you two have been having fun in my absence."

Apparently, I wasn't his only eyes and ears in Austin. "We've been hanging out."

"Well, I'm here now, so you can stop."

It was unlike Jamie to be so decisively bold, and it rather startled me. "I'm not sure I want to," I said.

Jamie took my hand. "I'm sure enough for both of us. I came back as soon as I heard about you two."

I felt flattered by that grand romantic gesture, except, "Why did you bring along Mindy Cotillion?"

"I didn't *bring* her," he said. "When I told her I wasn't going to Europe, she asked if she could come down and film the show."

"Is that all she wants?" I asked. "Because she kissed you hello."

"That's how she is. It's nothing."

"Like your fling was nothing?"

Jamie exhaled hard, then appeared to reconsider what I assumed would be another dismissal of that night that broke my trust and all but ruined our relationship. He drew me to him and kissed my hair. "I can't undo that night, so all we can do is move forward." He held me at arm's length and looked into my eyes. "I love you, Poppycakes, and I miss you in my life."

"I know, but let's not do this tonight, okay?" I said. "I'm here with Drew."

Jamie nodded in a way that meant he didn't like what he heard, then left for the Field.

———

I returned to the privacy of the storage pantry to call Mitch and tell him about Dana, but before I redialed my father's number, Randy Dove blew in.

"Inspector Poppy," he said, sounding more sober than I thought he should after a couple of hours of pity-party wine drinking. He looked behind me at the shelves. "I need a wrench," he said. "Loose wheel on my cooler."

I moved aside, but stayed close. The storage pantry was the only buffered zone that let me see faces—most importantly those of Drew, Jamie, Mindy, Nina, and Ursula—and have a quiet phone conversation, and I didn't want to lose it.

He looked at me, then leaned away. "Are the measles making a comeback?"

"I hope not," I said, and meant it. A city-wide outbreak would bring the health department to its knees. "Are you feeling better?"

"I'm dandy. Dandy Randy Dove." He laughed. "But I hear Dana's not doing so good."

I didn't want to assume what he had heard, so I threw out some bait. "Well, she wasn't too happy after you sent that bottle—correction, sent Colin Harris to deliver that bottle—of champagne. It really upset her."

"Good," Randy said. "She deserves it after trying to ruin me and firing Colin."

"Fired? I thought Colin—" Randy tilted his head as if waiting for me to either praise Colin or diss Dana. "—will make a fine sales rep."

"No, he won't. But that's not why I hired him." Randy picked up a pair of needle-nose pliers from their nail on the wall. "These'll do," he said, then left.

Dana's cooks had told me Colin quit, but Randy thought Colin had been fired? One of them had bad information, but had it come from Dana or from Colin? Colin could have quit but told Randy that Dana fired him. For what reason though? To get a job with him? And Dana could have fired Colin, but told everyone he quit. That made more sense. If Colin was beloved among their employees, she would look like The Donald for firing him. And if Colin was that upset with her, he couldn't have exacted a more perfect revenge than to go to work for her arch-enemy.

Jamie needed to know about this new twist. I flipped open my phone to call him, hit Send, then immediately hit End when Mike Glass stepped into the storage pantry.

"Sorry," he said. "I figured this was a quiet place to make a phone call." His bulk made the room seem smaller. "I see you had the same idea. We both had the same idea." He peered at my mouth. "Is that a bee sting? I'm allergic to those."

"It's a non-communicable strain of buccal measles," I said, then before he figured out I had made that up, I said, "Sorry y'all lost the election. You did a good job as vice president."

"We were counting on another year," Mike said. "Who did you vote for? Because everyone I've talked to said they voted for Randy. Did you vote for Randy?"

"I didn't have a chance to vote this year."

Well, I did have a chance. Several chances, in fact. The election had been elevated to The Topic the week before, and I'd had the best intentions of getting my ballot in the mail, but other things captured my time—a stakeout at a butcher shop reportedly selling pig eyeballs to Santería practitioners, and making an in-person protest of the ludicrously high tax value of my house with the county appraisal district. I would have marked my X for Dana.

"Randy's going to ask Perry for a recount," Mike said, "and I think that's a good idea. Don't you think that's a good idea?"

"Checks and balances is always a good idea," I said. Mike hadn't mentioned Dana, but I wanted her name to come up. Dana's win meant his loss in this election, too, which was another story I could hand to Jamie. "Did you hear about Dana?" I asked.

"That she tried to make Randy choke? I think that's a terrible thing to do. Don't you think that's terrible? I saved him. Did you see I saved him?"

"You're a hero, Mike." I decided that Mike Glass was too dumb to be the subject of an article on Jamie's website. "The parking lot might be a good place to make your phone call," I suggested.

After he left, I pressed Redial, then had to hit End when Perry came around the corner. "Whatcha doing?" he asked.

50

"Trying to make a phone call," I said. "It was either here or the chicken coop."

He frowned and pointed to my mouth. "Is that contagious?"

"No," I said. "Am I in your way?"

"Nah. Just making the rounds. Tomorrow's a pickup day, and I don't want my interns dealing with a sink full of vomit like they did last year after the dinner."

"Do you think it's a good idea to tell that to a health inspector?" I said.

"Tell what to a health inspector?" He winked. "Going to put the chickens to bed."

I stepped out of the shed to see who else was on their way to interrupt me and saw Megan coming from the office. I thought she would continue on to the party, but she came into the washing shed with her face down, so she didn't see me.

"Hi, Megan," I said.

She reared back and brought her hand to her heart. "What are you doing out here?" Her tone was scolding, and she caught herself. "You should be enjoying the party," she said more gently.

"I'm taking a breather," I said.

"Are you feeling okay?" she asked in her concerned-mom voice.

"I'm a little hungry, but yeah, I'm okay."

"No, your face is blotchy."

"It's a sunburn, I think."

I thought she would mention that I hadn't had a sunburn a couple of hours ago, but she said, "Thank you for helping tonight."

"Happy to do it," I said. "Do you know if Dana is okay?"

"We haven't heard," she said, "but I should call and find out."

"Mom!" I heard someone call as she walked toward the office. I looked out and saw Brandon hurrying through the archway. "Mom!"

I waited for him to pass before I dialed Jamie again. On the first ring, however, Cory loped into the washing shed, so I closed my phone. Pretty soon, Jamie was going to come and investigate me and all of my hangups.

"Hey, Core. I haven't seen you all night."

"I … uh … what are you doing back here?"

"Trying to make a phone call," I said. "You'd think the party had been relocated the way people keep popping in."

"Like who?" he asked.

"Everyone in your family for starters."

"Were they looking for me?"

"Not that I know of," I said. "Was that you I heard arguing in here with your dad while dinner was being served?"

He shook his head. "I made up a couple more boxes, then Uncle Ian called me to help him with the fence. Probably Brandon." He examined the shelves behind me.

I moved aside. "Did you want something from here?"

"I thought I left my phone on the shelf. Have you heard it ring?"

"No, but I can call it for you."

He looked at the archway and saw Bjorn intent on one of us. "I think I left it in the office," Cory said.

Bjorn had been smiling like a bounty hunter, but his face hardened when the youngest Vaughn escaped to the office. Bjorn stopped when he saw me. "That kid," he said. "Impossible to pin down."

"What do you need him for?"

"What do you care?"

Well, that just got him this: "Does it have anything to do with you quitting the farm to work for Dana White?"

Bjorn rolled his eyes. "I told you—" He stopped and grimaced at my mouth. "That's disgusting."

52

"Bjorn!" Kevin called, stepping out of the kitchen.

"Oh, great," Bjorn said, then hurried toward the Field.

I didn't want to talk to Kevi either, so I slipped into the storage pantry and waited for him to pass, except he didn't, and I found myself being asked, yet again, "What are you doing here?"

"Wondering if humans can get hoof-and-mouth disease," I said. "You?"

"I was . . . never mind."

He about-faced and huffed off, and I followed a couple of steps behind him, curious to see whether Kevin snared Bjorn or Bjorn snared Cory, but my eyes landed on Drew walking toward me, and, more specifically, the full glass of wine in his hand.

"Is that for me?" I asked.

"Yes, but first tell me what's wrong."

I covered my mouth. "It's nothing."

He pulled me to him. "No, it's in your eyes. Did Sherwood upset you?"

"I'm worried about Mitch. Nina said he isn't coming because he doesn't like to drive in the dark," I said into his warm chest. "Do you know anything about that?" Before Drew answered, my phone vibrated in my hand and I checked it behind his back. Jamie. I withdrew from his embrace and said, "I have to take this."

"I found out where Dana is," Jamie said when I answered. "I'm coming out of the Field."

I looked at the archway. "I see you."

"Meet me in the parking lot."

"What's going on?" I asked, but he had hung up.

I watched Jamie stride down the plywood, his eyes as serious as a runway model's, oblivious to the hopeful smiles and sighs of the female Friends on their return trip from the bathroom. Drew watched him, too, a heavy strain on his face. He offered the glass of wine to me, but before I took it, Jamie seized my hand.

"Jamie!" I complained as he dragged me away from Drew like some romance novel he-man. I looked back at Drew to plead an apology with my eyes, but he had turned his back to us to rejoin the party.

When we reached the first row of cars, Jamie stopped and faced me. "It's not good," he said.

"You were so *rude* back there!" I said, wiggling the fingers he had crushed. "Is Dana at St. David's?"

"Poppy—"

"Can she have visitors? I have tomorrow off and—"

"Poppy!"

"Pipe down. I'm right here."

"Dana's at the morgue."

EIGHT

Jamie let me sit quietly for a moment to process that idea, but it didn't make sense. "No. She's alive," I said. "I kept her alive."

"I talked to a dispatcher I know. Dana died on the way to the hospital."

"What else did they say? Was it foul play?"

He rolled his eyes. "Not every dead person is taken out by foul play."

"Why all the grouch?"

"I'm sorry," he said softly. "Dana was a friend."

I touched his arm. "To a lot of us."

"They're going to do an autopsy," Jamie said, "but it was probably another heart attack."

"She was fine earlier," I said. "Better than fine. Radiant."

Jamie shrugged. "This was an emotional night for her—winning the Friends election, arguing with Bjorn and Dove. It makes sense."

A reasonable explanation, but I couldn't quite accept it. Running a kitchen is a high-stress endeavor. Chefs toggle between high and low emotions every day, sometimes minute-to-minute, and Dana had been through much worse. Plus, there were the strange welts on my face and knees that came from Dana and had yet to be explained.

"Are you okay?" Jamie asked.

"I'm thinking about Mitch," I said. "He's known Dana and Herb a long time."

"Isn't he here?" Jamie said.

"He's golfing," I said. "I came in here to call him and tell him about Dana, but I got interrupted by everyone and their chef coming into the storage pantry."

Jamie held up his phone. "You dialed me instead."

"That was on purpose," I said. "I have a scoop for you. Remember how Dana's cooks said Colin quit a couple of weeks ago? Well, Randy Dove just told me Dana *fired* Colin."

"Did he say why?"

"No, but you could go ask him." I paused. "Unless Mindy needs you for *A Foodie's Taste of Cow Patties*."

Jamie smiled sarcastically, then said, "Michael Douglas and Brittany Murphy."

We play a trivia game where one of us names two actors, and the other names the movie they starred in. Jamie has an amazing memory, but I have to study movie websites to keep up. With Jamie gone the past few months, other things had distracted me.

"You win this round," I said.

"*Don't Say a Word*," he said.

"About Dana?"

He nodded. "It'll just cause a lot of trouble."

"You mean it'll shut people up before you can get your stories," I said. He arched a warning eyebrow at me. "You can count on me," I said.

Jamie shook his long curls in disappointment. "You could have said that with Laura Linney and Mark Ruffalo." He started up the gravel drive, but stopped after a few steps. "Coming?"

"You go on," I said. "I still need to call Mitch." And inspect the kitchen for anything suspicious before it was lost during cleanup. If one of the most famous chefs in Austin had died from food poisoning on my watch, my boss would bust me down to septic inspections.

As soon as Jamie passed out of turning-back-to-see-me range, I ran to my Jeep, grabbed my badge from my backpack, clipped it to my waistband, and zipped to the kitchen.

———

Good Earth's kitchen was never intended to support high-volume table service, so they don't have a commercial electric dishwasher, and everything has to be washed by hand. When I entered, Tarzan and the other male cook were elbow-deep in a three-compartment sink of steaming water filled with bubbles and dinner plates. The two chicks stood at the prep table eating leftover skewers.

"Y'all doing okay?" I asked.

The girls nodded sadly. I put my hand on my hip to draw their attention to my badge. "I'm with the health department and—"

Cheri stopped in mid-bite. "We normally don't eat in the kitchen."

See? Everyone *knows* the rules; they just don't abide by them.

"I'm not here for that," I said. "I'm investigating what happened to Dana."

"Was it food poisoning?"

"I don't know yet," I said. "Right now, I'd like to exclude the possibility of an outbreak."

Technically, to be deemed an outbreak there has to be more than one case of the same illness reported by a doctor or a hospital—except in the case of botulism, which requires only one incident to be considered an outbreak—but the word is loaded and gets people's attention.

"Can I ask y'all some questions?" I said.

They nodded and resumed eating. I addressed the blond one who earlier told me Dana had fallen. Kelly was her name. "You told me she made a joke, and then her eyes got wide and she dropped." Kelly nodded, and I continued. "Did she clutch her chest like she was having a heart attack or double over like she had stomach pain?"

The girls exchanged glances then Cheri said, "She sort of… crumpled."

That's what happened to Mitch when he had his heart attack a few months ago, but he had strained his heart picking up a large tray stacked with dirty dishes.

"Did she lift anything heavy during the day?" I asked.

"The guys carried in all the catering tubs, but she could have earlier."

"While you were with her today, did she eat or drink anything that no one else did?"

They both shrugged. "It's possible," Cheri said, "but Chef doesn't eat while she's working, except to taste stuff we make. We all ate the same today."

Kelly said, "She got really upset when—"

"Kelly!" Cheri said. "That has nothing to do with food poisoning."

"It could help eliminate food poisoning," I said. "If she had a heart attack, then being upset may have triggered it." I addressed Kelly. "What upset her?"

She looked at Cheri, then at the floor. "Colin … you know, her old sous … brought her a bottle of champagne. He said it was from Randy Dove."

"And Dana got upset?" I said. I knew the answer, of course—saw the answer in the Field.

Kelly nodded. "We were all happy to see Colin again. We thought he might want to come back, until Chef started yelling at him. She called him a traitor and said he'd never cook in Austin again."

"What did Colin do when she reacted like that?" I asked. "Was he mad?"

"He's used to it. He said he was sorry, then he left."

"Did you see where he went?" Because he didn't return to the Field until after Dana had gone in and yelled at Randy.

They shook their heads.

"I'll need to see that bottle of champagne," I said.

"It's in the walk-in," Cheri said. "She didn't drink any."

After she left to fetch it, I asked Kelly to describe what happened before Dana went down.

"It was a normal busy night, except in a different place," she said. "It took us a little while to get the hang of things, but then we were rolling. Chef was in a really good mood, actually, even before she won the Friends president."

"Was that unusual? The good mood."

"I guess. Yeah. She's always real serious when she's cooking. When we first got here, she had us unpack the supplies while she talked to Mr. Vaughn. She was gone for like thirty minutes, then came back all happy."

I assumed Perry had given her advance notice she won the election. "So she was in a good mood," I said, "then Colin delivered the champagne and she got upset." Kelly nodded. "And she left the kitchen, correct?"

"She was gone like five minutes," Kelly said, "but I don't know where she went."

"And she was in a good mood when she came back?"

Kelly frowned.

"You said she made a joke that y'all were laughing at right before she went down."

"Oh, yeah."

Cheri returned from the walk-in unwrapping two bread rolls sealed in foil. "I can't find it," she said. "But I know it was in there earlier. I put it on the shelf."

"Are you sure Dana didn't drink it?" I asked.

"We're sure," Kelly said. Cheri handed her a roll and she used her index finger to hollow out the center to make room for a couple of pieces of pork. She took a bite of the sandwich then said, "Chef was drinking a lot of water all night. We were all dying from the heat."

A cook's uniform is not designed for comfort. Good coats and pants are made from heavy twill cotton, cheaper ones a cotton/polyester blend, which makes them supernova hot. Add to that an undershirt to soak up the sweat, socks and full-coverage shoes, and some sort of hair restraint, and the entire outfit becomes the opposite of comfortable. Its first job is as protection against burns, scrapes, and grease splatters. However, most cooks try to get some relief from this fabric suit of armor by rolling up their sleeves when they work, which exposes their wrists and forearms—the very body parts most susceptible to burns, scrapes, and grease splatters.

If Dana had snacked on bad food, other people would also be sick, but the only solid lead I had was that she had been drinking water. Unless the rumor Jerry told Daisy that Dana started her day with vodka was true, which could contribute to a heart attack. But did she indulge on a night as important as this?

"Where is the glass she was drinking from?" I asked.

Kelly reached under the counter of the prep table and removed a glass measuring cup from a lower shelf. Everything about her seemed guilty, and I thought she had realized she had no choice but to confess that her boss was an alcoholic, but she said, "Chef doesn't like to drink from a straw."

I remembered seeing that measuring cup on the floor when I helped do CPR on Dana. Owing to the pour spout and handle, the cup hadn't laid completely on its side and still had close to half an inch of liquid in it, which fizzed when I sloshed the cup. That explained where the champagne went.

Jamie was looking more right, because a heart attack was seeming more likely after Dana had gone through the high of the Friends win, the low of Colin's betrayal, and a couple of mugs of bubbly in a room as hot as a bonfire.

"Found it!" Cheri called from the dry storage area. I met her halfway. "The guys started packing up stuff we were done with and pulled it from the walk-in."

The bottle still had its foil wrap and cork. "You're *sure* that's the bottle Colin brought?" I asked.

"Positive," Cheri said. "The label was wet and peeling off a little."

If Dana hadn't been drinking champagne, then what was fizzing in her cup? Soda water or Sprite? Neither of those would cause her to pass out, unless she had splashed in a few jiggers of vodka. I sniffed it, but didn't detect any offensive fumes, so I dipped my pinkie into the liquid. I didn't taste it because I felt the same burning sensation on my finger as on my mouth and knees, and then I saw white foam.

There was only one thing in the kitchen that would cause that.

NINE

Food-grade hydrogen peroxide. Not the 3% or 5% percent solution anyone can buy in a brown bottle at the grocery store for first aid and hair highlights. This is a concentrated 35% solution that comes with all kinds of warnings against using it full-strength, including cautions against direct contact with skin and consuming it. It's as clear as vodka and has no odor. It's recommended that food-grade peroxide be diluted with water to a 3% solution before using it as a natural household cleaner or blood therapeutic, and even then, it fizzes when it comes into contact with the microorganisms on organic material like skin or raw ingredients.

Full-strength would eat something alive.

How did *that* get into Dana's cup?

To make sure it was what I thought it was before I violated anyone's civil rights, I picked up a raw green bean that had fallen to the floor and broke off a piece. I dropped it into the liquid and watched it fizz. It quickly resembled a little ball of cotton. Soda water or Sprite would not have attacked the green bean like flesh-eating bacteria.

Ingesting the stuff would have made Dana nauseated, but not immediately, and it wouldn't have killed her, not even eventually. Well, it wouldn't have killed a healthy woman.

I tried to imagine myself in Dana's place: gulping what I thought would be refreshing water, surprise at drinking something harsh and fizzy, shock that someone had filled my cup with it, and alarm that it might prove immediately hazardous to my life. The panic would have revved my healthy heart and made me flush. But Dana? It would have revved her diseased heart and made her dead.

This was no accident. Everyone knew about her heart condition, and whether the peroxide was intended to kill her or simply incapacitate her was irrelevant. The end result was the same.

The kitchen was a crime scene, I realized, and everyone in it was a suspect. I raised my badge into the air and yelled, "Hold it!"

No one held anything.

Tarzan and the other guy couldn't hear me over the running water, and the girls must have left the kitchen while I conducted my experiment. It was just as well. In light of Dana's death being intentional, Jamie would be more than a little unhappy that I spread the news she had died.

I decided to keep an inspector's eye on everyone and notice if they acted suspicious. So far, no one seemed concerned to see me handling Dana's cup, but I had seen enough guilty restaurant employees pretend to know nothing about nothing to take that at face value.

I clipped my badge to my skirt, then placed the measuring cup on the prep table. Had I known I was going to find malice aforethought when I asked to see Dana's drinking cup, I would have worn gloves so as to preserve any fingerprints, but not even *I* possessed the ability to turn back time. Besides, you can pour anything into a cup without handling it, which Dana's killer may well have done.

And if they were safety-conscious, they followed the manufacturer's recommendation to wear gloves while handling the stuff.

This was a mystery I *had* to solve. Dana would never have won the Nicest Chef in Austin award, but she was a friend and mentor to as many people as she rubbed the wrong way, and lots of both were at the dinner.

I covered the cup with the foil that had contained the bread rolls so the peroxide didn't spill or evaporate, and because over time, food-grade peroxide loses its potency when exposed to air and light. By the time the police got around to testing it in a month or two, it could have lost a few molecules and reverted to nothing more dangerous than water.

I took the evidence to the five-foot-tall upright freezer against the far right wall. Like alcohol—both rubbing and drinking—peroxide does not freeze, so because an airtight freezer is usually the consistently darkest place anywhere, that's where most people keep it. I wanted to store the cup in a safe place, but I also wanted to check on the bottle of food-grade peroxide Good Earth kept inside, wrapped in a red plastic bag on the bottom shelf. I had seen it during inspections.

The first thing I noticed was the freezer's combination lock on the floor, which meant that the freezer's contents were accessible to anyone. I opened the door to find shelves of frozen dinners, coffee beans, phyllo dough, and raspberries, but no peroxide. They could have been out, but I suspected the killer had taken it. I placed Dana's cup on the bottom shelf, then shut the door and locked the lock. Dinner had ended and I assumed that no one needed inside the freezer again.

My stomach yelled at me as I thought through my next move. Good Earth also used food-grade peroxide to clean the office, the washing shed, the chicken coop, the bathrooms, and their homes, so the kitchen wasn't the only place to find it. I left the cooks to their cleanup and went to the storage pantry in the washing shed. I explored the shelves, moving aside spades and trowels, pliers and seed packets, until I saw a small white bottle on the top shelf. I didn't see any gloves on the shelves and didn't have even a crumpled bevnap on me, so I used a pair of garden shears as tongs to gently lift the bottle and bring it down to eye level.

It was an oxygenating plant additive called OxyGrowth. The label listed hydrogen peroxide as the first of many ingredients, so this was another possible murder weapon. Did this mixture have an odor? Would Dana have noticed if it had? When you're that busy and that thirsty, you grab your glass and gulp. I couldn't open the bottle and sniff without leaving my fingerprints all over it, and especially not since my prints were already on Dana's cup, so I would have to come back later and test it.

I noticed dirt on the bottle, which wasn't that unusual because, as I reminded Nina earlier, we were on a farm, but my thumb slid across a smear of soft mud, which meant that it had been wet recently. Brandon and Cory wouldn't have used it for the washing demo, but I remembered hearing something thud on the ground when Perry argued with one of them earlier. Perhaps they had handled the stuff for some reason.

I returned it to the top shelf, hung the garden shears on their hook, then set out to tell Jamie about my discovery. I was intercepted again, however, but this time I welcomed it.

Trevor Shaw—Ursula's twenty-five-year-old sous chef and secret sometimes-boyfriend whom Nina would have a herd of cows over if she knew—ambled out of the Field. With his long dark blond hair, slow smile, colorfully illustrated arms, and bad-boy vibe, he looks like the audacious flirt that he is. He wore faded blue jeans and a once-black vintage Rolling Stones T-shirt, drained to gray from many launderings.

He stopped in front of the archway, placed his hands on narrow hips, and watched me walk up to him, his blue eyes starting at my boots, lingering on my skirt, and finally resting on my face.

"Evenin' sheriff," he said, tipping an imaginary hat. "I just rode into town and want no trouble with the law."

I still had my inspector's badge clipped to my waistband, and I put it in my pocket to forestall Jamie jumping to all kinds of correct conclusions about me investigating before I had a chance to tell him the facts. "Good," I said. "I've got a nice, quiet farm community here, and I aim to keep it nice and quiet."

Trevor bent down and peered at my face. "Are you an extra in a horror movie?"

"Still?" I said to the welts as I patted them with my fingertips. I looked down at my knees, and so did Trevor. "Don't say a word," I said. "It's from hydrogen peroxide."

"Whatever you say, Popstar," he said in that slow Texas drawl of his.

"Where's Nina?" I asked, wanting to establish her whereabouts to make sure I avoided her.

He chuckled. "Tryin' to find me a nice girl to date. She doesn't understand why Ursula won't help her. I thought I'd take a walk and let Ursula get her talkin' on something else."

Trevor doesn't "walk" without a cigarette. "They won't let you smoke on the farm," I said. "You'll have to go to the parking lot."

He held up both hands. "I quit."

"Since when?"

He removed his phone from his pocket and illuminated the time. "Goin' on ten hours and thirteen minutes," he said. "Ursula and I were preppin' for brunch, and I misidentified mace as nutmeg, and she said my palate was polluted and suggested I quit."

Ursula York does not suggest. She commands, she makes, she insists, she demands. "She crushed up your pack and threw it in the trash, didn't she?"

"The sink," he said. "We were thawin' scallops in there."

"And then you discarded that contaminated food, right?"

"That's the first thing I said to Ursula. 'This food is now contaminated, and we must discard it at once.'"

He did no such thing.

He plucked a cigarette from behind his ear and smiled. "She missed one. Got a light?"

"You might find some matches in my backpack in my Jeep. Second row, all the way down on the left. Doors are off." I lifted the hair off of my neck to let it cool. "What took y'all so long to get here?"

"She wanted to stay and work on her salmon cake recipe for the cookbook."

"The one Markham's serves?" I said. "Because that's *my* recipe."

"Hey, I'm just the sous."

"Did Drew find our table?"

"Yeah, and he's sittin' at it, poutin'." He laughed. "Why did you invite both of your boyfriends to the same party?"

"I didn't. Where's Jamie now?"

"Talkin' to some little guy in a blue hat. Ursula said his name, but I don't recall it."

"No, where exactly in the Field?"

"By the bandstand last time I saw."

In the rear-right corner. Our table was in the front-left corner, so Drew and Jamie were already as physically far apart as possible. "And Daisy?" I asked.

"Who?"

"My cousin."

"*Ha!* I thought she was you when I saw her at the bar. She almost slapped me when I came up behind her and asked if she heard the one about the blonde who tiptoed past the medicine cabinet because she didn't want to wake the sleepin' pills."

I laughed. "I guess Daisy's not one for sneak attack dumb blond jokes, but that's pretty good. Is she still at the bar?"

"That was awhile ago," Trevor said.

"Thanks. I'll leave you to your walk."

As I started for the archway, he called after me, "Tell Nina I like thirty-five-year-old redheads."

One redhead in particular, who had a place at our table next to her mother.

I entered the Field, using my health inspector skill of looking for Jamie without appearing to look for him, so I didn't see Candy Fitzhugh, a former waitress at Markham's I'd had to fire a few years ago after she followed a customer to his car to return the five-cent tip he left her, until I almost crashed into her. After she asked about my father, she said, "A *ginormous* roach crawled across my table the other day at the All-Night Flashlight."

She's lucky it was just one, and it was just a roach. First, that place has the worst food, service, and ambiance of any 24-hour restaurant in the city—nothing but greasy meals, greasy waiters, and greasy walls. How they stay in business could be explained only by a tarot card reader. Second, bugs in the dining room are a harbinger of unbelievably careless health practices. If a restaurant doesn't keep their public dining room clean, it means they don't keep their kitchen clean.

This week, the Flashlight would get an extra surprise inspection by me. I know I'll find a colonial empire's worth of roaches in the kitchen and probably a significant population of mice or rats. But the owners (who have actually prompted me to ask my boss, Olive, for the authority to issue four-figure fines for poor personal hygiene) will clean up fast and reopen their doors with promises to do better. My colleague, Gavin Kawasaki, calls them the All-Night Frightblight.

"Thanks, Candy," I said. "I'll look into it."

As she rejoined her friends, I approached our table and saw Nina pointing to a couple of nubile girls at the bar and Ursula shaking her auburn curls.

Drew stood when he saw me, a dispirited smile on his face. He knew that Jamie's early return was sure to upset the balance of our provisional relationship.

I went to Drew's side of the table, accepted a quick kiss on my neck—nowhere close to my mouth and the blisters—then we both sat down. I pointed to an empty wine glass in front of him. "Opus One?" I asked.

"It was," he said. "Is everything okay?"

"Poppy," Nina interrupted, "you have friends, don't you?"

I knew she meant friends she could set up with Trevor, but Nina is under the mistaken assumption that what she says is so important and compelling, everyone listens to her and follows her plot. "Not a single one," I said.

"Mother, please," Ursula said, sounding bothered by Nina for the first time since *ever*. "Trevor can find his own girlfriend. Drink your wine and let's enjoy the band."

I returned my attention to Drew. "I lost Daisy and Erik. Have you seen them?" I asked, hoping he would think I was looking around for them instead of Jamie.

A woman dressed in black moved to the right when she hugged a friend and I glimpsed Jamie, still by the bandstand, still talking to Jerry Potter.

"I didn't know they were here," Drew said. He pointed to his cell phone on the table. "You can call her."

"The only call Daisy will answer when she's on a date with Erik is from her kids."

"Do you want me to look for them?"

I almost said no because I didn't want Drew roaming the Field, coming upon me talking to Jamie again, but if he stayed at the table, he would watch me walk across the Field to him, and while I had a good reason to do it and Drew was a big boy, I didn't want him to see me leave our table specifically to talk to his rival. "Would you, please?" I said. "I have something I need to do."

Drew looked toward the bandstand. Of course he knew where Jamie was. And Jamie knew where Drew was. "Sure," he said, giving me that sad smile again, now with a cherry of anger on top.

Daisy was right. I couldn't handle this.

TEN

I'VE NEVER HAD TWO boyfriends at the same time in my life. I've never even casually dated more than one guy at a time. Growing up in a restaurant, the guys I met were either customers or employees, and I learned early on—and with some wise advice from my mother—that I could expect technical difficulties if I dated either. Plus, I didn't have time to cuddle with my cat, never mind juggle multiple demands for affection. Yet there I was, in love with two good men, and having to make a choice under duress.

Drew knew where I intended to go and would watch me anyway, but I didn't want to rub it in, so instead of taking the straightest route through the Field, I circled to the right, saying hello to friends and Friends, keeping my eyes clamped on Jamie. Jerry Potter's story must have been compelling, because instead of glancing up at every passerby, hoping to find a convenient excuse to break away, Jamie had given Jerry the gift of his full attention. He had that intense expression on his face, the one where he's listening and composing his article at the same time. Jamie doesn't get that look for just any story.

The musicians, a four-boy hair band wearing over-dyed black clothing and metal spikes in their eyebrows, noses, and lips, approached the stage, so I went around the back of it and came up behind Jamie. Jerry clammed up when he saw me, and Jamie turned to see why. He took my hand and tugged me into their conversation. "Keep going," Jamie said.

Jerry removed his cap and scratched his sweating scalp. "That's all I know about it," he said. "You going to, you know … "

"I'll get you the money this week," Jamie said.

Jerry nodded. "I'm gonna get me a beer."

When Jerry left, I said, "This story must be incredible if you're paying a source."

"Just twenty bucks," Jamie said. "He had some information about the farm."

Jamie looked everywhere but at me, and I knew there was more to the story, but I didn't push. When Jamie knows a secret, he likes to keep it to himself for a while, form his own ideas and conclusions before they can be polluted by another person's.

Unlike me.

"I need to tell you something," I said. "New facts have come to light and I *guarantee* my headline is bigger than Jerry Potter's headline."

"Okay, wow me."

Wow me? Where did that come from?

The band started their sound check, so I put my arms around his neck and brought his ear to my mouth. "Dana was murdered," I said. He tensed and tried to pull away, but I held on. "Someone filled her cup with hydrogen peroxide."

I released him and we took a few steps away from the band.

"Peroxide," he said flatly.

"Food grade," I said, then put my finger on my upper lip. "That's what burned me."

"How do you know this?"

I have heard Jamie sound skeptical before, but that was the first time with me. He always questions my theories and postulations to help me solidify them, but I could tell he thought I was grasping, if not making it up entirely. I took him farther away from the crowd and the band, then detailed my investigation. "I tested the remains of her cup," I concluded. "It can't be anything else."

Jamie searched my eyes, wanting to buy this admittedly far-fetched story, but not quite coming up with the cash.

"You don't have to believe me right now," I said, "but accept the premise and help me discover who did it." I pointed to the center of the Field but kept my eyes locked with Jamie's. "Everyone knows about Dana's heart condition, and someone here filled her cup with peroxide. By the time the police investigate, the evidence will be gone."

"Maybe it got in there accidentally," Jamie said.

"How do you accidentally pour food-grade hydrogen peroxide into someone's glass? Or your own glass? Besides it was a measuring cup. She had it when Perry announced her as president. Everyone saw her drink from it."

He put his hands on top of his head and blew air from his lower lip, a physical expression of his mental frustration. "Are you sure enough to take this to the police?"

"Yes."

He pulled out his cell phone. "Then we're going to."

I waited while he left a message for one of his detective friends. "Why not nine one one?" I asked. "I said I'm sure."

"I want to run it by Baxter and let him decide what to do." Which meant he still didn't believe me and didn't want to look foolish in case I was wrong.

"Fine, but in the meantime, we're on the scene. Nobody knows Dana is dead, not even the killer, so we can look for evidence and interview perps. Plus, all these people have been drinking for a couple of hours and will have loose lips. *In vino veritas* and all that."

"Perps?" he asked, finally smiling. When Jamie gets focused, he can get broody as a hen.

"I have a few in mind," I said. "Randy Dove being *numero uno*. He lost the Friends election to Dana, and they had words over him hiring Colin Harris."

"As a motive, that's kind of thin."

"Really? You wrote a four-article series on that filthy campaign. After Randy hired those high school kids to let loose a couple of ferrets in the Wolff's dining room, you think he'd have a problem putting peroxide in her cup? He also accused Dana of trying to kill him when he choked during dinner. Maybe he didn't intend to kill her. Maybe he wanted to get even."

"Maybe. Who else?"

"Bjorn Fleming. When I asked him about approaching Dana for a job, he called her Hitler and said he'd never work for her."

"Maybe he *didn't* ask her for a job," Jamie said. "Maybe it was for something else."

"Dana's cooks said it was about a job. They also said Dana called Colin Harris a traitor when he delivered the champagne from Randy. And we still don't know whether Colin jumped or was pushed."

"How come Dana's cooks are spilling all this info to you?"

I showed him my badge, which made him frown and smile at the same time. "I wanted to rule out food poisoning," I said.

"That's two *perps*. Didn't you tell me one of Perry's sons didn't want her to be Friends president?"

I thought that was pretty thin, but kept it to myself. I couldn't chase after that many people alone and needed whatever help Jamie would give me. "I overheard the conversation, but listen to this—I asked them if they argued with their dad and they both said it wasn't them."

"Then maybe it wasn't."

"Perry called him son, so one of them is lying."

"Why?"

"Exactly."

"I don't see how any of this leads to suspecting them of murder," he said.

"It's a place to start. We can ask questions and follow where it goes."

Jamie rubbed his jaw and squinted at me.

"What?" I said, getting a little annoyed with all the unromantic attention my mouth was receiving. "You know what it is now. It's not contagious."

"No," he said. "I'd feel better if we waited to hear from Baxter."

I sighed and rolled my eyes inside. Outside, I said, "You know that meantime I mentioned earlier? We're in it. You're not the only reporter here with contacts. One of them is going to find out Dana is dead, and once that happens, a judicial gag order won't stop it from spreading. We have an advantage right now. Let's make the most of it."

Jamie rubbed his jaw again, then said, "As soon as Baxter calls, we let the police take charge and we're done." He looked at me meaningfully. "Done, done."

"Done," I agreed. "How do you want to work this?"

"Like you said, start talking to people, asking questions about Dana, and see what comes up."

"Who first? Randy or Bjorn?" I asked.

"We can cover more ground if we split up," he said. "Which one do you want?"

"I have more pull with Bjorn, so you take Randy."

Jamie nodded and went to the bar while I stood on tiptoe, scanning the drunk, sweaty, noisy throng for Bjorn's ghostly figure. The band was a couple of songs into their first set, and several couples bounced around on the unfinished plywood dance floor.

"Poppy," a female voice said.

Gah! I had been so intent on trapping Bjorn, I had forgotten I was another hunter's quarry. "Ursula," I said. "Can't talk now."

"Okay."

The simple fact that she let me go so easily made me ask, "What's wrong?"

Ursula narrowed her eyes and I knew that whatever her grievance, she had already laid the blame elsewhere. It would turn out to be trivial, like when her cooks petitioned for time-and-a-half for helping her test cookbook recipes on their day off, or a guest sent back their gazpacho soup at brunch complaining that it was cold. She took a breath, preparing for a torrent.

I held up my hand. "The short version, please."

"Mom is trying to find a girlfriend for Trevor."

Oh, that. Trivial compared to a criminal maniac on the loose. And how could she expect me to care one whit after she drove out with Trevor on his motorcycle just so she wouldn't have to take Nina home? "Tell her he likes redheads," I said.

"Funny."

"Then tell her y'all are dating already."

"Are you crazy!" she said, as if I had proposed that she convert to a raw vegan diet.

"I don't understand why you're trying to keep your relationship a secret. Even Mitch knows."

"She'll start planning our wedding."

I waited to see a playful smirk on her face, but she looked as earnest as an executioner. "You two aren't that serious," I said.

"It doesn't matter," Ursula said, sounding uncharacteristically desperate and whiny. "She does it with everyone I date. She wants grandbabies."

Nina? Grandkids? Un-people brimming with unfriendly bacteria, emptying snotty nostrils onto her designer blouses, wiping jam-sticky fingers on her Queen Anne chesterfield, bawling over the milk they spilled on her Italian marble countertops, grabbing fistfuls of fur from Dolce and Gabbana—well, not fur, because they're Chinese Hairless Cresteds, so grabbing snouts or ears or tails—spilling drinks full of red dye number 789 in her pearl white Lincoln Town-car, wailing when their demands are not met? Those things?

No, Nina's desire for grandbabies did not well up from any grand-maternal feelings, because way down deep inside of her are thorns and crickets. More likely she felt left out of the brag-a-thons among her country club cronies who had grandkids and were always going on about how smart and funny and special they are.

Nina probably saw her potential new title spelled, capitalized, and inflected as "*Grand* Mother."

And that would make Mitch a grandfather. Stepgrandfather. And me a stepaunt. Babysitting, diapers, bottles. And oh, no! Ursula would go on maternity leave, and who would have to run Markham's kitchen until she came back? Ursula and Trevor *both* gone on maternity leave.

"Poppy?"

"Not me, that's who," I said. "Just indulge Nina in her matchmaking game, and tell Trevor to veto anyone she picks."

"I already tried that. Trevor's going along with it because he wants to ingratiate himself with Mom because he wants her to like him because he wants me to tell her about us, too." She glared at Trevor and Candy on the dance floor. "He thinks the whole thing is funny."

"Tell him the truth, then."

"He'd think that was even funnier and act worse."

I had thought to suggest that she flirt with Jamie to get even with Trevor, but then remembered that we weren't in ninth grade. I also finally saw Bjorn, sitting alone at a table in the center of the Field, so I was done wasting time with Ursula.

"It'll all work out," I said.

I headed for Bjorn, who stood suddenly when I approached his table, upending the can of soda in front of him. I almost gave him credit for being a gentleman until I saw Cory Vaughn passing by on the other side, hugging an armload of used tablecloths to his chest.

That was the second time I had seen Bjorn become animated at the sight of Cory. What was it he said in the storage pantry when Cory escaped him? He was hard to pin down. And then Bjorn refused to answer my perfectly innocent question about why he wanted to talk to him. I thought that was a mystery for another time until Bjorn twisted up a handful of the back of Cory's T-shirt.

ELEVEN

Cory wrenched out of Bjorn's grasp and spun around to face him, using the mountain of white linens as a physical buffer between him and his attacker. What on earth was so important that Bjorn refused to wait until after the party to talk to him? They both lived and worked at the farm and saw each other more regularly than a married couple. I doubted Bjorn wanted to know if Cory wanted his breakfast eggs scrambled or poached, or to ask after the health of the pumpkin crop for their Great Gourd preserves.

I needed to get close enough to hear, yet not so close that they would notice, but that was impossible due to the din of inane conversations that had increased with free alcohol consumption. "I love how green this grass is!" "*Shazam!* I poured beer in my wine and made it fizzy!" "What do Cornhuskers taste like?"

I wouldn't hear a syllable unless I stood right next to them.

I have seen enough arguments—had enough arguments—to know that the one who picks the fight is the most invested and therefore the least aware of who is listening and taking notes. Also, Bjorn couldn't see me over that mound of linen, so I stood with my back to Cory and pretended to be interested in Betelgeuse and Rigel in the night sky.

"Look," Cory was saying, "I did what you made me do, and it didn't work."

"Then who voted for her?" Bjorn insisted.

"I don't know."

"You better not be lying to me, kid. You know I still got—"

"Bjorn, I told you I don't know! And now everything's all messed up. Just leave me alone!"

Cory took a step back and we connected rump to rump. "Excuse me," he said, not seeing me as he escaped with his dirty white burden.

Which left me standing in front of Bjorn, but he didn't notice me because he was trying to set Cory on fire with the laser beams of his hateful gaze.

"Hey, Bjorn," I said. "Enjoying yourself?"

He grunted, then turned to me with residual combustion in his blue eyes. I admit I flinched, but I didn't back off. The first two times I had talked to Bjorn, I was a nosy party guest and had tried to be nice. But my friend was dead and the time had come for me to be a nosy investigator, which meant that I was done with nice. "What were you and Cory talking about? What vote? The one involving Dana?"

Dana's name acted as an accelerant, making his eyes burn hotter, but he didn't answer me.

"Why are you so against Dana being president of the Friends?"

He cocked his head. "How is this your business?"

"Simple curiosity," I said. "Like I'm curious whether you've solved that fly problem Valdes keeps citing you for."

"It doesn't matter now." He picked up the empty soda can, crushed it in his hand, then rabbited through the grass without speaking with anyone else.

Jamie was still conferring with Randy at the bar, but he had stayed tuned in to me and Bjorn. The next time he glanced over at me, I took an imaginary sip from an imaginary glass—the universally recognized mime for *bring me a drink*—then stationed myself by the back hedge to wait for him.

He joined me a couple of minutes later.

"Where's my wine?" I asked.

"Wine?"

I repeated the sipping motion.

"Oh, I thought you were telling me your mouth hurts," he said. "It's looking a little better, but it could just be the light."

I said, "Bjorn killed Dana," at the same time Jamie said, "Randy's acting guilty," then we both said, "Really?" and then, "You first."

Jamie Sherwood is the only male in the civilized world who is not a fan of the Three Stooges and was already frustrated with this mild hijinks.

"Go," I said.

Before we even interviewed our suspects, Randy had the most reasons for wanting Dana out of the way, so I expected Jamie to tick off ten fingers' worth of facts he had gathered to support his assertion, but he said, "Randy's hiding something."

"The fact that he put the peroxide in Dana's cup?" I asked.

"He's acting nervous."

"Because he knows we're onto him?"

"No, when I walked up to the bar, Randy was telling Colin he wanted him to finish working the dinner on his own so he could leave. Colin was having none of it, saying he was too new and didn't want to be left alone."

"So because Randy wants to leave early, you think he killed Dana?" I asked. "Are you sure you're not just trying to compete with me—my perp is guiltier than your perp."

"No," he said. "It's all the stuff we know from before—the dirty campaign, the personal attacks between him and Dana, the Friends loss."

"Did you uncover anything new?" I asked.

"Okay, why did your perp do it?"

"Uncross your arms and be nice," I said. "Bjorn is super ticked that Dana was elected president of the Friends."

"Why?"

"No idea, but he cornered Cory and wanted to know if he voted for her. Cory said he didn't and didn't know who did."

"So because Bjorn is upset about the Friends election results, you think he killed Dana?"

I ignored his sarcasm. "How could one vote make a difference? It's not like a real presidential election where the popular vote decides the Electoral College votes."

"That's why it doesn't make sense that the election would rankle Bjorn," Jamie said. "Dana being president wouldn't affect him. It's the farmers who have to work with her."

"Election or not, he has strong negative feelings for Dana," I said. "You saw him after she told him he was a one-trick pony and she'd never hire him."

"Actually, I missed that."

"Well, I told you. Bjorn was furious, and no doubt embarrassed that everyone heard her say it. Plus, Dana died on Bjorn's turf."

"What did Bjorn say about that?" Jamie asked.

"He took off before I could ask."

"Let's get back to Randy," Jamie said. "He had motive, too, but did he have opportunity?"

"Randy stormed off with Mike Glass after the choking incident," I said.

"That certainly can be called opportunity. Did you see where they went?"

"No, but none of Dana's cooks mentioned seeing Randy or Mike in the kitchen."

"Why would they?" Jamie said. "They don't know Dana died, and they don't know you think it's murder."

I gave his arm a few quick taps. "Oh! I'm remembering something! After I checked on Dana's cup, I tried to find the bottle of peroxide they keep in the freezer, but it turned up missing, so I hunted up other sources. I found some OxyGrowth plant food in the outside storage pantry. The main ingredient is peroxide."

Jamie smiled. "You suspect the plants? Think they were taking revenge on Dana for cooking their comrades?"

"Don't be silly," I said. "Plants aren't homicidal."

Jamie laughed. He looked adorable.

"Before you told me Dana died, I was in the storage pantry trying to call you to tell you that Randy thought Colin had been fired, but kept getting interrupted—Randy, Mike, Perry, Megan." I paused, thinking back to whether I had seen Brandon or Cory in the pantry and remembered Brandon carrying the tray of dirty linens right before that. "Cory, Bjorn, and Kevin. All of them came back there. Maybe they were looking for the OxyGrowth."

"Do you know for sure it was OxyGrowth in her cup?" Jamie asked. "And why would they need it if the deed had already been done?"

"No, I don't know for sure it was OxyGrowth," I said. "Maybe they were returning it. Not everything is logical. I just think it's significant that they went back there with some excuse or another, especially Randy, Bjorn, and Cory."

"Our perps," Jamie said.

"You're getting a lot of mileage out of that word," I said. "And why are you so resistant? It's like you don't want to know who killed Dana."

"Of course I do," he said. "But we don't know for certain it's murder, and there are people whose job it is to find killers."

I opened my mouth to refute that, but heard, "Jamie!" and saw Mindy waving her arm as if she were going the distance on a mechanical bull.

"Hold that thought," Jamie said to me.

I closed my mouth and waited for Mindy to herd herself through the Field. When she reached us, she extended a full glass of red wine to me. I had a warmhearted feeling for her until she said, "Hold this for me." She pulled a cell phone from her space-age purse and started texting as she asked, "We all set for tomorrow?"

Jamie recognized that she had started to multitask and answered, "The major players are in place and everything's a go."

"Capital!" she said. She slid her phone closed and held out her hand to me for the glass of wine, which is when someone bumped my arm, sloshing most of the liquid out of the glass and onto Mindy's new boots.

The look she gave me—a mix of disbelief, accusation, and hatred—stopped my apology. Like the looks Pam Ewing flung at Sue Ellen Ewing.

"I'm sure it was an accident," Jamie said, taking the almost-empty wine glass from me with a look that was a mix of disbelief, accusation, and confusion. He took her elbow. "Let's get you to the ladies' room."

As they walked off, I wanted to open my lungs in an Olympic scream of frustration. That Jamie was here all of a sudden, at the party and in my life. That the night I had planned to devote to Drew had been ruined by Jamie's premature presence and now Dana's demise. That Jamie was more interested in schmoozing that East Coast interloper than discovering who killed his friend Dana.

But I'm a grownup, so I didn't scream. I fumed instead.

And then Drew was there with his arm around me. "You okay, Sugar Pop?" he asked. "You look kind of discouraged."

Drew! With all the excitement of working on the case, I had forgotten I had this ally. I didn't need Jamie Sherwood *or* his permission to find the murderer. I had a new helpmate. "Just the opposite," I said. "Let me tell you a story."

We moved to our dinner table, which was still empty and quiet for the moment while Nina and Ursula intercepted Mr. Amooze-Boosh and Ms. Foodie's Taste near the archway. I hadn't seen Daisy and Erik in so long, I figured they left.

I told Drew that Dana had died in the ambulance, then backtracked to explain about Dana winning the election; her altercations with Randy and Bjorn; Randy sending champagne and a message to her via her old sous, Colin Harris, who had either quit or been fired; and my suspicions that someone had probably killed her with food-grade hydrogen peroxide.

"Interesting," Drew said when I had finished. "I think you're right that Randy Dove and Bjorn Fleming have the best motives."

"You do?"

He nodded. "It could be anyone, though."

"Do you want to help me figure out who?"

"Sure," he said. "We'll be like Turner and Hooch."

I raised an eyebrow. "Who's Turner and who's Hooch?"

"*Woof*," he said. "Where's the cup with the peroxide?"

"In the deep freezer in the kitchen."

"Let's take a gander at it." Drew stood and held out his hand to help me up, but I didn't take it. "With our eyes," he said.

"I locked it with a combination lock."

"Make up some health reason you want to see inside, and we'll get one of the farmers to open it."

"Oh, good idea."

Moments later, Drew and I were standing in front of the freezer, but I didn't need to come up with a reason to have it opened. The lock was already off.

Dana's cup was gone.

TWELVE

DREW AND I DIDN'T have time to do more than look questions at each other because we heard angry voices on the other side of the wall. Now that everyone was a suspect, everything was suspicious, and two people arguing in the office during a party was on the high end of suspicious. We stood as still as totem poles, straining to make out their words.

I caught Drew's eye and mouthed, "*Anything*?"

He shook his head. "If we can't hear them, they can't hear us," he said in a normal voice.

I shut the freezer door, then squeezed between it and a butcher block, and put my ear to the wall. "Male and female," I said. "He's saying he can't believe she voted for Dana."

Drew leaned in, and I closed my eyes to listen harder.

"What are y'all doing?" a girl said. We looked back to see Cheri and Kelly standing in the doorway.

Drew loudly kissed the air in front of me, then said, "Picking the wrong place for some private time with my girl." He took my hand. "Come on, Sugar Pop."

The two cooks moved aside to let us leave.

"Did either of you take the measuring cup from the freezer?" I asked.

"No."

"Did you see someone else take it?" Drew asked.

"No."

"That would be too easy," I mumbled.

Drew and I left the kitchen for the washing shed but hadn't gone two feet before Babs Tucker, a sales rep with Lone Star Supply, stopped me. She held a napkin-wrapped can of Shiner Bock in one hand and an unlit cigarette in the other. "It wasn't you who told me," she said, obviously having enjoyed several free beers, "but Beefalo Bull's walk-in busted a coupla days ago, and they got all their meat in coolers on ice."

Old news. Gavin had already shut them down and made them destroy hundreds of dollars' worth of meat, then let them reopen after they fixed their walk-in and promised to study the *Texas Food Establishment Rules* handbook.

"I'll look into it," I told her, because I didn't want Babs trading on the truth with the next gossip she tripped over.

Drew and I watched her weave past the office and into the parking lot, then he went into the storage pantry while I stayed guard outside. "The OxyGrowth is on the top shelf," I said.

"Where?"

I joined him in the pantry, pointing up. "It's right … *dang it!*"

We searched the other shelves but found no white bottles. I thought Drew might have concerns that I was making the whole thing up, but he said, "We've got ourselves a right good mystery."

"It could get dangerous," I said, giving him a chance to take himself off the case.

"Whatever gets me away from listening to Nina and Ursula have a non-fight over Trevor."

I smiled, thrilled to have him not only helping me, but encouraging my efforts. I needed to be cautious, though. Drew was smart, but was he wily? If he didn't have the skill to do this on the Q.T., he might hamper me or possibly jeopardize the investigation. I decided to task him with something small to test his abilities.

"I'll hang around the office and see who comes out, okay?" Drew said, giving his own self something small. "What's your next move?"

I pulled my badge from my pocket. "I think I'll take a peek inside Randy Dove's cooler."

Which turned out to be more challenging than applying lipstick to a pig.

"No customers behind the bar," Randy said, trying to wave me away with the hand that wasn't pouring wine into his glass. "Go, go."

Were I an agent with the Texas Alcohol and Beverage Commission, I would have encouraged Randy to comply by reminding him who I worked for, but the health department has no jurisdiction over his business. Still, I tried. I took a step closer to him and brought my badge up to his eyes. "We've had a possible food poisoning incident tonight and I need to examine the contents of your cooler."

Randy stepped in front of a blue Igloo the size of an ottoman. "I didn't make the food, Dana did. Talk to her."

"I just came from speaking with her cooks," I said. "I need to inspect all consumables on the premises."

Randy looked at Dana's former sous chef. "Can she do this?"

Colin nodded. "She's a health inspector."

I pressed my lips together, trying to temper the triumph sneaking into my smile. "It won't take but a minute," I said.

"What if I refuse?" Randy asked.

I leaned into him, getting a whiff of wine mixed with sweat. "I'll put a Detained sticker on it, which means you can't access the contents, then I'll contact the police and get a search warrant."

The landscape of Randy's face changed from garden-variety annoyance to outrage. Jamie was right: he was definitely hiding something.

I made a show of looking behind him. "Is that Dana?"

Randy whirled around, and I used the pointy toe of my boot to flip open the cooler lid. If my open mouth hadn't prevented me from putting my lips together, I would have whistled at what I saw.

Colin whistled for both of us. "Where did *that* come from?" he asked.

The cooler was halfway full with ice, which is what coolers are designed to hold, but the ice wasn't chilling Chardonnay or champagne or a personal stash of oysters on the half shell. Sitting on top was a clear plastic bag stuffed with money.

Randy slammed the lid shut—as much as a plastic cooler lid can be slammed—and said, "It's nothing."

That's the opposite of nothing, I thought as I sat on the cooler and crossed my legs. "Randy, let me tell you a story," I said. "A couple of weeks ago, I was doing a routine inspection of a Cuban restaurant and saw a flamingo in the dry storage room. Yes, a live one. Not only do flamingos not belong in restaurants, they don't belong in the possession of the average citizen. Now, I didn't get too excited about it because maybe they had a really good reason for keeping a flamingo in the dry storage. So I asked the manager. He told me that the bird had a hurt leg, and sure enough, I saw a bandage on the standing leg."

I tapped the lid I was sitting on. "Something similar seems to be going on here. That much cash doesn't make sense at a private function, especially since you're not taking tips tonight, so maybe there's some other really good reason why you've got it."

"I won a bet," Randy said tersely.

I nodded. That was a good explanation, but the money could be a diversion from what he really had hidden inside—a bottle of food-grade hydrogen peroxide or OxyGrowth and a clear glass measuring cup. I had to see inside that cooler again.

"I'm not going to involve myself with your gambling activities," I said, "but the health department is concerned that this ice is contaminated and is the possible cause of Dana's illness."

Randy snorted a laugh. "Dana was EMSed out of here because of *food* poisoning? Sherwood told me it's her heart." He smiled at Colin. "Not that she has one." Colin looked away.

I stood and picked up a fresh plastic cup from the table. "I need to take a sample, and you'll need to set aside any open bottles of wine that were in the cooler, then dump the ice."

"No open wine has been in there, and I didn't poison Dana," Randy said. He took the plastic cup out of my hand, opened the cooler only as far as necessary to insert the cup, then dragged it through the slush of water and ice. In a real investigation, I would have taken the sample myself.

Randy closed the lid and handed the wet cup to me. "We won't serve this ice," he said.

"Code requires that you dump it."

He snatched the handle of the cooler and rolled it to the end of the bar. "I think I can handle it," he said when he saw that I intended to follow him.

"I need to watch you do it," I said.

Even though I was the one with the badge backed by the authority of the city of Austin, the county of Travis, and the state of Texas, Randy wanted confirmation from his new sales rep. Colin shrugged and nodded.

"This is *ridiculous*," Randy said. "I said I'll dump it. You don't have to shadow me."

If I had a strand of linguine for every time I have heard someone tell me they could be trusted to destroy potentially hazardous food, I could feed every capo in the mafia three meals a day for a year. In truth, people can't be trusted with a lot of things, but especially to destroy consumables and especially at a later time. A lot of things can happen between now and when they get around to it—a memory lapse, a shift change, a justification that it won't hurt anyone this one time. A lot of my job involves babysitting adults.

I said, "Let's dump it in the sink in the washing shed to make sure we don't accidentally contaminate any crops here at the farm."

Randy didn't have an obvious reaction to my mention of the washing shed, but he was already upset, so I wouldn't have noticed any subtle change in the essence of his anger. He towed the cooler across the grass, glancing back at me every two feet as I escorted him through the Field.

When we reached the archway, I turned and looked for Jamie. He stood by the dance floor talking to Mindy, Ursula, and Nina, but watched me, wondering, no doubt, why I was leaving the Field with Randy and a cooler full of who knows what. I gave Jamie an exaggerated wink to gloat a little. Jamie had a feeling Randy was hiding something; I had the something Randy was hiding.

If Randy really had won a bet, did it have something to do with the Friends election? And was it relevant to Dana's death? It looked like a few thousand dollars in $20 bills—not an insignificant amount. Randy could have bet against himself in order to win the money and then...no, that made no sense. If the person Randy made the bet with knew that Randy bet against himself, that person would have also known Randy would throw the election. Or was that the idea? Who was invested enough in Dana's win to do something like that? And why make it a bet? Why not a bribe? And since the winner of the money was here tonight, the loser of the bet had to be here, too.

Or! I had seen blood money Randy intended to pay to a third party to kill Dana, and I was jumping out of the frying pan and into the fire.

Once we reached the plywood walkway, the cooler rolled easier and Randy moved faster. Drew still manned his post in front of the kitchen, talking on his cell phone, or pretending to. He had his back to us while facing in the direction of the office, but he turned when he heard the rumble from the cooler's wheels. He took a step toward us, but I shook my head and he stayed put.

"Where are you going?" I asked Randy when he tried to zoom past the washing shed.

He stopped and dropped his shoulders before wheeling the cooler around and onto the dirt floor to the sink.

"It's just *ice*," I said to him as much as to myself. I wouldn't have played this hand and made him dump any product if his losses affected profits. I also would have used a foodborne illness kit and collected samples into sterile bottles rather than a plastic cup. "Why are you getting your nose out of joint?"

"I have a new sales rep who isn't ready to be left alone, and I already told you we weren't using this ice."

I knew that his first nose-disjointing reason was a lie because Jamie heard Randy tell Colin that he wanted to leave early. As for the second reason, "Why bring all that ice to the party if you're not going to use it?"

"We're not going to use it *now*, not after you told us not to."

I pointed to the sink. "Need some help lifting the cooler?"

"You can go," he said. "I'm here. I'm going to do it."

I still held the sample cup of ice I had carried from the Field, and set it on the counter. "Do you want me to hold the bag of money?"

Out of his mouth came a pained growl as he untucked his shirt. He put himself between me and the cooler with his back to me, then lifted the lid and put the money in his waistband. "*Ach!*" he cried.

"What's wrong?"

"Cold."

Randy maneuvered the cooler closer to the counter, then used a small white plastic bucket to scoop ice into the sink. He seemed to be in a much better mood all of a sudden. The only thing that had changed in the last few seconds, however, was that I could no longer see the bag of money. Why would that matter? I had already seen it once, knew it existed, so he must be hiding something else. Not wanting to miss him sticking other items in his waistband, like peroxide or OxyGrowth, I moved to the other side of the cooler to help.

I turned on the hot water tap to make the ice melt faster, but before it got too hot, I squeezed the sink's spray nozzle and "accidentally" squirted a stream of water at Randy's face and shoulders.

He dropped the bucket into the cooler and jumped back. "What is *wrong* with you!"

"Sorry," I said. "Didn't know she was loaded."

When he pulled up his shirttail to wipe his face, I bent down to dredge the bottom of the cooler with the bucket and get another peep at the money. I saw printing on the bag, something colored green, blue, and brown.

It wasn't the money Randy didn't want me to get a closer look at—it was that bag.

THIRTEEN

"HAPPY NOW?" RANDY ASKED as he dropped his shirt and slammed the lid on the cooler. Again, the aggressive intent of finality was there, but not the effect.

"The health department asks that you sterilize the cooler before you put it into service," I said.

"Anything else?" he asked, white-knuckling the handle.

"I'm curious about something."

"No, I won't give your stepmother a ride to Hyde Park."

"How do you know about that?"

"Her table is right next to my bar."

"What I want to know is, what happens if Dana can't fulfill her duties as president of the Friends?"

"Whoever she chose as vice president and treasurer," he said. "*If* she wants the job."

"She? Do you know who it is?"

"I assume it's a she. Dana White hates men." Randy rolled the cooler forward. "Now, if it pleases the health department, I'm going back to my bar."

"Thank you for your cooperation," I said, then checked the time on my phone. A little after 8:00 PM. If I wanted to solve this mystery tonight, I needed to expedite my investigation by keeping both of my assets employed in covert operations. I stepped out of the washing shed and looked to the left, but Drew was gone. Either he had caught the trail of whoever was in the office, or his cover had been blown and he aborted the mission.

I would have to dispatch Jamie, who, last time I saw him, was doing nothing more consequential than engaging in girl talk with Ursula, Nina, and Mindy. However, if Jamie thought he was helping me meddle, he might refuse the assignment. But not even Mindy Cornhusker could keep him by her side if he was chasing a story.

I called his cell phone. "Did you get Ursula to confess to killing Dana?" I asked when he answered.

"Not yet," Jamie said, "but I'm looking at Randy Dove coming through the archway, and he looks rattled."

"You were right that he's hiding something. Come on up to the washing shed and I'll tell you."

"I'm kind of in the middle of something."

"Something important with Mindy?"

"Not really," he said, quickly switching modes from business-man to boyfriend. "Give me two minutes."

I poured the sample cup of ice and water down the drain because I had never intended to have it tested. It was one thing to waste Randy's time, but I wouldn't waste the state lab's resources.

Jamie's two minutes turned into five, which turned out to be good because Colin Harris came through the archway, chin buried in his chest, his strides long and hard against the plywood. Jamie followed a few steps behind him. Colin went past the kitchen, then me, then the office. Was he leaving? No, no, no, he couldn't leave.

I rushed out to meet Jamie and rapid-fired my intel. "Randy is hiding a bag of money in his cooler. Colin saw it, but didn't seem to know about it. Randy said Dana doesn't have a heart and looked at Colin when he said it." I pointed at the parking lot. "Colin is leaving."

Even though Jamie was dying to pump me for money details, and I was dying to know what kind of conversation he could have possibly been having with that coven, I had handed him an enticing lead on a story that was now time-sensitive and he was activated.

"Ursula wants to talk to you," Jamie said as he turned to follow Colin.

I nodded that I heard him, but Ursula was last in line. First in line was the bottle of food-grade hydrogen peroxide missing from the freezer and the bottle of OxyGrowth missing from the storage pantry, either of which was hopefully with Dana's measuring cup. And if I didn't find something to eat soon, I was going to take to the herb garden and start grazing on rosemary.

At the thought of sustenance, my stomach grumbled, and I remembered the CSA boxes full of freshly washed vegan offerings. The washing demo ... of course! *That's* why the peroxide wasn't in the freezer. Brandon and Cory had used it to wash the vegetables. So what did they do with it afterward?

It wouldn't hurt to sift through the boxes while I was in the vicinity.

They rested side by side on the pallet on the dirt floor. Two of them. Brandon told me Cory had stayed behind after the demo to make up more boxes. Cory said he made a couple before Ian called him to help mend the fence. "A couple" can be anywhere from two to five, but there were definitely only the original two. No more.

Cory was racking up the circumstantial evidence against him. I knew I should be impartial, but I couldn't help wishing it was Kevin who had poisoned Dana.

And then I realized that I had been so focused on corroborating my suspicions, I hadn't given any thought to what it would mean to solve Dana's murder. It meant that someone I knew—had known for years—killed her. I had to suspect not just hardheaded Brandon and sweet Cory, but prickly Kevin, generous Perry and Megan who opened their hearts and their farm to strangers every day, hard-working Ian and Tanya who were mostly responsible for the growth of the farm, and talented Bjorn who had doubled the farm's prepared food sales.

Identifying one of them as the killer would take them off the farm, out of the world, forever.

Just like one of them had done to Dana.

Personal relationships have never swayed me as a health inspector, and they wouldn't sway me now. If the Girl Scouts awarded a Dirtbag Takedown badge, I was going to earn it.

And I would have to hurry. The night was getting on, and people like Colin who didn't live at the farm would eventually leave, so I didn't have the leisure of questioning people in my own time, and I didn't want to drive all over tarnation the next day, making up some excuse for wanting to talk to people I had seen the night before. I still needed to ask Dana's cooks whether they saw Randy or Mike Glass in the kitchen, and talk to Mike to determine if he had a beef with Dana. Jerry Potter, too—find out for myself what confidences were worth twenty bucks to Jamie.

I opened one of the boxes and saw the demo veggies of onion, peppers, and broccoli, but no peroxide. Same thing with the other box. I slid the boxes to the other end of the wooden pallet and peered through the slats in case evidence had fallen through. I thought I saw something in the dirt near the corrugated metal wall and reached around to pull my flashlight out of my inspector's backpack, forgetting my civilian status that night. No backpack, so no flashlight.

I looked around to make sure that no one had become interested in me, then flipped open my phone and shined the dim light between the slats. Something caught the light, but my arm wasn't long enough to reach it. I dropped to my knees on the pallet, tensing at the rough wood biting into the tender peroxide welts, stuck my butt in the air, and snaked my hand between the slats.

I was groping around for the item when a man said, "I didn't know there was a full moon tonight."

I jerked my hand back. "Tre-vor!"

"Don't get up for me, darlin'," he said.

I lifted up to sit on my heels, but they landed on the edge of the pallet, sending me bakery over biscuits to the dirt floor, which made me decide to never wear a skirt again.

"What are you doin'?" he asked, extending his hand.

"Yoga," I said, as he yanked me up to standing. "Puppy pose. It's good for the back."

Trevor turned me around and began dusting off my shoulders. "Looks like you were tryin' to grab hold of something."

"I can do the rest," I said, dusting off my fanny. "I saw something shiny in the dirt."

Trevor moved the CSA boxes to the dirt floor then lifted up the pallet.

I could have done that.

I moved closer to the wall and shined my phone along the edge. I picked up a coin about the size of a half dollar. Not money, though. A cheap gold disc with "1 Day at a Time" printed on one side and "24 Hours" on the reverse. It had other words and images, but I couldn't make them out.

Trevor replaced the pallet on the floor. "What is it?" he asked.

"Looks like kid's play money," I said, handing it to him.

"This is an AA medallion," he said. "For newcomers who've stayed sober twenty-four hours."

I tilted my head and looked up at him.

"Not me," he said. "My parents. It's what killed my dad."

"I'm so sorry, Trevor."

"It was a long time ago." He handed the coin to me. "Anyway, that's what it is."

"Sorry to bum you," I said. "What are you doing out here, anyway?"

"I'm on my way back to the matchmakin' drama," he said to me, then to a Goth-looking guy passing down the walkway, "Thanks for the smokes, dude. Catch you later."

"Smokes plural?" I asked.

Trevor ran both hands through his shoulder-length blond hair, bunched it into a ponytail, then let it go. "They're like potato chips," he said.

"Ursula's going to smell it on you."

"Only if she kisses me, which she won't do with her mama around," he said. "I know what I'm doin.'"

"Did you see a protein bar in my backpack?"

"This thing?" Trevor reached into his front pocket and pulled out a silver wrapper. "Tasted like cardboard."

I narrowed my eyes at him. "But you finished it anyway."

He shrugged. "We missed dinner."

When he left, I considered the medallion. Other than Jerry's highly suspect assertion that Dana drank vodka for breakfast, I hadn't heard any rumors in that vein about her. Even if she had a problem and was seeking professional help, it seemed unlikely that she would bring the coin with her to the party.

Bjorn said he hadn't had a drink in six years, so was Brandon or Cory a newly recovering alcoholic? Or someone else at the farm? It could belong to anyone, of course. A lot of people had crowded into the washing shed during the demo, not a few of them without substance abuse issues. It could also have been dropped much earlier, but it didn't have dirt on top of it, so I didn't think it had been there very long.

I couldn't figure an immediate correlation between alcoholism and cold-blooded murder or between alcoholism and Randy's money, but I saved the coin in my pocket in case it became relevant later.

I was so hungry, I could have eaten a sink full of half-thawed tobacco-marinated scallops. If I ate broccoli from the CSA box, I would mess up someone's delivery, so I went to the kitchen to demand food from Dana's cooks. I had paid for dinner, darn it. Well, Mitch had. But a meal had been purchased for me, and I wanted it.

At first I was so annoyed that I didn't see a single chef's coat when I walked in, I failed to see the blessing of having the scene of the crime to myself. My denseness continued as I entered the walk-in to find something I could eat unheated, standing up, and with my hands.

Earlier, Cheri had returned from there with bread when she went after the champagne, but all I found were raw eggs—presumably the ones the Friends had gathered during the tour—an unlabeled tub of something thick and brown that could have been either chocolate sauce or year-old beef stock, and a gallon bucket of shelled pecans dated two days earlier. Finally. Something that hadn't been laid or born.

I would violate health code if I laded out a handful with my bare, unwashed hands, especially after I had sifted dirt and handled an alcoholic newcomer's medallion. But oh, my stomach wanted them *now*. I searched the shelves for a box of rubber gloves or a cup to scoop them with. I didn't find any of those, but I did see a little white bottle on the top shelf. OxyGrowth!

FOURTEEN

THAT WAS A TWOFOLD whammy for Good Earth because aside from the possibility of it being the murder weapon, storing chemical compounds above food is a critical health violation, even if they are natural and organic.

I had the same problem as in the storage pantry—no way to lift it down without leaving my fingerprints. I left the walk-in to fetch gloves, a plastic bag to preserve the evidence, and a stepstool to reach it, but before the door clicked shut, I heard voices. Dana's cooks.

"And then she said, 'I asked for *cough* syrup, not *corn* syrup,'" Cheri said, and they all laughed.

"Remember that time we ran out of liver—" Tarzan noticed me. "Need help with something?" he asked.

"I missed dinner," I said. "Do you have any green bean casserole left?"

"We tossed it," Kelly said. "Sorry."

"And we're getting ready to join the party," Tarzan said quickly, probably to forestall me asking them to stay and make something for me, even though, as far as they knew, I had saved Dana's life and they should be falling all over themselves like Jewish grandmothers to feed me.

"I thought you had to do one more coffee service," I said.

"It's coffee in the kitchen if anyone wants it," Tarzan said. "Bjorn said he'd handle it."

"Poppy!" Ursula called from the doorway.

"Busy, Ursula," I said over my shoulder.

"I have a message for you," she said.

"Is that Ursula *York*?" the other male cook said, smiling like an aspiring backup dancer glimpsing Madonna. Was he interested in her as a chef and cookbook author or as an exonerated murderess? Perhaps he killed Dana and wanted tips from Ursula on how to beat the charges.

Oh, wow. I just heard my thoughts. One of Dana's cooks could have done it. I knew that Dana was gifted and manic—think Ursula, but with twenty more years of experience—but bad enough to incite someone to end her life?

Not impossible.

A restaurant kitchen is a lot like a department in a traditional business. The chef is the manager, and the sous chef, line cooks, prep cooks, and dishwashers are the employees. The manager gets indigestion over such things as costs, profit margins, and employee morale, and the employees make as little effort as possible to keep their boss happy so they continue to receive a paycheck.

Occasionally, managers do things that employees don't agree with—cut hours, dock pay, make unwanted romantic advances. And occasionally, every employee would make the same request of a wish-granting genie all three times: make my boss drop dead. Did one of Dana's cooks decide to grant that wish? And to what end? Dana White *is* Vis-à-Vis and the White Wolff Inn. Without her, the restaurants would probably close their doors for good, and those cooks wouldn't have a timecard to punch.

I didn't know of any motives yet, but they'd had several hours' worth of opportunity. And what better time to do it than on a busy night in an unfamiliar kitchen with a bunch of inebriated strangers on the premises?

"*Momentito*," I said to Ursula, then to the spellbound cook, "She's my stepsister. Why? Think you're going to be out of a job soon?"

"No. I'm … she's brilliant."

"So I hear," I said, then stepped outside to speak with her. "What's up?"

"Daisy and Erik left," Ursula said. "She wants you to call her as soon as they announce the winner of the recipe contest."

"Now that we're on the topic, I hear you're planning to include my recipe for salmon cakes in your cookbook."

She grimaced. "*Your* recipe?"

"If it's the one Markham's serves, then yes, *my* recipe."

"That's not yours," she said with certainty.

"It's not *yours*," I said at the same time my cell phone rang. "We were already serving it when you invaded my kitchen. Ask Mitch."

"I will," she said, then walked toward the Field as if Mitch were in there.

Jamie was on the other end of the line. "Where you at?" he asked. He sounded upbeat, so he must have gotten something good from Colin. Or maybe his stomach was full of food and wine. Satiation can have that effect on one's disposition.

"I'm in the kitchen dying of starvation," I said.

"Meet me in the washing shed."

"Right," I said. Thirty seconds later, I asked him in person, "What did you get from Colin?"

"He was driving off when I reached the parking lot," Jamie said.

"Where were you this whole time?"

"Having a smoke with the cooks."

Jamie doesn't smoke, but he'll hold a lit cigarette while he hangs out with people who do. He hears a lot of gossip that way.

"Did they admit to treason against Queen Dana?" I asked.

"They said she hasn't been feeling good lately, and she put Colin in charge of the Wolff this summer while she runs Vis-à-Vis."

"Dana handed Colin a hot downtown restaurant, and he quit to hawk wine for Randy Dove?"

"They thought it was strange, too, but none of them knew why he quit," Jamie said.

"Randy may be right that Dana fired Colin. He may have stolen from her or something."

"It's on my list to follow-up," Jamie said. "How did you get Randy to open the cooler?"

"I told him I wanted to investigate the possibility of food poisoning. He didn't want to play along, so I had to pull a fast one. When you saw us, we were on our way to dump the possibly contaminated ice so I could get a better look at the money. It's about five thousand dollars or so in a plastic bag. Randy told me he won a bet."

"That's some major wager."

"I thought so, too. Should be a good story if you can find out who, what, and why."

"*If* Randy told you the truth."

"Why else would he have that much money on him?" I said. "And don't say money laundering."

Jamie pressed his lips together.

"We also might need to look closer at Cory for Dana's murder." I told him that Cory used food-grade hydrogen peroxide during the washing demo, and that he was alleged to have stayed behind to make up extra CSA boxes, but the two from the demo were the only ones on the pallets. I pointed to them in the corner. "Maybe he stayed behind to kill her."

"Maybe," Jamie said in a way that sounded a lot like, "doubtful."

"Are you shooting down my suspects to stall for time until you hear from Baxter?"

Which reminded him to check for missed calls on his phone. "No, but Cory Vaughn? Why would he?"

"That's what we're trying to determine," I said. "Do you know who Dana was going to choose as her vice president? Randy told me that's who'd become president."

"Her husband, I imagine."

"And if Herb doesn't want to do it?"

"Why wouldn't he?"

"How am I supposed to know?" I said, crabby from lack of food and cooperation. "But what if?"

"I don't think there's a procedure for that," Jamie said. "Maybe another election."

"And Randy remains president in the meantime?"

"Probably, but why would he want Dana out of the way just to remain president for another month or two?"

"Maybe he wanted a do-over with an opponent he could beat."

"Maybe," he said, again in the tone of doubtful. "What else did you find?"

I pulled the medallion from my pocket, but he didn't see it because he was looking past me toward the archway. "Nothing," I said, making a fist around the coin. "Mosey on back to Mindy Corrosion."

Jamie frowned at me. "Have you eaten anything tonight?"

As if my annoyance was due to a lack of calories and carbs and not his fawning over that drugstore cowgirl! "I haven't had time, what with trying to figure out who killed Dana." I waved my hand dismissively. "Let me know when you hear from Baxter."

Jamie rolled his eyes and returned to the Field, and I placed a call to my other asset.

"Are you finished with Sherwood?" Drew asked.

"We were talking about Dana. He's gone now. Where are you?"

"In the parking lot. Stay where you are."

Drew joined me a few moments later, a scowl on his face that I thought was owing to Jamie, so I didn't ask if he was okay.

"Did you see who was in the office?" I asked.

"No." His gloom deepened. "The voices stopped, so I knocked on the door to, you know, pretend to be looking for the bathroom. No one answered, so I went by the parking lot to the other side and there's another entrance they must have gone out."

"That's okay," I said. "Not everything is going to go as planned."

Drew nodded. "What did you find?"

I quickly filled him in on Randy's claim that he won a bet, me making him dump the ice so I could examine inside his cooler, my theory that the money bag was important, and finding a bottle of OxyGrowth in the walk-in.

"I also found this." I showed him the medallion. "Trevor helped me get it from under the pallet the CSA boxes are on." I told him what Trevor had explained about its significance. "I don't think it means anything to us, but whoever lost it may have seen something."

Drew took the coin and rolled it back and forth across his knuckles, then dropped it into his palm. "Do you see that mark?" he said, pointing to a thin, bright-pink slash near the rim.

"Nail polish," I said. I knew then that the coin didn't belong to Dana because her fingernails were always short and natural. "Good catch." I put the coin in my pocket. "Let's both keep an eye out for pink nails."

"Did you say you found OxyGrowth in the walk-in?" Drew asked.

"Violating health code on a top shelf," I said. "Come help me get it down and test it."

We hadn't gotten past the kitchen's threshold before we encountered our first obstacle: Bjorn at the countertop plugging in a coffee pot. He looked up when he heard me groan. "You guys want some coffee?" he asked.

What was this? Bjorn Fleming being nice for no reason? "Sure," I said.

Bjorn walked over to the deep freezer, which had been locked again. Drew and I watched him scroll through the combination, but he couldn't snap it apart. He turned to the right to look at something on the wall, then tried the combination again and it opened. "New lock," he said.

I stepped closer to him in case he had the idea to steal evidence—or plant some—but he pulled out a bag of coffee beans. As he went about grinding the beans, I approached the freezer with the unreasonable hope that a Good Samaritan had returned the measuring cup I had safekept there earlier. They hadn't.

I glanced at the wall and saw three numbers written in pencil underneath the first aid kit. What was the point of locking the freezer when anyone with eyeballs and opposable thumbs could get the combination and open it?

I was glad to have time with one of our suspects, but that Oxy-Growth in the walk-in wasn't going to test itself. When the bean grinder stopped, I said, "Hey, Bjorn, I'm starving. Mind if I get something from the walk-in?"

"Help yourself," he said as he filled a carafe with tap water. "But we may be out of food after those storm troopers moved through."

"Do you have any gloves?" I called over the running water.

He used his elbow to point to a shelf under the prep table. I plucked a few from the box, then beckoned Drew into the walk-in with me. I handed him a glove, then pointed up to the OxyGrowth bottle.

Drew tugged a glove onto his right hand, then took down the bottle from the shelf. It looked like the bottle from the storage pantry, but it wasn't the exact same one, unless someone rinsed off the mud. But why? And why put it in the walk-in? The fact that nothing made sense was making this whole investigation much more difficult. Probably the killer's intent. It would take the police forever to catch up to the nuances of all this evidence. Lucky for them Drew and I were on the case.

"I think we should try to eliminate possibilities," I said. "Let me test this to see if it acts the same as what was in Dana's cup." I put on gloves, then opened the tub of pecans and pinched out a piece.

"I don't know, Sugar Pop … it's one thing to talk to people, but this … "

"It'll be fine," I said. I handed the pecan to him then opened the bottle and poured a quarter teaspoon of the OxyGrowth into its little red top.

Drew was right, though. There were so many things wrong with what we were doing. Conducting a chemical experiment in the walk-in would be a critical health violation for Good Earth if they got surprise inspected at that moment. We hadn't officially reported any crime, so investigating Dana's death on our own instead of waiting for the police might result in a charge of obstruction of justice. And then there was the small matter of tampering with evidence.

I made eye contact with Drew and nodded for him to drop the pecan into the liquid. "It takes a few seconds," I said. I lightly sloshed the lid to wake up the action. Still nothing. I poured more liquid from the bottle into the top.

"Maybe it's diluted too much," Drew offered.

I brought the lid up to my nose and sniffed, drenching my olfactory senses with a most foul, disgusting, stomach-churning stench. I drew back and extended my arm to get the vile stuff away from me.

"Chemicals?" Drew asked.

"Gin."

FIFTEEN

"WHY ALL THE THEATRICS?" Drew asked.

"I got sick on gin when I was fifteen." I laughed. "At this very farm, actually. Me, Daze, Brandy, and Kevi drank gin and orange juice that Kevi snuck from his parents' house. I threw up in the car on the ride home and Goodie Luke Shoes told my parents why. They put me on restriction for two months."

"Poppy Markham broke a rule?" Drew said.

I shrugged. "It wasn't a rule until the next morning."

"Gin's used in cooking, right?"

"Stored in an OxyGrowth bottle?" I've seen liquor decanted into everything from a turkey baster to an old fire extinguisher. "No, this is a secret stash."

"The newcomer's?" Drew asked.

"That's what I'm thinking, so it probably isn't related to Dana's death."

"Someone may have tried to give Dana gin, but mixed up the OxyGrowth bottles and poisoned her instead."

"Okay, yeah, that's a workable theory," I said, "but I'm still not sure if she drank OxyGrowth. Let's see if we can find a real bottle of the stuff and test it."

Drew nodded. "In light of this stash, the lush has to be someone at the farm."

"It could also be a one-time thing," I said. "Whoever it is may have wanted something harder than beer or wine tonight."

"A normal person carries it with them in a flask," Drew said. "Do you think it's Bjorn's?"

I shook my head. "I heard him tell Dana he's been sober six years."

"Alcoholics have been known to lie," Drew said.

Bjorn knocked on the walk-in door and called, "Coffee's ready."

Drew poured the tested liquid down the floor drain, then popped the gin-drenched pecan piece into his mouth. "Yum," he said as he screwed the top onto the bottle and returned it to the shelf. He removed his gloves and shoved them in his pockets, and I did the same.

"After we drink coffee," I said, "I'm going to stick around and talk to Bjorn and look around a little more."

Then I must have sighed out loud because Drew said, "What?"

"I can comb through the kitchen pretty good, but what if it's not here? There are a *squillion* places to hide stuff on this entire farm. The killer could have buried it or poured it out. It could be in the chicken coop, in their car, at their house. Heck, Dana's cooks could have taken it." I waved my hand in the direction of the hard-to-find evidence. "*It*," I repeated. "I don't even know exactly what I'm trying to find."

Drew put his hands on my shoulders and waited for me to meet his eyes. "You're looking for a bottle of food-grade hydrogen peroxide or OxyGrowth, or the measuring cup Dana was drinking from." He kissed me on the forehead. "You need to eat something."

"But we're running out of time," I said. "In a couple of hours, the party will be over."

"You want to solve this *tonight*?"

"Sure. I'm getting pretty good at catching killers. If I could just catch a break. I have too many suspects and I can't be everywhere at once."

"How about I go into the Field and watch everyone?"

"You know what they all look like?"

"I know Randy Dove. He's giving me full glasses of Opus because he wants Markham's business. Mike Glass is our Waterloo rep, and I recognize the family from tonight, Perry, Cory, and Brandon."

"And Kevin," I said. "And see if you can get Mike to tell you what happened after Randy choked at dinner."

"Roger that," he said.

I felt better after talking to Drew. He has that effect on everyone, which is what makes him such a good restaurant manager, and a good man. Everything always has an answer, and if you can't see it right away, Drew somehow makes you believe you will eventually.

Before I could push the safety bar on the walk-in door, it flew open. Nina stood on the other side, her purse in hand, another purse on her lips. I was already cold, but I swear her presence dropped the temperature ten degrees.

"I've been to the *moon* and back looking for you," she said testily. "I want to go home."

I looked past her at Bjorn sitting on a stool at the prep table, three white ceramic cups of coffee in front of him. "I'm in the middle of something," I said.

"I'll be happy to take you home, Nina," Drew said.

Nina looked up and smiled. "Oh, Drew, I didn't see you there." She patted hairs that are never out of place. "If you don't mind."

I would be nicer to her if she talked to me that way.

"It would be my pleasure," he said, easing us both into the kitchen. "Do you need anything before we go?"

"Maybe one more trip to the ladies' room," she said, then to me, "You might want to take a look in a mirror some time tonight, Poppy."

After she left, I said, "How's my mouth?" I lifted my chin to give him a better view. "Feels like the welts are going down."

He gave my face a thorough inspection. "Almost unnoticeable."

"You know she's not my mother, right? You don't have to be that nice to her."

"I'm being nice to my boss' wife," he said. "Besides, she brings me coffee from Dolce Vita whenever she comes to the restaurant." He gave me a light peck on the nose and said softly, "I'll be back in an hour. Watch yourself."

Ick. Gin.

I saw Drew to the kitchen door, then went over to Bjorn at the prep table and picked up a cup. "Smells good," I said.

"My own blend," Bjorn said. "Did they leave any food in there?"

"Not really."

"I can make you an omelet," he said.

Bjorn seemed like a different person, more relaxed and at peace. Perhaps the stress of having intruders in his domain had twisted him up earlier and their departure allowed him to unwind.

"I'm vegan," I said.

"Oatmeal?" he suggested.

"With some raisins?"

"I can do that."

Bjorn slid off his stool and crossed to the dry storage shelves on the far wall. He had been unattended in the kitchen while Drew and I experimented in the walk-in and could have occupied himself with anything, including, I realized, poisoning my coffee. Is that why he was being so nice? I wanted to get something in my stomach, but I also wanted to survive the evening, so I poured my coffee down the sink drain.

Bjorn returned with a tin canister of oatmeal. "It'll be a few minutes. More coffee?"

"I'll never sleep," I said, then didn't know what to say next. I wanted to ask him about Cory and Dana and the vote, but didn't want to set him off and be banished from the kitchen, or worse—make him want to take revenge on my food. Can you imagine the things that could go undetected in a bowl of oatmeal? I decided to work up to it with something neutral. "How's Tanya?" I asked.

"Haven't seen her." He reached under the stove for a saucepan, which brought him eye-to-eye with my knees. "Did you fall down?" he asked.

It's not often that a fish throws you a line with which to catch it. "You heard Dana passed out, right? This happened when I knelt on the floor to resuscitate her."

He stood and emptied oatmeal into the saucepan, then went to the sink and poured water into it. "Looks like it's from the floor mats," he said. "Indentations from the pressure."

"That's what I thought at first, but they wouldn't last this long. Plus, it stings a little." I waited a significant beat. "Like from a chemical."

He ignored the beat and the imputation and fired up a burner, then placed the saucepan on the stove. "We're all organic out here," he said. "No chemicals."

"Don't y'all use food-grade hydrogen peroxide as a natural cleaner?" I considered that I might be on dangerous ground mentioning the murder weapon to the possible killer, but Bjorn didn't know I suspected foul play, and cleaning habits were a perfectly legit conversational topic for a health inspector to have with a cook.

"Not lately," he said. "Kevin says it's too expensive." He poured himself more coffee, then indicated the dry storage shelves on the other side of the kitchen. "Bring me the raisins."

"Sure," I said. Out of habit, I took my time walking over there, glancing the compass, west, north, east, and south, but only with my eyes. Health inspectors have to act just as sneaky and clever as restaurant staff. If a cook saw me twitch my head to look at a half-eaten plate of French fries on the counter, it would have disappeared by the time I washed my hands and looked again. Nothing caught my attention until I saw a bulging linen bag in front of the shelves.

A full linen bag is the perfect place to conceal small contraband—a fifth of vodka for a quick nip here and there throughout the night (or morning, depending on how close you are to needing a newcomer's medallion); stolen cash, wallets, clothes, jewelry, pens, drugs, or credit card receipts from waiters, managers, cooks, and customers; frozen steaks or seafood, especially right before a full bag is exchanged for an empty one; and murder weapons.

Even though restaurants know that the linen bag is a good hiding place, things still go missing that way. Most restaurants make the dishwasher or one of the wait staff rummage through the contents looking for accidentally discarded flatware, plates, bowls, cups, ramekins, and the aforementioned stolen items, but the inspection is perfunctory. Think of the things you have put into a napkin—chewed-up gristly meat, mucous, coughed-up phlegm, puke, blood, smushed spiders or roaches. Now imagine you're a waiter assigned to dredge through the napkins at the end of your shift. And now imagine how much effort you're going to put into it.

I didn't want to dig through the linen either, not only because I had left my haz-mat suit at the office, but because I would have to explain it to Bjorn. It would be something else entirely, however, if the bags fell and spilled their contents. I wedged a leg between the bag and the shelves then threw my hips back to dump it over. It's a thin metal frame under a canvas sack, so it should have made as much noise as a Las Vegas blackjack dealer dispensing cards. However, the bag's strings had been tied to a small, lidless tub of flatwear on the shelf, so that came down with it, making as much noise as a dollar slot machine paying off a jackpot.

Bjorn rushed across the kitchen. "What are you doing?" he demanded, sounding like the Bjorn of yore.

I smiled innocently. "I guess I'm not as skinny as I thought. I'll clean this up."

"I got it," he said, swatting at my hand that had reached for the bag. He put his leg against the spilled contents as he stood the bag up and all the whites went neatly back inside.

"Why are the linens tied to a bunch of forks?" I asked.

He dropped to one knee and started clinking the forks into the tub. "To alert me in case they came to pick it up and I wasn't here."

It made sense that Bjorn wanted to know if a vendor had come into his kitchen when he wasn't around. It's not unheard of for them to throw a few loose items into the linen bag before hauling them to their truck. However, my guess was that he wanted to know that the peroxide and measuring cup he had hidden within would soon leave the farm.

"They're right there," Bjorn said, pointing to a low shelf.

"What?"

"The raisins."

"Wait, do you . . . " I sniffed the air. "Is something burning?"

Bjorn jumped up and dashed to the stove. "See what you did!" he cried, snatching up the smoking saucepan.

Um, no. "It's okay," I said, walking up to him. "I'll wash the pot and we can make some more."

The pot clanged when he flung it into the sink. "That was the last of it."

And why shouldn't that be the last of it? Maybe I wouldn't be so hungry if I considered my time away from food as a fast to help purify my system and make me more virtuous. "Can I have some of those shelled pecans in the walk-in?" I asked.

He clasped his hands in front of his belly then nodded toward the other side of the kitchen. "Grab a bag so you can *take them back to the party with you.*"

I returned to the storage shelves and slipped a plastic bag off the top of the stack.

It was the same kind of plastic bag that held Randy's money.

SIXTEEN

It had the word GOOD encircling a green and blue image of the earth. It was the farm's old logo, which is why I didn't recognize it when I saw it in Randy's waistband.

Ten or so years ago, the sons convinced their parents to bring their business into the modern era, which included putting up a website for e-commerce, switching the newsletter from black-and-white printed copies to full-color copies delivered via email, and modernizing the logo. In the newsletter, we learned that the boys wanted something completely different, but Perry and Megan said their logo had become a recognizable trademark. They ran a contest for subscribers (they love contests) to design a new one with those two directives. The one that received the most nods was an updated version from the rounded hippie image to a graphic woodcut style.

This development triangulated into the only people with access to the kitchen, and thus, those old bags: the farm's owners, employees, and guest cooks. But since I already had a list of suspects, I narrowed them down further to people who had both a reason and an opportunity to have dealings with Randy, which meant that whoever gave Randy all that money was either a Vaughn or a Mc-Dougal. Or Bjorn Fleming.

If the money was a payoff on a bet, was it related to the farm? Had they wagered on the success of the garlic crop? The number of people to attend the dinner? How many eggs a particular hen could lay in a month? No, I was thinking too small. This was thousands of dollars. What sort of bet would be worth risking that much money? Yesterday's Texas Longhorn's game, certainly, but why didn't Randy just say so?

I passed Bjorn on my way to the walk-in and smiled to assure him that I didn't suspect him of dirty dispensations. When I stopped in front of the door and pulled a glove from my front pocket, the gold newcomer's medallion came out with it. The coin tinkled as it hit the concrete floor, then rolled to Bjorn's feet.

He bent down and picked it up. "What are you doing with this?" he asked quietly. It was more of a menacing quiet than a sad, thoughtful quiet.

I went with the truth. "I found it in the washing shed."

"Where in the washing shed?"

"In the dirt under the CSA boxes from the demo."

Before I could ask why he wanted to know where I found it or discover its relevance to Dana's death or call finders-keepers, Bjorn made a fist around it and raced out of the kitchen. By the time I decided to follow him—because with an exit like that, where else would he go except to hunt down the person who lost the coin—he had vanished.

My amateur investigation was forcibly and prematurely concluded, however, when two police cruisers and two American-made black sedans prowled into the parking lot. No sirens or lights, so they weren't in a hurry.

I retreated down the walkway and called Jamie. When he answered, I said, "You finally talked to Baxter, I see."

"Not yet."

"Well, somebody talked to somebody because four cop cars just pulled up. Did you tell anyone Dana died?"

"No, did you?"

I hesitated.

"You told Cooper, didn't you?"

"I needed his help, but he wouldn't have said anything. Maybe the police are here for some other reason."

"I thought you needed *my* help."

"Not as much as Mindy does, apparently."

"Where are you?" Jamie asked, annoyed.

"My new headquarters, the washing shed."

"Meet me by the bandstand," he said. "Perry and Megan are getting ready to announce the winner of the recipe contest, and I need to tell you something I found out."

"I think I'll stick with the cops." Two uniformed officers stayed near the parking lot, while two others followed two guys in suits past me on their way to the Field. "Belay that," I said. "See you in two shakes."

I hung up and followed the officials to the archway where the uniforms paused, legs wide, both thumbs hooked into the fronts of their utility belts. They blocked the escape of a few guests who had panicked at the sight of the law, but none were my suspects.

Most everyone had kept their eyes on Perry and Megan on the stage. Perry shuffled some papers in his hand, then bent down to put his mouth to the mic and said, "Bear with me." Megan smiled at the audience, her glittering eyes turning overcast when she registered the official uniforms.

One of the cops pointed at the bar and the four men started walking. Megan thumped Perry's arm to indicate the new arrivals, so of course two hundred faces turned to see the cops approach an odd foursome consisting of Randy Dove, Bjorn Fleming, and Brandon and Cory Vaughn.

The eyewitnesses fell as hushed as a snowfall, so we all heard one of the detectives announce, "Corrigan Jeremiah Vaughn, you're under arrest."

SEVENTEEN

HOLY LONG ARM OF the law! How did they even begin to suspect Cory, much less assemble enough evidence to make an arrest? Had Dana's dying words fingered him before she died? Or maybe someone at the farm dropped a dime on him. I didn't think his family would do it, so that left Bjorn. But how did Bjorn know Cory killed Dana? Were they in it together and Cory placed the AA medallion under the CSA boxes as a signal to Bjorn that Dana had been discontinued? Or did I see a falling out earlier, and Bjorn decided to burn Cory? Or did Bjorn falsely accuse Cory to the cops to create a smokescreen?

The detective produced a pair of handcuffs, turned Cory around, and began, "You have the right…"

Cory didn't seem surprised, but I was. Or more like disappointed. It now appeared that I had sacrificed dinner and drink to snoop for evidence and interview perps for nothing.

Before the full Miranda had been recited, Perry and Megan were on the scene, Megan already crying, Perry not smiling for the second time that night. "What is the meaning of this?" Perry demanded of the cops.

"Dad," Cory said, the word loaded with resignation and apology.

Perry glared at his son. "What did you do?"

"It's nothing," Cory said, as much as admitting to it.

Perry stood in front of the detective who now held him. "What did he do?"

Your kid murdered Dana White, I thought, at the same time the detective said, "Possession and distribution of marijuana."

Whoa! Cory? A stoner? Dear little Cory Vaughn who used to hang upside down from the tire swing in the pecan grove with his mouth open to catch the shelled peas we threw at him. This made him a less likely suspect for Dana's death, but I wasn't ready to pull him out of the lineup. Perhaps Dana stumbled onto Cory's secret garden and threatened to expose him.

In the time it took Megan to understand what that meant—her baby boy growing an illegal crop of marijuana on the family farm—she skipped from worried to wrathful. "You're selling pot!" she screamed. "What are you thinking!" She slapped his cheek with every ohm of anger she could generate. "How *dare* you, Cory! How *dare* you do this to us!" She raised her hand to slap him again, but the detective moved Cory aside while a uniformed cop stepped in front of Megan.

Perry intercepted her raised hand. "Not now, Meg."

She turned her anger on Perry. "You think this is *okay*? We're going to lose our certifications, our business license—"

"No, I don't think it's okay," Perry said gently, "but now is not the time."

Megan shook her finger at Cory, then squeezed her eyes shut and let out a strangled mewl.

Perry said to Megan, "I'm going with Cory. Call Harv Gross, please. Tell him what's happened, and ask him to meet me downtown." Megan nodded, wiping her tears with the back of her wrist. Perry hugged her. "We'll get it worked out," he said.

"What about the party?" Brandon asked.

Perry watched the detectives escort Cory through the archway. "Find Ian," he said. "He'll handle it."

———

I didn't know how much time I had before Ian arrived and broke up the party, but I knew it would happen before Drew returned from dropping off Nina, so I called him.

"Hey, Sugar Pop," he said.

"Did you get *La Niña* home okay?"

"Yes, and I'm on two-ninety, passing Congress. I'll be there in twenty-seven minutes."

"The party's breaking up," I said. "Cops came and arrested Cory Vaughn."

"*Cory* killed Dana?"

"Marijuana farming."

"That doesn't surprise me," he said. "I've heard his name mentioned."

"Why didn't you tell me?"

"I thought everyone knew," he said. "Do you want to meet for a late dinner? Magnolia or Taco Xpress?"

"I would love to, but this is my last chance to investigate tonight."

"With Sherwood?" he asked, sounding a little pouty.

"Probably not. We'll talk tomorrow, okay?"

He sighed. "As you wish, Sugar Pop. Remember I'm working at Markham's in the morning."

After we hung up, I saw headlights floating over from somewhere behind the Field. When they stopped by the archway, Ian hopped out of the four-wheeler, his face covered with sweat and irritation. Half the partiers were already atwitter—"I heard they had a meth lab in the barn." "He grew some good stuff." "Got a light?"—and the other half was either drunk or dancing, so Ian had to work to get their attention. Not mine, though. I couldn't take my eyes away from him. His waist-length red dreadlocks had been chopped off and shaped into a buzz cut, long sideburns the only remains of his shaggy beard. I wouldn't have recognized him if I didn't know Brandon had gone to fetch him. Even his tie-dye T-shirts and jeans had been swapped for plaid and khakis. He looked a lot like his son, Kevin.

Ian jumped onto the stage and pushed a surprised lead singer aside, then commandeered the microphone. It took a few moments for the rest of the band to catch up to this, so Ian's first words were accompanied by guitars and drums. "Attention, people!" he said. "Give me your attention!"

Only the dancers and immediate bystanders gave him what he asked for, so Ian wrested the microphone out of its stand and placed it against one of the speakers, creating a piercing screeching sound that shut everyone up and turned their faces to the stage.

"Party's over," Ian said into the mic. "Time to leave."

Like me at first, most people probably didn't recognize Ian, either, which meant they didn't recognize his authority, so they resumed their drinking, talking, and dancing. In the Live Music Capital of the World, Austinites are possessed when it comes to music, and they don't need much more than the tempo of their own heartbeats to keep a rhythm going.

Ian jammed the microphone against the speaker again and let it squeal for what felt like a minute, then said into it, "Go *home*! The party is over. *Now!*"

Ian vaulted off the stage, and he and Brandon began herding people toward the archway. Some moved out of their way rather than move to the exit, confusing the situation and buying me time for one last run at a suspect. I had maybe half an hour before Ian cleared the farm, so I had to work quickly.

The bodies amassed into boisterous congregations, and I grew frustrated that I couldn't zero in on someone to Spanish Inquisition. But then my eyes landed on the perfect solution to my problem.

The former Cornhusker marching band staircase hovered near the chicken coop where it had been stationed earlier during Perry's farm tour talk, which meant that a good view of most of the farm's territory was as simple as climbing eight feet off the ground. Except I have a fear of heights. Or had one until a few months ago when I had been forced into a grudge match with it.

I'm sure it's no surprise that I don't like to be deficient in word or action. A deficiency is a weakness and a weakness can be exploited. I almost lost my life due to that particular weakness, so I determined to overcome it. I also like to solve my own problems, so going to a professional who would call it by it's official name, acrophobia, and then charge me enough money to pay for a run for Congress to help trace my anxiety to a childhood incident involving a kitten, a spatula, and a yellow balloon is not something I would ever do.

So I read some books and learned "coping mechanisms." My fear wasn't completely cured, but now my entire being didn't fast-forward into raw panic when I was higher off the ground than God intended humans to be. Well, I hadn't panicked during my experiments in controlled environments. This would be my first road test in the wild.

I scooted out of the archway and along the hedge, then backed up to the stairs, making sure I wasn't followed or paid attention to. Ian looked my way, but the cloak of darkness was pretty dense where I stood so I doubted he could see me. I broke for the staircase, slipping in the mud, regretting my skirt again.

I reached the stairs and ran up the first three steps, but the hard leather soles of my boots banged against the metal and made a racket that startled the chickens into squawking, so I tiptoed up the remaining ones.

My terror glad-handed my intestines as I neared the top, and I grappled with the techniques I had researched, which mostly consisted of controlling the physical symptoms of queasiness, sweatiness, dizziness, and the mighty desire to evaporate like steam. One technique is to remind yourself that your fears are irrational, but when does telling yourself that you're crazy ever help make a situation better? Another technique is to avoid the predicament altogether, which is how I had coped all these years, but as I already stood closer to heaven than to the earth, it was what you would call *too late*. Plus, I needed to do this for Dana. So I did what usually works when I want to ignore myself, which is take slow, deep, calming yoga breaths, inhaling as I placed my foot on a step, exhaling as I placed the other foot up next to it.

At the top, I dropped to my knees on the small rubber-lined platform, then crawled toward the edge, unreasonably proud that I hadn't fainted from fright. I could see well enough from where I crouched, so standing wasn't necessary. Besides, somebody might notice my blond hair reflecting the moonlight.

In the Field, Randy wheeled his cooler behind him, followed by Mike carrying a cardboard box of bottled wine. They waited a few feet from the archway while the clot in the exiting artery thinned out. I watched Randy open the cooler and drop something into it. Dana's measuring cup? The AA medallion? One for the road?

Dang it! From now on I'm bringing my inspector's backpack with me everywhere I go. I could have used the small monocular I keep in it. It comes in handy for stakeouts, festivals, and really big commercial kitchens.

I shifted my attention to the buildings and saw Ursula yelling at Trevor as they walked the plank path. Bjorn stood outside the washing shed, speaking with someone who was in shadow. And farther down, in front of the office, Perry pow-wowed with Kevin, probably issuing some last-minute instructions before he left to meet Cory at the jail.

I more carefully scanned the couples and clusters for Jamie and Mindy Cottonweed, but they were either buried in the sea of bodies or had broken camp earlier.

Randy was still my prime perp, so I decided to zero in on him. I would tell him I knew the money came from someone at the farm and confront him about his conflicting story about how Colin came to be a reduction of one from Dana's employ.

I faced the stairs, reminding myself that yoga had made me strong and flexible, and if I fell, it would be nothing more than a series of *asanas* on the way down. But before I took that first step, I saw light and movement near the barn. It was too dark and I was too far away to make out whether it was a man or a woman, but they were holding a flashlight and moving confidently from the direction of the public buildings. Metal squeaked as one of the barn doors rolled open.

Was this the killer? Was that the hiding place? And me a world away on the staircase!

The beam of light wiggled around the barn, disappearing once in awhile as the lurker moved behind equipment or to the other side of the space. Nothing happened for a few moments, then I heard the faint sounds of a bell dinging, a door closing, and an engine coming to life. Four wheelers don't have doors, so it had to be a car.

I gripped the handrail as I watched a dark, late-model SUV drive out of the barn without its headlights on. I didn't think they were valet parking cars in the barn, so this mystery individual was no doubt a resident of the farm. They jerked to a stop, then opened their door. I strained to get a glimpse of their face when the interior light came on, but the car remained dark inside. They closed the barn door, then got in the car and cruised slowly toward the parking lot.

If that was the killer, I figured they were either hiding their instruments of death or they had hidden them earlier and I had witnessed a rescue operation. I bet the thought of the police searching the grounds spooked them, so I went with the latter. With any luck, they were spooked enough to leave something behind.

I began to back down the stairs and became aware of the sound of…nothing. No laughter, no complaints, no one shouting, "Keep moving, people!" I looked at the Field, which was empty except for the band breaking down their equipment and Brandon stacking folded chairs on a rolling cart near the archway.

Good. No one would notice me.

When my foot touched the ground, my back touched the front of someone who said, "What are you doing?"

EIGHTEEN

I FLINCHED AND TURNED to meet the angry visage of Ian McDougal. Telling him the real reason I had climbed the stairs would put a crimp in things, so I deflected him with a woman's most effective weapon. I put my face in my hands and pretended to cry.

"What's the matter?" Ian asked.

"Jamie" I said. "With another woman. I watched them ... I ... I ... "

I peeked through my fingers and saw Ian grimace, then he said, "They left."

"Together?" I wailed, actually quite annoyed that Jamie didn't say goodbye.

"I don't know," Ian said, already desperate. "Everyone left. The party's over."

I sniffled extravagantly. "Why?"

"Family emergency," he said. "Can you get to your car by yourself?"

I sniffled again. "I think I can manage."

Ian stayed five paces behind me, which forced me to keep up my charade until we reached the parking lot. Once I climbed into my Jeep, I slumped against the seat and reviewed my situation: most of my suspects had left, both of my deputies had gone off-duty, the evidence was probably halfway to Mexico by now, and I was hungrier than a member of the Donner party.

Before I turned the key in the ignition, I heard voices and saw Tarzan and the other male cook in the parking lot. Each of them carried a large plastic tub professionally printed with "Hungry Like the White Wolff." They were headed for a paneled white catering truck that advertised the same words.

I hadn't thought to check the dishes they had been washing earlier, so they may have washed Dana's cup and packed it in one of the containers.

I swung out of my Jeep and ran after them yelling, "Stop!"

They did.

"I'd like to see inside those containers," I said when I reached them.

"What for?" Tarzan asked.

I displayed my badge. "Just open them, please."

"Fine," Tarzan said, "but don't mess anything up."

They placed them on the gravel and peeled back the lids. I knelt on one knee, changing to a squat when the rocks bit into my peroxide welts, and inventoried the contents. Small clear containers, ladles and spatulas, metal tins.

"Is this going to take long?" the other cook asked.

I stood and took a step closer to him, then stared at him for a couple of seconds before I said, "What's your name?"

"Paul."

"Why are you in such a hurry, Paul?" *Because you offed your boss and need to get rid of the evidence?*

My intimidation tactic worked a little too well, and instead of confessing, Paul said, "My girlfriend's waiting for me."

"Oh, well, let me hurry, then." I squatted again, which isn't easy to do and stay modest in a short skirt and boots, and ran my eyes over the second plastic tub. Knives, graters, basters, more metal tins.

"Are you looking for something special?" Tarzan asked.

I stood and looked at them because I wanted to see their reaction when I said, "I need to see the measuring cup Dana was drinking from tonight."

They didn't jujitsu me and sprint off into the night, but Paul asked, "Why?"

I addressed Tarzan. "Is Paul always this curious?" I wanted to make a point, not get an answer, so I continued, "Something she drank tonight may have made her sick."

Paul huffily dropped to his knees and removed the lid from one of the smaller plastic containers. Inside were linen napkins embroidered with *WWI*, long metal spoons, and a measuring cup! Paul stood and handed it to me, but I didn't take it because, "That's not the one she was drinking from." Dana's had red lettering on it, and this one had blue.

"That's the only one we have," Tarzan said.

"If it's all the same to you, I'll check for myself."

I went through the contents of both tubs, but Tarzan was right. No other measuring cups. And no peroxide or OxyGrowth.

"Do you want it or not?" Paul asked, dangling the cup from his index finger.

"Not," I said. If I couldn't get evidence from them, I could at least get information. "Do y'all know who Mike Glass is? Vice president of the Friends."

Tarzan nodded. "He used to be our Waterloo rep." He looked at Paul. "I got this. Go ahead and load up the truck." Paul began repacking the items I had disturbed.

"Did he go into the kitchen tonight?" I asked.

"A few times, yeah."

"Oh?"

"He supplied all the linens for the party."

Oh. "And Randy Dove? Did he go in there?"

"I didn't see him during service," Tarzan said, "but I was back and forth to the dinner a lot. He was for sure in there awhile ago with Mike."

"What did they want?"

"Randy said he wanted to make sure Chef got the champagne he sent." He dropped his eyes and said quietly, "We told him about her passing out."

"And Mike?"

"He wiped mud off his shoes with some dirty napkins."

"What time was this?"

Tarzan hugged himself to stretch his shoulders. "I don't even know what time it is now. Maybe an hour ago, maybe three."

"Did either of them open the deep freezer?"

"Why would they?"

"Why does anyone do anything?" I said. "Did they?"

"Not that I saw."

"Okay, thanks," I said. "Have a safe trip back."

I surveyed the parking lot for more of my suspects, but saw nothing except bright headlights and red brake lights. The evening that had started with the promise of dining, drinks, and Drew had ended in death, dismay, and disappointment. And hunger.

I couldn't do anything else at the farm, so I drove to my house using back streets to avoid the traffic from Cats and Bats. All the cat fanciers should have arrived home by then, but I heard breaking news on KUT that the Animal Liberation Front had shown up to emancipate the animals. Anyone with catnip or a love trap was asked to bring it to the auditorium.

In my kitchen, I went straight to my refrigerator, inhaled the last batch of rice and beans I had made earlier in the week, then rinsed off in the shower and dissolved into bed.

————

The sip of wine I had consumed at the party wouldn't have made a marmot need to sleep in, so I awoke the next morning as usual at 5:00 AM. I stayed in bed, waiting for all the thoughts kicking up dust in my head to settle into something cohesive so I would know where to consolidate my efforts on this rare day off.

My original plan was to take a long walk around Town Lake, something I never get to do, then meet Daisy at Namaste Y'all for a yoga class at 11:00 AM, also something I never get to do, then spend the afternoon at my house with Drew, playing Scrabble and waiting for the furniture store to deliver my new couch. After a killer attempted to incinerate me in my house a few months ago, I'd had it rebuilt and remodeled, and had recently begun to refurnish it.

But how could I sleep, sweat, or snuggle when Dana's killer was free to do the same?

I needed to begin where things had ended: Good Earth Preserves. I knew I could gain access to the kitchen with my excuse of investigating food poisoning and manhandle the linens if they were still there, see if Mike Glass stuffed anything but muddy napkins into the bag. Getting into the barn was another matter I would have to finesse once I got onsite.

I took a proper shower, dressed in my personal inspection uniform of black T-shirt and black pants, then browsed the Internet for developing local stories on Dana's death or Cory's arrest. I saw almost nothing but. Most of Dana's headlines were subdued: "Dana White Dead" and "Award-Winning Chef Cooks No More."

The media had more fun with Cory's: "Yes, But Is It Organic?" and "Good Earth Ganja." Also, volunteers for the new Found Feline Hotline were standing by to help reunite cats with their owners.

I had just sat down to a breakfast of guacamole and coffee, which was all I had in the house, when my phone rang. Other than telemarketers, my boss, Olive, is the only person who calls my landline. And since telemarketers are prohibited by law from making cold calls before 8:00 AM, and there was, as yet, no law forbidding bosses from disrespecting their employees via the phone lines, I figured Olive forgot that I had taken the day off.

Yes, I had a backlog of restaurants to re-inspect, but it wouldn't hurt them to wait another day. Half of them weren't open on Mondays, anyway.

It was Jamie. "I took a chance you'd be up this early," he said. "How's your face?"

"Welt-free," I said. "You didn't say goodbye last night."

"Yeah, sorry. I looked for you when Ian told everyone to leave, but couldn't find you."

I didn't ask why he hadn't called me because I didn't want to hear Mindy's name that early in the morning. "Why are you calling my home number?"

"You didn't answer your cell." He sounded put out, which didn't compute until he said, "Is Cooper there?"

Ah, a simple case of jealousy. "No, I was in the shower," I said. "I'm getting ready to take off and do some inspections." I didn't say what I intended to inspect. No way would I tell Jamie my plans. He would caution me to let the police handle it, and then remind me that curiosity killed the cat, but he would make it more clever, like inquisitiveness incinerated the inspector.

"How about breakfast?" he said. "I'm meeting Mindy at Taco Xpress at seven o'clock for our first shoot on location, then we're going over to—"

"Thanks, but I already ate," I said. "Before you run off to that woman, Dana's cooks said Mike Glass was supplying the linens last night and came into the kitchen a few times. Did Mike have a glitch with Dana?"

"Leave it alone, Poppy."

"What ever do you mean, Jamie?"

"The police are on it now."

"Yes, but they haven't gotten past thinking it's a suspicious death, and we know it was at least manslaughter. I've already narrowed down the suspects and know all of them personally. I'm not the police, and I'm not working a bunch of other cases, and I don't have to follow protocol. And I have a good cover story for being out investigating."

As loud as his sigh was over the phone, he probably blew his Donald Westlake hardbacks off the shelves in his living room. "At least make sure you're not alone with anyone."

"The killer poisons people, Jamie. Even if I was alone with him, I'd lose my job if I accepted any free food or drink from a customer. Then I'd have to go back to Markham's, cooking under Ursula. I'd be exhausted and cranky all the time, and I wouldn't have near enough time to solve all these crimes that pop up along my route."

"You wouldn't have to work at Markham's."

I laughed. "Mitch would disown me if I worked at another restaurant."

"Come work for me," he said.

"Sitting in a plush chair in an air-conditioned office all day writing blog posts?" I said. "I wouldn't have anything to complain about. And I'd lose my tan."

"I'm in the field a lot more than I'm in the office," he said defensively. "And I need someone I can trust to keep the blog going while I'm on the road."

That casual statement stopped me for a moment. Jamie had just informed me about his future plans rather than consult me so we could discuss it and decide together how his travel affected our relationship. But now, with Jamie dashing off to breakfast with that poseur and me gearing up to catch a killer, was not the time to get into something heavy.

"I don't mean that's all you do," I said. "It's just that I like seeing the look on a cook's face when I make him eat the lettuce he chopped right after he scratched his sweaty armpit."

"Give it some more thought, okay? We make a great team."

"I like things the way they are."

"Just think about it," he said. "I have to go. Mindy doesn't like people to be late."

"Sure, but Mike and Dana?"

Jamie hesitated, then said, "Dana quit using Waterloo at the same time she quit using Weird Austin Spirits."

"I bet Mike's boss wasn't very happy that Mike lost Vis-à-Vis *and* the White Wolff Inn."

"He still has hundreds of other accounts," Jamie said. "That's no reason for murder."

"Not for a sane person."

A distracted silence came across the line, then he said, "Call me if you learn anything about Dana, okay?"

I didn't know if reporter Jamie or boyfriend Jamie wanted to hear from me. "Sure thing, hoss," I said.

We hung up, and as I finished my breakfast, I used a pen and paper to get clear on possible suspects and motives. I had hoped to eliminate some of them, but by the time I scraped up the last bite of guacamole, I had enough names to initiate my own street gang.

Randy Dove—because Dana hurt his business and "stole" the election. For whatever reason, being president of the Friends meant a lot to him, and Dana had taken it from him. So, she had damaged both his finances and his ego.

Bjorn Fleming—because Dana refused to give him a job, and she embarrassed him in front of colleagues and friends. Ditto on the effects to both his finances and his ego.

Colin Harris—because he used to work for Dana, and she had either made him mad enough to quit or he had done something so awful, she fired him. Or worse—he had been a model employee, and she fired him for some trumped-up reason. Yep, finances and ego.

Mike Glass—because he was Randy's ally, and Dana's win affected him, too. So that would be finances and Randy's ego.

And Cory Vaughn—because of his strange involvement with Bjorn and the Friends vote. And because he's an unpredictable dopehead.

I also couldn't rule out Dana's cooks, the McDougals, and the rest of the Vaughns for reasons possibly to be uncovered.

I called the furniture store to reschedule my couch delivery for another day, but they weren't open yet. Then I called Daisy to cancel our yoga class and to find out where she and Erik disappeared to the previous night, but she didn't answer her home phone. I tried their plant nursery and her cell phone, and got the same non-response. Strange. One of the Forrests usually answers somewhere. I left a message on her cell that I might not make yoga and would call her later.

I opened my front door and heard a lawn mower rumbling next door. I automatically waved to my neighbor, John With, my nice neighbor, the one *with* all the cuteness, sweetness, style, height, and dark wavy hair. Except it wasn't John With and he wasn't mowing the grass next door.

It was John With's boyfriend, John Without, the one who thinks that bright yellow wrestler's trunks are appropriate attire for lawn maintenance, who substitutes cattiness for charisma, who thinks being short and muscular makes him adorable, who has more hair sprouting from his back than from his scalp—the one *without* a single abidable quality. *That* one was pushing the lawn mower. And he was cutting *my* grass!

I have a small crush on John With, and even though the Johns have lived together for fifteen years, John Without feels threatened by my harmless flirtations—which is the reason I do it. He would never in seventeen lifetimes do something for me out of the goodness of his heart, so he was either drunk and confused about the property line, or he didn't want his house value to decline because of the jungle next door.

Regardless of the reason, my grass was getting mowed, so I tossed my inspector's backpack into the passenger seat, started the Jeep, and pulled out of the driveway. When I drove past my front yard, I glanced in my rearview mirror, then slammed on the brakes before I swerved into a neighborhood frat boy's parked car. Maybe *I* was the one drunk and confused. My neighborhood arch-enemy was standing near the sidewalk, smiling and waving goodbye to me.

Had he plotted to ruin my day off by messing with my mind? Because it would work. That grotesque image of him would sniper attack my thoughts all day, like a mental version of Chinese water torture. It would prevent me from solving Dana's murder and eating solid food.

I had to reset my world.

I had to make him stop.

NINETEEN

I SHIFTED INTO REVERSE and backed down the street and onto my lawn, missing my driveway on purpose. "You look like an organ grinder's monkey in that getup," I said as I got out of my car.

He waved again, then shut off the mower. "What did you say?"

"You better get inside before the frat boys capture you and take you back to the zoo."

He frowned and looked around as if I might be addressing someone else.

The second half of my insult didn't sound quite as insulting without the first half, but repeating it would dilute it. "What are you doing?" I asked. "No, wait. I can see *what* you're doing. *Why* are you doing it?"

"Just being neighborly," he said.

"You know I'm the neighbor, right?"

"Obviously," he said, a hint of harrumph in his tone. "I can't bag the clippings until tomorrow, okay?"

"No, it's not okay."

He checked his watch. "I guess I could do the entire front today before the HOA meeting, then do the back yard tomorrow."

"Wait, is the homeowner's meeting tonight?" I asked, distracted for a moment while I made plans to arrive home after 5:30 PM. Sometimes, if they see your car in the driveway, they knock on your door and guilt you into attending.

John exhibited his teeth and extended a hand sheathed in a bright yellow gardening glove. "I hope I can count on your support for president." His words sounded rehearsed and stilted.

"*You're* running for president of our homeowner's association?"

"I'm announcing it tonight," he said. "I need your vote, and I may need your advice."

And all became transparent. I had been president of our Little Depth Creek HOA when the Johns moved into the house to my left a few years ago. They have since upgraded and sold that house and bought the house on my right, which they work on when they're not at their downtown art gallery, Four Corners, which is why they have never attended an HOA meeting.

John Without knew that I had served two terms as president, but he didn't know that the job is nothing but listening to endless complaints about barking dogs and loud music, moderating, and sometimes refereeing, fervent discussions about community swimming pool hours and privileges, and issuing warnings for illegally parked boats and RVs, and unauthorized lawn art (e.g., flocks of plastic flamingos and motorcycle muffler sculptures). Sometimes a board member brings cookies to the meeting, but not always.

Nobody actually wants the job. The only reason I had been elected to a first term was because I had mentioned to *one* person at a meeting months before that it might be fun to be in charge of something non-food related. They changed the time on the next election meeting without telling me and voted me in unanimously. I finally got rid of the job by forging a note from Olive saying that a Travis County health inspector could not hold an elected office.

"Who are you running against?" I asked.

"I don't know," he said. "Tonight will be my first meeting."

I surveyed my lawn. "You're going to edge the sidewalks, right?" He nodded and I decided to press my advantage. "I'm having a couch delivered today. If I'm not here, can you let them in?"

A scowl brewed on his forehead, but he fake-smiled it away and said, "No problem."

"It's supposed to come between one and five," I said, then took off again, wondering what made him want to be HOA president.

———

As soon as my tires crunched onto the gravel parking lot of Good Earth Preserves a little after 8:00 AM, I hit my first wall—a big blue one. Several marked and unmarked police vehicles, along with a CSI van, were parked close to the buildings. For the second time in as many days, the cops had come between me and my investigation.

Uniforms and guns wouldn't deter me so easily, however, mostly because Prince William would be King of England before I had another entire day off, and thus the leisure to do whatever I wanted to do. I had to at least try to get onto the farm.

I drove through the lot and parked next to one of the most iconic hippie vehicles in the northern hemisphere: a 1972 Volkswagen Microbus. The farm has two of them, both bright green with the farm's name and blue and brown earth logo painted on the side. Due to Ian's mechanical skills, they both still run.

As I crossed the parking lot, I searched for a dark SUV like the one I saw leaving the barn at the tail end of the party, but the car was either off the farm or back in hiding. I also didn't see Nina's car, so Mitch must have driven her out this morning to pick it up. Strange that they would both be up and about so early.

I made it as far as the sidewalk before a baby-faced police officer stepped out of the shade of the overhang. "Farm is closed today, ma'am."

I flashed my badge. "Health department," I said, matching his official tone. "Routine inspection."

He nodded and I thought I had him, but then he said, "You'll have to come back tomorrow."

I became aware of activity farther down the sidewalk past the policeman, and saw Perry speaking with another man. I figured him to be a detective until I registered his jeans and plaid shirt. Ian. It would take longer than one evening to get used to his new yuppie expression.

"Ma'am?" the cop said, stepping closer to me. "Tomorrow?"

"Are y'all here for Cory Vaughn or Dana White?" I asked.

He shook his head, not because he didn't have the answer but because he wasn't going to tell me.

"I have some information about Dana White," I said, assuming that those magic words would get me through.

"Give me your card and we'll call you if we require your assistance."

I did as he asked, then said, "I need to use the ladies' room."

He pointed toward the parking lot's exit. "You'll pass several gas stations on your way back to Austin, ma'am."

I returned to my car, planning to wait for the cop to take a break, but he had nothing else to do except stare me off the farm. I started the engine and approached the exit, then braked to a stop when my cell phone rang. My boss, Olive. *Ugh.*

I had every right not to answer, because as I said, it was my day off. One that I had scheduled several months ago and reminded Olive thrice a week in the month leading up to the day off, and then twice a day the week before the day off.

But if I didn't answer, she would keep calling and assaulting me with voicemail messages, and then I would have to deal with an interrogation the next day about why I avoided her calls, and possibly accusations of testing her patience, which would lead to threats of assigning me to permit inspections. So I answered.

"It's my day off," I said.

"I got a hot one for you, Markham," Olive said.

"It's my day off."

"We got a tip about Colonel Chow's."

"It's General Chow's, and it's my day off."

"They're making sundried chicken in the Dumpster."

"That doesn't even make sense, and it's my day off."

"I want you out there," she said. "Today."

Good Earth had the highest number of suspects, but I had other people to talk to, including Jerry Potter who lived behind General Chow's. I could score points with Olive and use this as a bargaining chip with her some time in the future. "It's my day off," I said, trying to sound put upon, "but okay."

Olive usually says something snarky before she hangs up, and sometimes I don't even get that, but she broke protocol when she said, "Good." And she still didn't hang up.

Maybe she was experiencing an attack of some kind. I listened for gurgling or whimpering, then said, "Do you have something else for me, Olive?"

"You're a girl, Markham." Her voice sounded different, less bull-dog and a little hesitant.

"I'm a grown woman with her share of other people's problems."

"So you know about … things."

"Some things," I said. I didn't want to brag in case I needed to get away from wherever this was going. I thought that would make her hang up, but she didn't. "Olive?"

"I'm thinking of changing my name," she said.

"Did you get married?"

"Not my last name, Markham. My first."

She wanted to girl chat? With me? No. "You know it's my day off, right?"

"How do you see me?" she asked. "Name-wise."

Olive has brown hair she keeps short and moussed, flabby, pale skin she sometimes tries to dress up with a spray-on tan, and a torso that begins with shoulders like a defensive lineman, widens at the middle, then tapers into spindly legs that resemble little plastic swords. "I think Olive suits you," I said.

"Do you know what it's like to go your whole life named after a color, Markham?"

"Actually, I do."

"Or a snack?"

"Well, in my case, a flower."

"You always get something colored olive for your birthday and Christmas."

"Red and black for me."

"I hate that color green. And I hate olives. I have a hundred jars of olives in my garage right now."

"Give them to a food pantry," I suggested. "Or regift them to other friends. You have other friends, right? Friends who could help you work through this major life decision."

As usual, she didn't listen to me. "I just want to get away from the whole olive thing."

"So do I," I said.

"So you'll help me?"

"With what?"

"Think of a new name," she said. "I want something that reflects my personality, something fun and exotic."

"I'm already having to work on my day off," I said.

"What do you think about Genevieve or Vivian?"

"Well, they're not drab colors or briny snack foods."

"I want to wear a name for a day or two before I decide," she said. "We'll try Genevieve first, so call me that every time you report in today."

"You mean the *one* time I report in after inspecting General Chow's on my day off?"

"Sounds good," she said, then hung up.

————

General Chow's is your typical budget Chinese food restaurant near the University of Texas main campus in south central Austin. They do a lot of lunchtime and takeout business, and most of their customers come from a few-block radius. The area is a mix of current UT students, former UT students, and miscellaneous other people who don't have a lot of money to spend on rent. It's not seedy, but it's not an area you want to put down roots in.

A few months ago, the owners of General Chow's had erected a ten-foot-tall wooden fence around the entire rear area—to keep vagrants out of the Dumpsters, they claimed. Now I knew that they wanted to keep their customers ignorant about how their food was prepared, and Zeus knows what else they were doing.

A trip north to the Health Department offices to review their previous violations would have eaten up too much time, so after I pulled into the back parking lot of the restaurant close to 9:00 AM, I called Olive/Genevieve to get a quick report. "Hey Gen, it's Poppy," I said when she answered.

"Who's Gen?" she asked, biting into something lightly crunchy that sounded exactly like a pork rind.

"It's short for Genevieve," I said. "You said that's what you wanted me to call you."

She grunted. "I didn't think about nicknames. I don't like Gen. Let's go with Vivian next time." She swallowed loudly. "Who's Poppy?"

"Markham," I said.

"Oh, right. It's your day off, isn't it?"

"Thanks for remembering," I said. "I'm at General Chow's and need to know their last few health scores."

"Hang on." A couple of minutes later, she said, "I can't find anything for Colonel Chow's."

"It's General, not Colonel. Never mind. Transfer me to Gavin."

I had thought to call my colleague in the first place because he spends Monday mornings in the office filing reports from any weekend inspections he does, but honestly, I wanted to try out Olive's new name. This was the most interesting thing she had ever done. I wouldn't say I felt honored that she had asked for my help, but I wanted to make sure she picked a good one. If she chose a name that reflected her real personality—which is the opposite of fun and exotic—I might have to start reporting to Bloodfang.

"I'm not your secretary, Markham," she said and hung up.

I called Gavin myself. "Hey, Poppy," he said a minute later. "Looks like trouble followed you to Good Earth last night."

"Have you written a new ending yet?" I asked. Gavin is a collector of bizarre restaurant news stories and likes to give them new endings.

"Dana White dying is sad, but not strange," he said.

"What if someone poisoned her with food-grade hydrogen peroxide?"

"That's not what the news sites are saying. Or Amooze-Boosh."

"Jamie has to report what the police report or he'll lose their cooperation," I said. "I was there. I saw the peroxide in her cup."

"Poor Dana," Gavin said softly. "That must have been awful for her. Do you know how it happened?"

"I'm not sure yet," I said. "Vis-à-Vis is yours, right? What do you know about her sous, Colin Harris, leaving?"

"Rumor is Herb fired him, but I don't know why."

"*Herb* did? I thought he ran the Wolff. What's he doing in Vis-à-Vis's business?"

"I'm sure he had Dana's blessing."

"That's very helpful," I said. "Now can you do me a favor? Can you pull up General Chow's and tell me what's going on with them?"

"That's in Bennett's area," he said, implying that I should call the new gal to discuss them. She had transferred from Washington State a couple of months ago.

I related the anonymous tip we received. "Apparently, she missed a few things," I concluded.

"You know tips, Poppy. It's probably some day spa darling getting even for not being allowed to bring her therapy dog into the dining room."

"It's not dirty fingernails or a dead moth in a Caesar salad," I said. "Besides, it came from Jerry Potter. He told me last night at the party."

"You think Bennett's on the take?"

"Anything's possible."

"That reminds me," Gavin said, "did you read the story about the girl who got fired from her pizza delivery job and wanted to get even?"

"She ordered a pizza and then robbed the delivery man, right?"

"When the police took her mug shot, she said, 'Hold the cheese.'"

Gavin has done better, but I laughed anyway. He asked me to hold, then came back on a few minutes later. He told me that General Chow's scored in the nineties on their most recent inspection four months ago, but in the seventies on the several before that. They had been cited for rodents, insects, improper storage of raw meat, slime in the ice machine, no hair restraints, and smoking in the walk-in. Page two is where inspectors document items that are lacking or gross or strange, but don't affect the overall health score. Those comments indicated that cooks must wear both shoes at all times.

"Yet they've never been the source of a foodborne illness," Gavin said.

"That bewilders me, too," I said. "Thanks, Gavin."

With those low health scores, General Chow's should have closed their doors and cleaned up their operation, but that fence told me they had gotten more dirty. Why do people enter a business with clearly established rules and regulations, and then refuse to follow them? It's much cheaper and easier in the long run. A chicken carcass can be cleaned and dried as easily inside the kitchen as out by the Dumpster. Unless fly larvae was one of their secret ingredients.

The chances of them flouting health regulations at 9:00 on a Monday morning were actually pretty good—fresh week, fresh deliveries, fresh food prep. I got out of my Jeep and applied my eye to a space between the slats and saw more wood. A double fence? They really wanted some privacy. I tried the gate, but they had locked it from the inside, so I moved closer and listened. I wanted to stay on the stealth as long as time allowed, so I didn't ring the delivery bell.

Sixty seconds later, however, my cover was blown.

TWENTY

"POPPY! HEY! POPPY!" SOMEONE yelled, then punctuated the words with one of those shrill fingers-in-the-mouth whistles that signals the beginning of an illegal dog fight.

I searched the vicinity, but saw no one in the parking lot or on the street.

"Up here!"

Up there was Jerry Potter, standing on the mini balcony of his apartment, dressed only in jeans. Even from that distance, I could tell that he hadn't bathed or shaved. He motioned with the hand holding a white coffee mug, "You can see better up here."

I gave him the okay sign, then put my index finger to my lips to hopefully get him to stop vocally spotlighting me.

He held up an apologetic hand, "Oh, right, sorry," he yell whispered. "I'm in number four oh six."

A few minutes later, I crossed the threshold into Jerry's tiny, smelly one-room kennel that also hadn't been shaved or bathed, like *ever*. It confined a futon, a new flat-screen TV leaning against the opposite wall, and in between, a wooden coffee table that also served as the dining table as evidenced by all the cardboard containers and plastic utensils collected on, under, and around it.

"You still get takeout from General Chow's after you've seen their food prep?" I asked.

"What they're doing is against health code," he said, "not common sense."

There was some logic that refused to be argued with.

"Coffee?" he asked, stepping into the galley kitchen, which was strangely debris-free.

"I'm good," I said.

He pulled a pint of cheap bourbon from his jeans pocket and poured it into his cup, then topped it off with coffee. "It's my day off," he said, stirring his drink with his finger.

"So, you can see General Chow's from up here?" I said.

He pointed to the open sliding glass door and I walked toward it, but stopped before I stepped onto the balcony. The previous night on the Cornhusker's staircase had been enough of a vanquish-my-fear-of-heights exercise. Besides, I had a decent view of the fenced area from where I stood in the apartment. It remained as inactive as a séance.

"Have they washed the chickens this morning?" I asked.

"I just got up," he said. He moved past me and onto the balcony, then turned to face me. He placed both elbows on the railing, putting his scrawny chest and bourbon-for-breakfast belly on display. "That was a great party, huh?"

"Are you a Friend of the Farm?" I asked.

"Friend of Cory's," he said.

I.e., stoner. "What time do they wash the chickens?"

"Various times," he said, then sipped his coffee. "Sure you don't want some?"

"I'm good. Have you seen them doing anything else?"

"Like what?"

"Come on, Jerry, you've worked in restaurants. You know the critical health violations."

"I don't spend all my time snooping over the fence," he said. "Washing the chickens is the worst I've seen, and I reported it. Do I get a reward or something?"

"Is *that* what this is about? You want money?"

"No," he said, hurt by my assumption, which nine times out of ten would have been spot on. "I was just wondering."

"The health department appreciates your tip, but there's no reward."

"You can hang around here if you want and wait for 'em to do something," he said. "We could watch a movie."

I wanted to wait, and I would have even done so in Jerry's apartment, but it seemed like I was the first female he had ever had in his personal space. People who don't know what to do in social situations can be counted on to do inappropriate things, like giggle in church or take more than one drink at a time at an open bar. Or throw a girl down on a futon and exhale whiskey-scented coffee breath in her face.

"That's a nice offer, Jerry," I said, "but my other restaurants aren't going to inspect themselves." I made for the door, then remembered I had another reason for talking to him. "What did you tell Jamie Sherwood last night?"

He smiled, showing coffee- and cannabis-stained teeth. "I guess you guys didn't do much pillow talk, huh?"

"We're not ... no, we didn't."

"Sure you don't want some coffee?" he asked.

"Did you roast it yourself or something? Yes, I'm sure. Now tell me what you told Jamie."

"I told him what I knew in relation to some nefarious acts," he said.

I rolled my eyes. "This is Austin, Jerry. Nefarious acts are a requirement for residency."

He pulled out his pint and splashed another shot into his coffee mug. "This one's of particular interest to the food community," he said, obviously trying to be cryptic and enticing.

I found it tedious and repellant.

"Fine," I said, backing up. "I'll ask Jamie."

Jerry bolted off the railing and into the apartment. "Hold up, hold up. I'll tell you." He indicated his futon covered with a pilly beige blanket and drool-stained pillow. "Have a seat."

Not even discovering that they were serving Soylent Green at the Governor's Mansion could be worth sitting there, but I did. On the very edge. He sat next to me and I scooted over a little. I wasn't scared of Jerry, just grossed out. "So tell," I said. "Quickly."

"That farm is using pesticide."

"On their crops?" I asked. "Their legal crops, I mean."

He nodded.

"How do you know this?"

"Cory told me last night after him and Brandon washed the vegetables. We went to the barn and, uh, chilled."

Using pesticide was more dishonorable than nefarious, but wait, "I thought Cory went to help his uncle mend a fence."

"Maybe after," he said, "but we were inside awhile."

"Did you see anyone else in the barn while y'all were chilling?"

"Kevin came in looking for Cory, but we hid behind some hay."

I stood. "Thanks, Jerry." If he had been smoking pot with Cory, I was lucky he remembered that much.

"Then Mike came in," he said.

"Mike Glass? Was he looking for Cory, too?"

Jerry shook his head. "He was with that bartender guy."

"Randy Dove?"

"I think that's his name. He was all ticked off at Chef and the dinner, yelling that she wouldn't get away with it and he wanted a recount."

So that's where those two went after Randy choked. But why go all the way to the barn? "What else did they talk about?" I asked.

"Nothing really. Mostly Mike listened, then he gave Randy something that settled him down."

"Like a sedative?"

Jerry laughed. "No, something bigger. It was in a plastic bag."

"A bottle of something?"

"I didn't see what it was," he said. He leaned back against his pillow and grinned up at me. "If you give me your number, I can call you when I see 'em doing the chickens."

I pulled a business card from my backpack and gave it to him. "I'd appreciate that."

I took one last look through the sliding glass door at General Chow's before I left, but saw no one. Thanks to Jerry's Broadway show earlier, they knew I was in the area, so they were probably waiting for my Jeep to leave. Normally, I would have done exactly that, then driven down the street and hoofed it back to the restaurant, but Chef Dana's murder trumped General Chow's chickens.

I left the apartment and descended the four flights of stairs slowly, mulling Jerry's new item of intel. It had to be Randy's VP and treasurer, Mike Glass—not someone at the farm—who gave Randy the money. But before I went all Marcia Clark on Randy and accused him of killing Dana, I needed to build a stronger case against him. Randy could have been telling me the truth when he said he won a bet. I doubted the money had relevance to Dana's death, but Mike had given it to him in secret and Randy had tried to hide it, and I could use it as leverage when I questioned him about Dana. I hadn't eliminated Mike as a suspect, so I could use that same leverage against him, too. I practically skipped to my car, excited that I finally had something solid to work with.

I sat in my Jeep and called Olive/Vivian. Where did she come up with these names?

No answer, so I left a message. "Hey, Viv. I'm at General Chow's right now. It looks like the chickens have the day off, too. I'll try again tomorrow when I'm *at work*."

———

Before I drove thirty plus miles to Waterloo Linen, I called to make sure that Mike Glass hadn't taken the day off and would be somewhere I could find him. Like health inspectors, he travels around the city talking to restaurant owners, managers, and chefs, but unlike inspectors, he isn't avoided, glared at, and lied to. Or at least not as often.

The receptionist, Tina, told me he was due in at 10:00 AM, so I headed for the far north side of town. I made good time and arrived at ten till. Mike had not yet arrived, so I waited inside by the front desk, reading framed newspaper articles hung on the walls lauding Waterloo Linen as the greatest linen supply company in all the land, and, of course, bragging that they were voted #1 in the *Austin Chronicle* reader's poll. I have yet to be in a service establishment that *hasn't* won first place in that poll.

Five minutes later, Mike came through the front doors, wearing pressed jeans and a burnt orange polo shirt, his shaved head shiny with sweat. "Is Sammy here yet?" he asked. "Where's Sammy?"

Tina smiled at him, then picked up a microphone attached to a coil. "Base to Sammy," she said. "What's your ETA?"

"Twenty minutes," came the reply. "We're leaving Good Earth now."

"Thanks," Mike said to Tina, then looked where she pointed, which was at me.

"Hi, Mike," I said. "Problem with the party's napkins?"

"No, no," he said. "Everything is fine. The party was good. Everything is good."

"Do you have a few minutes?" I asked. "I'd like to ask you about some things that happened at the dinner last night."

"No time right now. Make an appointment, okay? I don't have time."

Linen suppliers aren't under the jurisdiction of the health department, so I had to encourage his cooperation in a different way. "Shall we meet at Markham's? I believe it's that time of year when Drew Cooper decides whether we keep using our current vendors."

He squinched up his face as a prelude to a protest, but when he correctly inferred my implication, he said to Tina, "Give her a visitor's badge."

Mike waited at the double doors leading to the back as Tina handed me a black badge with a big red V on it, then asked me to sign in.

He opened the doors and the sound of several powerful industrial washers and dryers hit me so hard, I felt a little dizzy. Mike pointed to the right, and I followed him into a large break room filled with picnic tables. The place wasn't entirely soundproof, but we could talk.

He went over to a counter and lifted a brown ceramic cup from a tray. "Coffee?" he asked.

"Sure," I said, trying to sound agreeable and friendly to put him at ease. "Why are you waiting for Sammy to return from Good Earth?"

"We, uh, used our better linens for the party. I want to make sure we get them all back."

"They're not coming back today."

"Sammy said he was bringing them."

"Sammy said he was on his way back," I said. "I was there earlier. The police aren't letting anyone onsite."

Mike stopped shaking powdered creamer into his cup. "Police?"

"Dana White died last night, Mike."

He looked up at me. "Died?"

He sure was answering a lot of questions with questions—a billboard of guilt, in my experience. "They think it's foul play," I said. Actually, I didn't know what the police thought, but lying to Mike wasn't a crime.

"Someone did it to her? They think someone *killed* her?"

"How did you feel when Dana kicked you and Waterloo out of her restaurants?"

He shrugged. "Accounts come and go."

As a health inspector, I never forget that the element of surprise is my constant sidekick, so I round-housed him with, "Why did you give Randy all that money last night?"

Mike might be a salesman, but he's not slick. He handed me my cup, then brought his coffee up to his lips with a shaky hand. "What money?" The lie is always in the voice, not the words.

"The money you gave him in the barn."

It's hard to predict how an individual will react when confronted with a very large truth. If Mike ran through the door and into the laundry room, finding him would be a challenge. At that point, though, I would let him escape. I already had enough to take to my

159

interview with Randy. The fact that Mike had essentially denied the existence of money told me that it probably had *not* been a payoff on a bet. He also didn't make up a lie about it being a business transaction, which would have been a better deflection. No, this money was the key to something, and if Mike was the type to make assumptions, he thought I witnessed the payoff.

"It was in a plastic bag with the farm's logo on it," I said for an extra dash of authenticity.

Mike dropped his eyes to the scuffed white floor, then sighed.

"Tell me, Mike."

He sat on top of one of the picnic tables and put his feet on the bench. "Randy'll ruin me if I tell you. Like seriously ruin me."

"He won't have to know," I said, unsure if we were still talking about the money or something that carried a long prison sentence.

"You think so? That'd be great if he didn't know. I mean, he knows. He's the one who did it. I just helped. But I didn't want to." He searched my eyes. "I *swear* I didn't want to."

TWENTY-ONE

I USUALLY HAVE ENOUGH time, and once in a while enough patience, to listen to a guy kvetch until he eventually blabs the truth—it was their manager's idea to use expired ground beef in the Bolognese sauce, or they used the hand-washing sink as a urinal only the one time—but I really didn't want to listen to Mike flubber over this. If I got a confession out of him, I might could still make the morning yoga class with Daisy.

He seemed more delicate than the cooks and managers I normally deal with, however, so I softened my approach. "It's okay, Mike. Whatever it is can be fixed."

He closed his eyes and shook his head deliberately, looking more like a toddler refusing to share his toys than a muscle-bound bouncer on Sixth Street.

"I can try to help you if you tell me what's going on," I said.

After a long pause, he said, "We've been borrowing money from the fund. Randy has."

I quickly put that together to mean, "The Friends of the Farm treasury fund?"

"Randy's going to *kill* me."

I tapped the table to get his attention. "Forget Randy and tell me about the money."

"Randy's business was tanking with the election and everything, you know, so he borrowed a couple of thousand from the fund. He said he'd pay it back, but he didn't. And then he borrowed a couple more."

"And he didn't pay that back either, did he?"

"I didn't want to do it!" he cried. "I swear I didn't want to do it."

I believed Mike, but he was still as guilty of embezzlement as Randy. "Were you giving him more money last night?" I asked.

"No, not that. No. Randy thought he might lose the election, so he was paying it back. He gave me the money when we first got there for the tour, but then he asked for it back before dinner."

"*After* Perry announced that Dana was president? Why?"

"He said he had a better idea."

"Did he tell you what it was?"

"I didn't ask him," he said. "I was just glad Dana was elected and I was finally done with Randy."

Not for the first time in my life did I ask the obvious. "Why didn't you quit, Mike?"

"I tried, but Randy said he would tell everyone I took the money. I didn't take the money. Randy did."

"I understand," I said. "Why was the money in one of the farm's plastic bags?"

Mike ran his hand over the top of his head. "Randy gave it to me loose, and I couldn't carry it all, so I put it in a bag I found in the kitchen."

Oh. "After you gave him the money, did you and Randy leave the barn together?"

"Yeah, but he went to put the money in his car."

Oh, no he did not! Unless ice chests had become street-legal vehicles. I now had another reason to suspect Randy of killing Dana, but not even the threat of exposing his theft to the Friends would get me an audience with him. I knew someone he would talk to, though.

———

I wasn't so lucky with traffic on the trip down south, and arrived at Markham's at 11:17 AM. Our family restaurant is closed on Mondays, but Drew was there. I hadn't lied to Mike when I told him that Drew was assessing all of Markham's suppliers to make sure we were getting the best product, service, and price. Since Ursula had determined to exceed the food budget while finalizing the recipes for her cookbook, Markham's had been special ordering items from other vendors, which isn't cost-effective. Drew had worked extra hours charting all of that on a monster spreadsheet every Monday morning for the past few weeks.

I drove around to the back expecting to see Drew's gray truck and only Drew's gray truck, but I had to park on the street for all the other vehicles—Ursula's, Trevor's, Mitch's, Nina's, Jamie's, Daisy's. Daisy's? And several others belonging to employees.

What could everyone be doing? And without me. I turned thirty-nine last month, so they weren't holding a super-secret surprise party planning meeting. A family council? But why include Jamie, Drew, and Trevor? Perhaps they had finally scheduled an intervention for Ursula's bad attitude or Mitch's ongoing love affair with golf or Nina's snobbery and reckless spending. Regardless of the target or the issue, I had plenty to say and should have been included.

I put my hand on some of the car hoods on my way to the back door. They still felt warm, so whatever they were doing, they hadn't been doing it long. I had to use my key to unlock the door, then stepped into the kitchen.

Someone yelled, "Cut!" Then everyone turned to look at me.

Jamie and Ursula stood together at the silver prep table, a mess of ingredients in front of them and large bright lights above them. Several cooks wearing radiant white chef's coats and checked pants manned the stove and grill, wrapped in clouds of steam and enticing smells. The rest of the car owners formed an audience behind two cameramen, each positioned at a tripod near the corners of the table.

Mindy Collision, dressed in a similar cowgirl getup as the night before, except for the hat, glared at me. "I thought I told everyone to come in through the *front* door," she said. Her black hair pulled into a tight ponytail added extra severity to her words.

"Apologies, Mindy," Nina said with an obsequious twitter. "She's not familiar with filming."

How would Nina know what I'm familiar with? She doesn't even know the name of the agency I work for. And how was I supposed to know they were filming? "Next time," I said.

Mindy rolled her eyes, then said. "Take five, people."

I can't stand being addressed as "people," but no one else seemed to mind. Trevor approached Ursula and together they sniffed something in a pot on the stove. Nina produced a hand mirror from her purse and made faces into it, Mitch and several others pulled out cell phones, and the rest began to graze from a tray of cheese and fruit set up near the walk-in.

Jamie smiled at me, then raised a *momentito* finger while he spoke with Mindy, who stood by the sink conversing with a girl with a blond pixie haircut and a clipboard in her bent elbow. Mindy's minion.

Logan rushed up and hugged me. "TeePee!" she squealed, using the accidental nickname she had christened me with as a two-year-old trying to say Auntie Poppy.

"Hey, honey, are you helping out today?" She wore a small white chef's coat and black-and-white pinstriped pants, a present her father gave her for her fourteenth birthday after she announced that she wanted a career as a professional chef.

"That lady's filming Ursula and JJ, and JJ told my mom last night that I could be on the show, but now she won't let me." JJ came out of Jamie requesting "just Jamie" the first time Logan called him Mr. Jamie.

"Your *mom* won't let you?" I asked.

"No, the lady."

"Oh, honey, I'm sorry. Did she say why?" Logan is quiet and mature, so I knew it wasn't because she had busted onto the set full of attitude and assumptions. And if that were the deciding factor, Ursula shouldn't appear on camera either.

I caught a brief shake of Logan's head before Daisy came over and hugged me. Like me, she wore all black, but she looked chic and poised, while I looked shabby and practical. "I got your message this morning," Daisy said. "I meant to call you, but we had to get here early."

"And for nothing, it appears," I said. "Logan said Mindy changed her mind?"

"When Jamie told us last night, Erik and I went straight home to tell her." She smoothed Logan's hair then gave her shoulder a squeeze. "She's *so* disappointed."

"Jamie should have some say in this," I said, "being that he's the star of the show."

Daisy said, "He tried to talk to Mindy when she first said no, but she started to get mad so he backed off. He said he'd try again later."

"You're sure she didn't give a reason?" I asked.

"No," Logan said. "JJ said I could be Ursula's assistant and hand her stuff when she asked for it. We did it twice, then they didn't want me anymore."

I watched Mindy scan her film set like a lightning bolt searching the horizon for a place to land—Ursula measuring out sea salt at the prep table, Jamie now talking to one of the cameramen, the minion tasting a spoonful of something Trevor offered her. Mindy stopped when her eyes landed on me, then she shifted them to Daisy, then to Logan, then to me again. She got that look people get when they realize that my cousin and I look enough alike to be confused for each other.

I tapped Daisy on the arm. "I think I know why Mindy doesn't want Logan. She thinks you're me and Logan is my daughter."

"Why does that matter?" Daisy asked.

"Mindy has designs on Jamie, and Jamie canceled his trip to Europe because of me, and she's jealous."

Daisy smiled. "Jamie didn't go to Europe because of you?"

"He said he came back when he learned that Drew and I were dating. Except we're not dating."

"You're dating," Daisy said. "How romantic of Jamie!"

"Yes, very romantic that I have to choose between him and Drew six weeks early."

Daisy let out a hard sigh.

"Okay, yes, it's romantic. And I'm flattered that he came back for me. Shocked, actually."

"Can you do something, TeePee?" Logan asked. "I *really* want to be on teevee."

"I'll talk to JJ," I said. "We'll get it worked out."

Logan sprinted up to Jamie then tugged him away from the cameraman and over to me. "Here he is," Logan said.

I looked at Daisy, who guided Logan to the snack table.

Jamie kissed my cheek. "I'm glad to see you," he said.

"You, too. Why didn't anyone tell me y'all were going to film here today?"

"I tried to this morning, but you interrupted me."

"Oh. Sorry. Thank you for getting Logan on the show."

Jamie laughed. "She keeps stealing all the scenes."

"Is that why High Cotton decided to keep her behind them?"

Jamie glanced at Mindy. "It's the weirdest thing. Mindy was really chuffed to present Logan as an up-and-coming young chef, but after a couple of takes, she changed her mind for some reason."

"I'll tell you the reason," I said, then repeated to him what I had told Daisy.

"Mindy's not interested in me," Jamie said. "She's my boss."

"Since when does that matter? Ursula is Trevor's boss."

"Trust me, she's not interested," Jamie said.

"Do you have another explanation why she suddenly overturned her decision?"

"Mindy's a professional. I'm sure she has a good reason."

"Can you please find out what it is?" I asked. "Logan is crushed, and I think she would feel better knowing that Mindy thinks she's too short or too immature or too whatever to hand Ursula a spatula on camera. And if Mindy is too immature herself and doesn't want whom she thinks is my daughter on the show, well, we would all feel better knowing that."

Jamie brought up his hand to run fingers through his curls, but stopped.

"Keep going," I said. "I won't cite Markham's for improper employee hygiene."

"No, Mindy's concerned about continuity. She wants us to look the same from shot to shot."

Mindy, Mindy, Mindy! "Please go talk to your boss about Logan before you start shooting again."

As soon as Jamie left, Daisy and Logan returned. "What did he say?" Logan asked.

"He's talking to her," I said.

We three looked over at what to Logan had to be the most important discussion since her parents debated whether to let her put a pink streak in her hair when she was ten. I admit to feeling a little fluttery myself. To stop us from rubbernecking, I asked Logan to tell me about her latest original recipe, but she was too absorbed in the small drama on the other side of the room to mumble anything other than "Sour cherry tart."

A few minutes later, Jamie walked up to us. "She wants to talk to you."

"Daisy or Logan?" I asked.

"You," Jamie said.

TWENTY-TWO

"Me-ee?" I said. "Why?"

"She didn't say," Jamie said.

What could Mindy want with me? I wasn't even supposed to be at Markham's. And how did a plea for Logan's guest spot on the show earn me a summons into judge's chambers? Considering the situation, the best thing I came up with was that Mindy wanted to barter with me—if I give her Jamie, she'll give Logan her fifteen minutes. "I have nothing to say to her," I said.

Logan grabbed my hand. "TeePee! Go talk to her!"

"Maybe she wants you on the show, too," Daisy suggested.

"Pleasepleasepleasepleaseplease!" Logan whined.

I sighed dramatically. "Only for you, little one."

"Yes!"

I never hurry through a commercial kitchen and I didn't this time. I stopped to examine the contents of every bowl, tin, and platter between me and the prep table. Nobody said I had to be nice to Mindy, but I was anyway. "Hello, Mindy," I said when I reached her. "I like your plaid shirt. Do you need anything?"

"An apology," she said curtly.

"From?"

"You."

"For?"

"Spilling wine on me last night."

What! She knew I hadn't spilled the wine on purpose. And really? That's why she subpoenaed me? For a stupid apology? "That was an accident," I said. "Someone bumped my arm."

She tried to insert her hands into her front pockets, but her jeans were so new and stiff, she couldn't make the gesture look nonchalant, so she put them on her hips.

An apology would essentially be admitting that I soaked her in spirits intentionally. And then what? Would she use that against me with Jamie? Wait ... I was being paranoid, and almost as childish as she. I crossed my fingers behind my back and said, "I'm sorry."

Her face acquired an expression that could only be described as victorious, then she clapped her hands twice. "Places people!"

"Logan, too?" I asked.

"Of course," Mindy said.

I turned to my cousins and gave them a thumb's up. The smile on Logan's face was worth all that crow I would have to pick out of my teeth.

"Ursula!" Mindy's assistant yelled across the kitchen. "Is it time to take the salmon cakes out of the oven?"

Salmon cakes! *That's* what Ursula was making on the show! I whipped my head around and saw Mitch skulking through the swinging doors that led into the wait station. I took off after him and caught up with him in the second dining room.

"That's *my* recipe for salmon cakes," I said as he unlocked the door to his private office. "Ursula stole it for her cookbook!"

"It's the restaurant's recipe." His quick response told me that Ursula had already gotten to him.

"*I* created it."

"You improved on Rolly's version, who got it from Dana, who got it from your mother." He went behind his desk and sat on his throne.

"Well, it's not fair for Ursula to make the entire world think it's hers by cooking it on network television." I knew I sounded like a six-year-old, but it's hard not to do when I'm emotional about something—especially when my stepsister gets to do whatever she wants all the time.

"It's cable television," Mitch said, "and she's making her venison stew for the show. The salmon cakes are for the crew."

"Oh."

Mitch indicated that I should sit. "This is good for us," he said. "We need people to stop thinking of Markham's as the place where Évariste Bontecou died."

"Ursula wouldn't even have a cookbook deal if she hadn't gotten herself arrested for killing him."

"Nevertheless, she's worked very hard. She deserves this."

I agreed with Mitch that Ursula had worked hard, but I didn't necessarily agree that she deserved this notoriety. The decision wasn't up to me, though, and I accepted the futility of my position.

"Why weren't you at our family affair?" I asked. "Nina said you don't like to drive in the dark."

"Honey, there are two kinds of people in this world. Those who Monday-morning quarterback, and those who accept the final score."

"I'm not trying to change last night, Daddy. I just want to know why you didn't show up."

Mitch picked up his signed Babe Ruth baseball. "My heart meds are affecting my eyesight."

My father is not above telling a white lie to get me off a topic he doesn't want to discuss, but he had already tried to deflect me once, so that may have been the truth. I would check later when I cross-referenced his medications with their side effects. "You can always get glasses," I said.

Mitch snorted. My old hippie of a father doesn't have many vanities, but ever since Nina made him cut his ponytail and shape his bushy white beard into a goatee, he has become strangely concerned with keeping up the appearance of vital youth.

"You'd look good in some trendy black ones with rectangle frames," I said.

"Not my style," he said, squaring some invoices into a neat pile.

"Glasses might improve your golf game."

He stopped rustling papers while he considered that, then said, "Still not my style." Then, because he's so good at changing the subject, "Jamie Sherwood is back in town, I see."

Mitch's interest in my personal relationship wasn't a father's for his daughter. Whether I chose the general manager or an influential food writer, Markham's would thrive regardless, so I had decided to leave the restaurant out of the equation as a tactical necessity. And because I'm equally as good at changing the subject, "Did he tell you I tried to save Dana White last night?"

"He did, and I'm proud of you, honey."

"Thanks, Daddy."

"Ironic that it happened at Good Earth," he said.

"Ironic how?"

"Dana was one of the founding members."

I scooched to the edge of the chair. "Of the *farm*? When was this?"

"Late seventies or so. Perry and Dana started the farm with Ian and Tanya."

"Dana was Perry's *wife*?"

"Girlfriend."

"How did Perry end up with Megan?" I asked.

"Ian brought his little sister to the farm a few months into their venture. Perry and Dana had a fight. Dana left and Perry eventually married Megan."

"Do you know why Perry and Dana fought?"

"That was a very long time ago," Mitch said. "It's all water under the bridge."

Trevor filled the doorway and rapped twice on the jamb. "Excuse me, sir. Mindy's askin' for you."

"Coming," Mitch said, standing up, then to me, "I expect you to support the restaurant, Penelope Jane. Ursula, too."

Penelope Jane is not the name on my birth certificate, but my father made it up when I was a kid to show that he meant business, and I should straighten up and fly right. I got called Penelope Jane for everything from forgetting to empty the cat's litter box at home to getting drunk on gin at Good Earth Preserves to quitting the restaurant and becoming a health inspector.

"I'll do what I can," I said.

Mitch raised an eyebrow at me, then went back through the dining room.

"Has the morning been as fun as I think it has?" I asked Trevor.

"Oh, yeah. Jamie's interviewin' Ursula about the restaurant and her cookbook, but what's goin' on off-camera is much more entertainin'." He grinned and lowered his voice. "Duelin' dames."

"Ursula versus Mindy?"

"Better," he said. "Ursula versus Nina."

"What's the glitch? Ursula always rolls over when her mom enters a room."

"Nina thinks Mindy's assistant, Tiffany, is *simply perfect* for me. Ursula's been huffin' and puffin' a lot, and I think she's aimin' to blow down the house."

"Ursula cooks better when she's mad," I said.

"Yeah, but she doesn't smile, and there will be a *television audience* as Mindy keeps remindin' her."

"I suppose you're already taking bets on the winner," I said.

"For a small wager of five dollars, you can choose whether Ursula leaves or she makes Nina leave. Winners split the pot."

"I'm in," I said. I fished an emergency $5 bill from my backpack and handed it to him. "Nina stays."

Trevor put the money in his pants pocket.

"Aren't you going to mark down my bet?" I asked.

He laughed. "You and Mitch are the only ones bettin' on Nina."

He turned to leave, but I caught the sleeve of his chef's coat. "Promise you won't try to influence the outcome."

"Like how?"

"Like flirt with Tiffany or tell Nina that you and Ursula are involved."

"Too late on the first one," he said. "And as far as Nina, I don't know what the big deal is. People date."

I squinted up at him. "You really don't know why Ursula doesn't want Nina to know you two are seeing each other?"

"I suppose she's ashamed of me." He displayed both tattooed forearms. "I'm not exactly country club material."

"That's not it," I said. "Nina's grandmaternal clock is ticking."

"So?" he said, then his blue eyes widened. "Oh!"

"Act accordingly."

We walked through the dining rooms, and I said goodbye to Trevor in the wait station. He slipped into the kitchen, and I knocked softly on the office door then let myself in. Drew was sitting behind the desk, dressed casually in a black short-sleeved shirt that showed off his fading summer tan. "Sugar Pop!" he said with a grin.

Even though the manager's office had been completely redone during the upgrade a few months ago, and even though Drew had been away from the restaurant for several years, it was as if no time had passed when I opened the door and saw him pondering a pile of paperwork. Some of my happiest times traced back to when he managed Markham's and I cooked. It felt familiar and comfortable.

"Hey," I said. He stood and came around the desk to hug me, then we sat in brown leather club chairs so shiny and taut they chirped. "How's the accounting going?" I asked.

"Close to done," he said, rubbing his left thigh. "We'll be making a few changes. How are you coming on your side work? You still think Dana was murdered?"

"Yes, and I need your help." I told him about my day so far, starting with being denied entry to the farm, then I described my visit with Jerry Potter, which led to Mike Glass's admission that Randy had embezzled thousands of dollars from the Friends. "I think Randy's better idea was to keep the money and blame the theft on Dana," I said.

"Then why kill her?" Drew asked. "She would have to take office for his plan to work."

I hadn't gotten that far in my thinking. "Well, then, his better idea was to kill Dana so he could stay president and not have to pay the money back."

"Wouldn't they hold another election? He could lose again."

"Well, then, his better idea was to kill Dana and run off with the money," I said. "Plus, there's all that other curdled milk between them. I'll bet Randy blames Dana for forcing him to embezzle in the first place."

"So what do you need my help with?"

"Randy won't let me near him, but he'll come out here because he wants Markham's account." I picked up the landline receiver from the desk and handed it to him. "It's 555-WEIRD."

"I don't know about this," Drew said. "Getting the restaurant involved."

I appreciated that he put Markham's first, but I didn't like his loyalty interfering with my investigation. "Make the appointment and I'll intercept him in the parking lot. He won't have to know you were part of this."

"He'll know."

"It won't matter," I said. "It's not like Randy's going to refuse to sell us thousands of dollars' worth of wine. He's in Chapter Eleven. Besides, he's fixin' to have other things to think about, like what he wants for his last meal."

Drew shook his head, but took the phone from me. "I already planned to call him. He's trying to get everyone to forget the campaign, so he's making a lot of good deals right now."

"Tell him you want to make a decision soon, and he has to come over right away," I said.

Drew talked to Randy, except he didn't tell him the lie I had proposed, then hung up. "He's finishing up at Mostaccioli's and says he'll be here inside of twenty minutes."

I leaned over and kissed him. "You rock like Bon Jovi."

"Van Halen," he said. "Do you want me there when you talk to him?"

Aw. "Thank you, but we should keep you and Markham's out of this as much as we can. I can stand the heat."

"I know," he said, then, "Have you seen what they're doing in the kitchen?"

I nodded. "Why aren't you watching?" I asked, realizing too late that he was probably avoiding Jamie.

"I was out there earlier, but Ursula kept flubbing, and I could only take so many repeats of Sherwood saying, 'So, Chef, tell me how you came to add green peppercorns to your venison stew.'" Drew dropped his voice to sound like a radio announcer when he quoted Jamie.

"I think they got past that," I said. "I'm going to watch until Randy shows up."

"I'll come with you," he said. "I need to stretch my legs."

We stepped into the wait station, but Drew placed a hand on my shoulder to stop me from going through the swinging doors. Apparently, he was familiar with the specifics of filming and that it shouldn't be interrupted. He was tall enough to rest his chin on the swinging doors, and the crown of my head came to his chin, so he went to the dining room and dragged a chair over for me.

I climbed onto it and saw Logan standing at the prep table, smiling up at Jamie while Ursula diced potatoes on the other side of her. Jamie said, "And what are some of your favorite ingredients to work with, Logan?"

Before Logan answered, Ursula slammed her knife on the prep table and cried, "Mo-*ther*!"

"Cut!" Mindy yelled.

TWENTY-THREE

I FIGURED URSULA'S OUTBURST had something to do with Nina standing next to a grinning Trevor, but I was with Drew on the sidelines in the wait station and didn't witness the exact offense. Perhaps Nina had whispered something into Trevor's ear while pointing to Tiffany. Actually, just seeing Nina standing next to Trevor would have been enough to make Ursula swerve off the road.

Mindy came around the prep table and stood boot-to-clog with her starlet. "Ursula, sweetie, I'd *love* to see you more focused. And *smile* more. Our one point two million viewers *love* to see chefs having fun." She backed up, saying, "Okay, wow me."

Ursula's face took on the color and quality of a calcium deposit. "Million?" she murmured.

Mindy rolled her eyes and yelled, "Take another five, people."

Seeing Ursula helpless stunned everyone into inaction, but finally Jamie put his hand on her back and handed her off to Trevor, who walked her through the swinging doors and into the wait station. Drew had already helped me off the chair, so Trevor eased

Ursula onto it. No one else came out of the kitchen, so it was left to the three of us to discover why Ursula malfunctioned.

Trevor knelt in front of her and said, "I don't know why I did that, babe. I'm sorry. I'll stop, okay?"

"Millions," she said again.

Okay, I knew what was going on. For all the attention General Ursula York demands and commands in her kitchen, she gets stage fright when the audience is much bigger than her crew, specifically an audience made up of strangers. And now, apparently, an imagined audience. She never leaves the kitchen during service to greet customers and accept compliments, not even from a former US president.

Trevor put his hand on her shoulder and some honey on his tongue. "You need to get back in the kitchen so they can finish filmin', okay?"

That wasn't going to work. Not fast enough, anyway. But I knew how to encourage her, and amuse myself in the process. "Ursula," I said sternly, "a word in the office."

I took her hand and pulled her behind me, then shut the door and locked it in case Trevor wanted to come in and spoon-feed her some more nice. I put my hands on my hips. "What are you trying to pull?"

"What?"

"First you steal my recipe for salmon cakes, and now you're trying to ruin the restaurant."

"Mitch said it's Iris's recipe, and I'm not ruining the restaurant."

"Mindy and her film crew don't have time for you to work through your personal problems with your mommy and your boyfriend."

"I'm not—"

"Not what? Acting like a princess like you always do when something doesn't go your way?"

"No, I—"

"This isn't about you, Ursula, this is about Markham's, which already has a black eye because you were arrested for Évariste's murder."

"That wasn't my fault. I—"

"And I suppose this passive-aggressive little stunt of yours—"

"*Stop* interrupting me!" she screamed.

Finally.

Someone jiggled the door handle, and I figured it was Trevor riding to her rescue, but Drew said, "Poppy? Randy Dove is here."

"*Momentito*," I called, then unlocked the door and said to Ursula, "That's *your* kitchen, Ursula. Cowgirl up and get back out there."

Ursula had a strange smile on her face as she opened the door, and I knew that the General was primed to execute a maneuver. "Come on," she said, as she took Trevor's hand and dragged him onto the front lines.

I looked over at an amused Drew. "I'm glad I wasn't working here when you two were cooking together," he said.

"It worked, didn't it?" I pointed at the still-swinging doors. "Fat lady hasn't sung yet, though."

Ursula's impulsiveness is more suited to sneak attacks than planned assaults, so whatever she had brewed up would go down immediately. We opened the swinging doors at the moment Ursula took Trevor's face in her hands and put her lips on his lips.

"Nothing good can come of that," Drew said.

The kitchen gushed with cheers and applause, mostly from the cooks. The look on Nina's face was every bit as stupefied as the one on Trevor's, then Nina rushed into the center of attention and wrapped bony arms around her daughter and her daughter's no-longer-secret-but-probably-still-sometimes boyfriend.

Mindy clapped her hands until everyone realized that she wasn't on the same rhythm as the applause, and when she had their attention, she said, "Let's get to work, people."

"I guess nobody wins the Duelin' Dames pot," I said to Drew. "Where's Randy?"

"I asked him to wait in the foyer while I located some paperwork."

———

Randy stood at the hostess stand, assessing his competition—our current wine list. Like the restaurant a few months ago, it, too, had been upgraded from a three-varietal listing of our cheap house wine tacked on at the bottom of the food menu to a leather-backed presentation with two columns' worth of red, white, and sparkling wines offered by both the glass and the bottle. No more half-carafes.

So absorbed was Randy in professionally judging our wines that he didn't notice me until I stood in front of him and said, "How many in your party, sir?"

He scowled at me. "I'm waiting for Drew Cooper," he said, no warmth in his voice.

"Oh, is that why you're here?" I said. "I thought you might be looking for me so you can confess your crime."

"I told you that money was from a bet."

"And Mike Glass told me it was money you took from the Friends of the Farm funds."

Randy became interested in the surroundings and said, "Borrowed."

"But you haven't paid it back, so if the Friends took an accounting today, they'd call it embezzlement."

"I borrowed it, and I'm going to return every penny," he said. "It's not like the money was going to needy little orphans."

"Needy little vegetables," I said. "Good Earth couldn't buy their mobile irrigation system this summer because the Friends didn't come up with their share of the money. And now we know why."

Randy waved his hand and tried to laugh it off.

"The reason the Friends exist is to support the farm, Randy. You cheated them, the farmers, and the CSA subscribers. If you think business is bad now, wait until everyone learns what you did."

"Anything else?" he said, examining his fingernails to demonstrate his weariness. "A lecture on how wearing fur is cruel or eating animals is wrong?"

"No, but taking a human life is wrong."

"I agree."

"And your method was especially vile."

That finally ruffled him. "What on earth are you blathering about?"

"You poisoned Dana White."

"*Poisoned* her!"

"You had lots of reasons," I said. "So she wouldn't find out you stole the money is one. A big one. You also wanted revenge for what she did to you and your business during the election."

"If I killed everyone who had a negative effect on me or my business, we wouldn't have many restaurants in Austin."

"Are you admitting to it, then?"

"Of course not!"

"Why did you ask Mike for the money back? He said you had a better idea."

"I don't have to explain myself to you."

Oh, yes you do. "Was your idea to get rid of Dana so you could keep the money?"

"Are you hard of hearing? I didn't do it. I wanted the money back so I could make it look like my company was giving a big donation to the farm."

I let the disgust on my face offer my opinion about that, then said, "Where did you go after you left the barn?"

"To my car."

"But not to put the money there, like you told Mike."

"Too many people were in the parking lot, and I thought it safer to keep the money with me."

"Oh, right. We wouldn't want your stolen money to get stolen," I said. "And not only did you steal money, you stole people."

"People?"

"Person. Colin Harris."

I didn't know the circumstances of Colin becoming an employee at Weird Austin Spirits, but I thought it best to keep lobbing accusations at Randy. In spite of his denials and dismissive attitude toward me and my interrogation, he still had the best motive.

"Now *that's* a guy who had it in for Dana," Randy said.

"Colin? How's that?"

"She fired him for reporting her to the labor board."

"Her own sous ratted on her?" A sous chef is the vice president to the president, the Tonto to the Lone Ranger, the Scully to Mulder, the Walter to el Duderino. They're not supposed to squeal.

"And then he came to *me* for a job," Randy said smugly. "Of all people."

"You didn't have to hire him."

"You're kidding, right? Listen, I'll admit I'm not above kicking someone when they're down, but I've never killed anyone."

If Randy was the murderer, he would never confess it to me, so I had to either come up with irrefutable evidence against him, like

183

Dana's measuring cup covered with his fingerprints, or move on to my next suspect, which had just become Colin Harris.

"You're still a cheat and a thief," I said, "and I'm going to report you to Perry and the Friends."

"The money will be back in the Friends account by close of business today," he said. "And to apologize for the small mix-up in communication between myself and Mike that resulted in a temporary reduction in funds, I'm going to purchase an irrigation system for the farm."

No doubt with Weird Austin Spirits splattered all over it as the sponsor. "With what money?"

"Not to worry, my dear."

"Where's Colin this morning?" I asked.

"At the Wolff, I presume. Herb hired him back as executive chef."

Blimey! Gavin said Herb fired Colin. Had I uncovered a conspiracy? Did Dana's husband and her sous chef plot to kill her? I didn't know of any professional or personal disputes between Herb and Dana, but Jamie would.

I left Randy at the hostess stand while I went to fetch Drew for their meeting, but I got distracted by laughter in the kitchen when I entered the wait station. I stepped onto the chair and peeked over the door, lest I interrupt filming.

My eyes immediately locked onto Jamie interviewing Ursula and Logan, and I saw what the world would soon see: poised, articulate, handsome Jamie Sherwood, as natural in front of the camera as a stag in the forest, being ogled and appraised by every doe-eyed woman in the room. And soon, by 1.2 million viewers.

I felt a hand on my waist. "Is Randy still here?" Drew asked.

"Yes, sorry." I put my hands on his shoulders and hopped off the chair. "He's waiting for you up front."

"He's not our killer?"

"He says he's not, but he's a scumbag liar. He as much as admitted to stealing money from the Friends."

"I'm not sure I want to do business with a cheat," Drew said.

"Randy would never cross Mitch, but it wouldn't hurt to get any deals you make in writing."

"Will do. Are we still spending this afternoon at your house? I've been reading the dictionary."

I wrapped my arms around his waist and gazed up into his hazel eyes. "You might beat me at Scrabble one of these days, but you won't have the chance today. I really want to keep going with my investigation. Randy was number one on my list, but I have others."

"You still like Bjorn Fleming?"

"And now Colin Harris."

"For reporting Dana to the labor board?"

I pulled back and punched him lightly on the chest. "You know about that? Why didn't you tell me?"

"I thought everyone knew," he said. "Isn't your new couch coming today?"

"John Without is going to let them in."

"Without? Really?"

"It's a long story. I'll tell you later."

"Sure," Drew said. "Now how are you going to get out of here?"

TWENTY-FOUR

ONLY *I* WOULD BE forced to choose between leaving through the kitchen where I would interrupt one of my boyfriends interviewing my stepsister for a cable television show, and leaving through the front door, which would out my other boyfriend as a co-conspirator to the restaurant supplier I had just accused of murder.

"I'll wait in the second dining room while you bring Randy back here to the office, then I'll leave through the front door," I said.

That was, so far, the only plan that had worked all day, and a few minutes later, I sat in my Jeep and called Gavin.

"You're awfully busy on your day off," he said.

"I'm trying to earn some extra credit with Golferina." Golferina is our secret nickname for Olive. Not because she regularly takes the afternoon off to go golfing, because she doesn't, but because we've never seen her dressed in anything but black polyester pants and one of her well-stocked supply of short-sleeved polo shirts from various golf courses throughout the US.

"You mean Bovina?"

"*Ha!* Where did that come from?"

He laughed. "I suggested it and she's trying it out."

"Oh, Gavin, you're terrible."

"Merely a small payback for calling me Kowsaki all the time."

"I didn't think that bothered you."

"Does it bother you when people mispronounce your name as Mark-*ham*?"

"Yes, but you're not as tightly wound as I am," I said. "What can you tell me about the White Wolff Inn's last inspection?"

"I did them in August," he said. "They scored in the high nineties. Drinking from open containers, ice scoop in the ice."

"I'd like to inspect them again if it's okay with you."

"For the case you're working on?"

"Yeah."

"Then you have my blessing."

———

The White Wolff Inn is not an inn in the Holiday or Ramada sense of the word. It's a tavern that pours frosty mugs of micro-brewed beer and offers fat gourmet sandwiches served with homemade herbed potato crisps and cucumbers in brine (don't call them pickles) and mascarpone cheesecake. To counter the formal atmosphere of white tablecloths, black-aproned waiters, and valet parking service of Vis-à-Vis, its big sister two blocks away in downtown Austin's Warehouse District, the Wolff has cherrywood tables and chairs, bartenders to take your food order, and a serve-yourself parking validation stamp attached to a brass chain at the bar.

I pulled into the alley and entered through the open back door, which had a hand-written sign that read Closed—Death in

FAMILY. A hatless Colin Harris sat on a barstool, a sink full of water filled with Idaho potatoes to his right, a tall gray trash can in front of him, and a deep tub of peeled potatoes on his left. His eyes and nose were red, but potatoes don't usually induce tears, so I figured he couldn't contain his guilt over poisoning Dana.

"Is it that time again?" he asked when he saw me.

"There's no set schedule for surprise inspections, otherwise they wouldn't be a surprise." I looked around the small kitchen and didn't see any cooks or dishwashers. "Are you alone this morning? Where's Herb?"

"Making funeral arrangements."

I nodded. "I'm surprised to see you here, Colin. Yesterday you were working for Weird Austin Spirits."

"Herb called last night while I was at the party and asked me back."

"Is that so?" I said. That must have been why he left early.

He used the tip of the potato peeler to dig out an eye. "He needs someone who knows what they're doing. You know... with Dana gone."

"Sure he does," I said. "Except Randy Dove told me you were fired for reporting Dana to the labor board. And now Dana is dead and your new title is Executive Chef."

He blinked at me. "What are you driving at?"

I shrugged. "Maybe you killed Dana to make it happen."

"That's not even close to how it went down."

"Why don't you start with why you reported Dana to the labor board."

Colin wiped his runny nose on his sleeve. "Chef's been really good to me," he said. "She's an amazing person when you get to know her, but lately, with the Friends election and all the stuff with Randy, she'd been making some bad decisions."

"Like what?"

"I guess it doesn't matter now," Colin said, telling himself it was okay to tell me. "She was making everyone work a couple of hours off-the-clock every shift."

"Everyone? Waiters *and* cooks?"

The minimum wage for tipped employees is $2.13/hour, so Dana wasn't saving much money, but neither were the waiters losing much. Cooks, however, typically earn in the $10-$15/hour range and can make as much as $20-$25/hour depending on experience and rank. Say seven cooks on a shift, that's a hundred or so dollars a shift, times twelve shifts because her restaurant serves lunch and dinner six days a week, and double that if she did it at both of her restaurants. It would add up to a lot of savings for Dana, but the interest she accrued on employee resentment would compound by the minute.

"We went around and around," Colin said, "but I couldn't change her mind."

"Yet she handed the Wolff over to you."

"That was before I reported her."

"What does this have to do with Randy and the election?"

"Nothing directly, but she wasn't in her right mind because of it."

"Why do it in the first place?" I asked. "Her restaurants are doing really well as far as I can tell."

"It's not that," he said. "I didn't know it at the time, but Good Earth voted for Chef to bring in a restaurant, and she wanted to cut payroll costs so she'd look more solvent for the bank. Even if I'd known, I still would have reported her."

"What do you mean, bring in a restaurant?"

"Bring in a restaurant," he repeated. "Tables, chairs, a dining room, cooks cooking food, waiters serving customers. A restaurant."

It happens so rarely that people begin at the beginning when they're explaining something that I've gotten good at backing into a story. "Are you saying that Good Earth wanted Dana White to open a restaurant at the farm?"

"That's what I'm saying."

Whoa! "And you reported Dana to the labor board in the middle of all this? No wonder she fired you."

"I had no choice," Colin said. "These people are my friends, and I had to do what was right for them. Besides, I wasn't really fired. More like a temporary leave, but Chef didn't know."

I was sure that made sense to him, but no clarifying questions came to mind, so I motioned with my fingers for him to keep talking.

"She was really ticked off when she found out and wanted me gone immediately, but Herb did the actual firing. That's when he told me they're opening a restaurant at the farm. Herbivore they're calling it. It's going to be all organic and vegan using the farm's produce."

My taste buds snapped to attention at that description. Austin has lots of vegan restaurants, and most have some organic offerings on their menu, but none serving recipes prepared by Dana White. And none had such a perfect setting! I imagined a solarium-type room with huge glass windows overlooking colorful fields bursting with earth's bounty. What a fantastic idea!

Except Dana was dead.

Colin lobbed a peeled potato into the tub, then dunked his hand into the sink and fished out another. "Herb said Chef would see how impossible it is to run three kitchens by herself, and he'd convince her to re-hire me. He told everyone I quit so it'd be easier when I came back."

"Why did you go to Randy Dove for a job?" I asked.

"Randy came to me. He heard I quit at an ABRA meeting and called me the next day." Colin shook his head sadly. "I knew he did it just to twist the knife in Chef."

Interesting choice of words from Colin. And another lie from Randy? "But you took the job anyway," I reminded him.

"I still have bills to pay, but I didn't want to start at another restaurant knowing I'd have to leave soon."

"Please, Colin. Cooks start and leave all the time."

"I don't want to get that kind of reputation," he said, then dropped his eyes. "And I guess I wanted to get back at Chef, too, a little bit."

"That wasn't the smartest move," I said. "Working for an enemy Dana hated as much as she hated Randy. She might never have hired you back, especially if she had lost the election."

Colin nodded. "I know. I wasn't thinking. I felt like such a jerk delivering that champagne to her. She thought it was an olive branch until I told her it was from Randy and she figured out what was going on."

Colin's explanations sounded believable, but he knew what he was doing going to work for Randy. He admitted that he wanted to get even with Dana for firing him. He knew she would be at the party and their paths would cross. He knew Dana would discover this second treachery on top of reporting her to the labor board. Did he want the ultimate revenge?

I didn't think so. Someone soft-hearted enough to risk his very good job to do right by other employees wouldn't kill his employer, especially when he believed he would eventually get his job back.

And now with this revelation about the farm and all that implied, I felt more sure that the answer was at Good Earth. But the cops were conducting their own investigation, so I would have to wait until the next day to get that answer. It looked like my day off was going to happen after all. I could still do a later yoga class, then kick Drew's butt in Scrabble.

"I just remembered somewhere else I have to go," I said. "You and the Wolff get a break today, which is good, because you're not wearing a hair restraint."

I left Colin to his spuds and drove to Markham's to check on the status of filming and to plan the rest of my day. This time I came in through the front door. You don't have to tell me twice not to do something.

"Cut!" Mindy yelled.

A dining room full of people turned their heads in my direction.

In addition to everyone from the morning, the players now included several of Markham's food servers, bartenders, and hostesses. They wore pants and skirts and collared shirts, and posed on barstools at the bar and at tables in the main dining room. It had the look and feel of a regular weekday lunch service, but was happening after lunchtime and was made up almost entirely of Markham's employees.

"I thought you were filming in the kitchen," I said.

"We're in the dining room now," Mindy snapped.

"Is that so?"

"We can use you," she said. "Sit there with Jamie and act like you're having a good time."

She pointed to Jamie sitting at a two-top decorated with a white tablecloth, two place settings, and two half-empty glasses of white wine. He didn't have any food in front of him, so I didn't know if he had made an appropriate wine pairing. He obviously hadn't planned to pretend dine with me because I drink red wine with everything from popcorn to kale salad.

"Actually, Mindy, I have a yoga class to get to," I said. I heard a man clear his throat and located Mitch sitting at a booth with Nina. My father shouted *Penelope Jane* with his eyes. I turned back to Mindy. "But I'll be overjoyed to spend my day off supporting the restaurant."

"Lose the backpack," Mindy said.

I handed it to the bartender, Andy, then walked up to Jamie's table. Ever the gentleman, he stood when I approached and held out my chair. "What's all this?" I asked as he settled me then took his place across from me.

"Mindy's doing some crowd shots," he said. "For cut-aways."

"Listen up, people!" Mindy said. "We're going to do another wide shot, then move among the tables for some random close-ups, filming from different angles. I'd *love* for you to act like you're having a good time. Talk about whatever you want, but keep your conversations to a murmur, and no big movements. And smile!"

"Expecting company?" I asked, pointing to a glass of wine.

"Mindy's been rearranging everyone and somehow Logan ended up with me, but Trevor pointed out that she was too young to be my date, so they moved her to Daisy's table." He dropped his voice. "So, what did Mindy want with you earlier?"

"She said she *loved* the authentic cowboy boots I was wearing last night and wanted to know where I got them. I told her I bought them at Target."

"Jim Carrey and Maura Tierney," he said.

Liar, Liar. "She wanted me to apologize for spilling wine on her, so I did. For Logan."

I turned all the way around in my chair so Jamie couldn't see me and looked for Drew. I saw him several tables away sitting with Trevor and two waitresses, like couples on a double-date. I smiled at Drew, hoping he had witnessed Mitch's strongly glared directive and knew that I had no choice but to have an intimate pretend meal with Jamie. Drew crossed the first two fingers of his right hand and put them over his heart, his nonverbal way of saying "I love you."

"Did you find out anything about Dana?" Jamie asked.

I turned back to him. "As a matter of fact, two things, and one of them is huge."

"Rolling!" Dana yelled from somewhere behind me.

"How huge?" Jamie asked.

"Scoop-of-the-month huge."

"Oh, yeah? Wow me."

I rolled my eyes at him repeating Mindy's refrain. "Dana made a deal with Perry and them to open an organic restaurant at the farm."

"Herbivore," Jamie said.

"You knew?" I shouted.

"Cut!" Mindy yelled. She marched up to our table and said, "*Quiet* discussions." Then returned to her spot and clapped her hands. "Rolling!"

Jamie put his forearms on the table and leaned into me. "That's what I wanted to tell you last night before the police arrested Cory Vaughn."

"You should have called me, Jamie, or told me this morning. That's a major motive to kill Dana."

"Not really," he said.

"Yes, really." I crossed my arms and leaned back in my chair. "But since you're surrounded by bright lights and beautiful women, I'm sure you're not interested in why."

"Come on, now. Of course I'm interested."

"Cut!" Mindy yelled. She walked up to our table again, then uncrossed my arms and put them in my lap. "This is a *fun* lunch for two." Hand clap, then, "Rolling!"

Jamie laughed, having fun like he was supposed to.

"Colin said Good Earth *voted* on bringing Dana and Herbivore to the farm," I said. "A vote means it wasn't unanimous."

I knew I had Jamie's attention when he abandoned the fluid flirty voice he had been using and said in his reporter's voice, "Which means someone didn't want her there."

"And that brings us to the second thing I found out." I relayed what Mitch told me about Dana being a founding member of the farm. "Don't tell me you knew that, too."

"No, but it will add some interesting flavor to my upcoming feature on the farm restaurant that never was."

I lifted my glass to eye level and swished the wine around like Jamie had taught me to do. The legs were thick and slow, like a dessert wine. I said, "All those conversations I heard—"

A cameraman moved in close to us, and Jamie picked up his glass of wine and held it up as if to toast. I clinked mine against his, then we both sipped.

Then I spit my mouthful onto the table.

TWENTY-FIVE

"Cut!" Mindy yelled. The cameraman stepped sideways to make room for his bossy boss. "*First* you interrupt filming," she said, "then you *shout* like a carnival barker, *pout* like a teenager, and now you're *spitting up* like a newborn!"

I didn't respond because (a) she had made several inaccurate statements, not asked any relevant questions, and (b) I was disgusted by the residue of oil in my mouth. Not even good oil, like coconut or olive. It felt and tasted cheap.

I wiped my tongue with my napkin, then asked Jamie, "Why is canola oil in this wine glass?"

"It's a prop," Mindy answered. "You're not supposed to drink it." She looked at her watch. "Especially not in the middle of the day."

My nostrils have not been known to flare in anger, but that time they did. Mindy Cottonmouth! Hissing at me like that in my family's restaurant! This fake drink belongs in her fake face!

Jamie stealthily moved my glass out of reach. "It's my fault, Mindy," he said. "I forgot to tell her."

Mindy flapped her mascara-caked eyelashes at her handsome apologist and patted his shoulder. "Oh, Jamie, that's fine. Rolling!"

"Do we have any real wine in the house?" I said when she clopped off. "Or is it all grape jelly and digitalis now?"

"Digitalis isn't purple," Jamie said. "You just have to get used to things on a film set."

"This is a restaurant dining room," I said. "And I don't want to get used to a debutante whose vocabulary is limited to 'take five, people,' 'rolling,' and 'cut.' At this rate, she'll be filming until those jeans of hers get worn in."

He steered me away from that with, "You were going to tell me about conversations you heard?"

"The ones I heard last night between farm people about votes had to be about the restaurant, not the Friends election."

"Maybe the vote was partisan along family lines. The McDougals wanted her, but the Vaughns didn't because of what happened between her and Perry."

"Except Vaughns outnumber McDougals four to three, so if that were the case, Dana wouldn't have gotten in."

"Maybe someone broke ranks," Jamie said.

"Or multiple someones. From what I heard between Cory and Bjorn, Cory voted against her. I also heard a man and a woman arguing in the office last night, but I never found out who it was. He was saying he couldn't believe she voted for Dana."

"Perry and Megan?" Jamie suggested.

"If Perry didn't want her there, I can't see Megan siding against her husband."

"Maybe what you heard really was about the Friends vote, so it could be anybody." Jamie slid my prop glass of oil back to me. "What else you got?" he asked.

"Bjorn. He lives in one of the little cabins out there. If Dana set up shop, he'd probably lose his job and his house. That's motive. He also had opportunity, seeing as he has the run of the place and it being his kitchen Dana was cooking in. I'm making a trip to the farm tomorrow."

I heard chairs scuffling and everyone started to stand and talk above a murmur. "Looks like we're taking five," Jamie said, no longer interested in me or my theories. He stood, then looked down at me. "Let—"

"The police handle it. I know."

"I was going to say, let me know if you find out who won the recipe contest."

"And when I find out who killed Dana, shall I tell you first or the police?"

He hesitated, as I knew he would, then responded as I knew he had to. "The police."

"Sure thing, hoss," I said.

I stayed in my chair and contemplated my approach at Good Earth for the next day. Finding out who voted to bring in Herbivore—or rather, who voted against it—would help sort the sheep from the wolves. But what if the vote didn't split neatly by last name? That added another layer to this cake of intrigue. With seven votes, at least four family members voted yes and won, which meant that, at most, three family members might have a reason to ixnay Dana. For sure Cory voted no because—oh!—Bjorn made him!

"There's that smile I love," Drew said into my ear. He kissed my cheek then sat in Jamie's chair. "What's the reason?"

I smiled. "I have the rest of the day off."

"Does that mean our plans for today are on?"

"Yes, if you still want to."

"I didn't read the dictionary for nothing," Drew said. "Let me tell Mitch we're leaving."

"You don't have to stay for filming?"

"I think we're done with the crowd shots. I heard Mindy say they're going to shoot the front, then do more filming in the kitchen. Besides, I'd rather be with you." He stood and came around the table to pull out my chair. "My truck's blocked in, so we'll have to go in your car."

———

By the time Drew pulled my Jeep into my driveway at 3:04 PM, I had told him my suspicions about the farmers and the votes, except I didn't mention they were the product of my forced lunch date with Jamie.

"Everything points to Good Earth," Drew said as he unlocked my front door and let us into the empty living room.

During the remodeling, I'd had the house finished out with warm wood panel walls and floors so it looked like a ski lodge, but I didn't want to choose any living room furnishings until I bought a couch to establish the style and color scheme, and that had taken months due to twelve-hour work days and my lack of interest in color schemes. I finally agreed to let Nina help me, not because she didn't have a place to sit when she visits, which is never, but because she works as an interior decorator when she's between husbands and actually has skills in that area.

Drew crossed into the kitchen to open the bottle of Gundlach Bundschu Merlot I insisted he take from Markham's as payment for me being a foodie extra under duress. I knew he would deduct it from his own wages later.

"I agree," I said, sitting on a fold-out chair at the card table topped by a Scrabble board. "All those farmers go way back with Dana, and any one of them could have a grudge against her."

Drew placed a glass filled with dark crimson liquid in my hand, then sat next to me. "That was, what, thirty years ago?"

I sniffed the bouquet. "Thereabout."

"Long time to carry a grudge."

"Time doesn't always heal a wound," I said. "Sometimes it makes it fester."

"And sometimes it makes the heart grow fonder."

"Is that in reference to the murder or to us?"

He smiled and handed me the bag of Scrabble tiles.

I pulled out the letter C and Drew came out with the letter M. We tossed our go-first tiles into the bag, then I chose seven new ones and handed the bag to him.

"What were you and Sherwood talking about?" Drew asked as he reviewed his letters.

"The case," I said, then kicked off the game with STORM.

"So you weren't giving him the heave-ho?"

I answered with an unhappy tilt of my head.

"You know I love you, Sugar Pop."

I nodded. If I knew anything, it was that.

"And you love me."

"I've never said that."

"You don't have to," he said, rearranging his tiles.

"Dana's husband may have done it," I said, wanting to put off that discussion. "For insurance money."

"Poppy," Drew said heavily. He put his hand on mine and held my eyes with his. "You have to decide. Me or Sherwood."

"Are you giving me a deadline?"

"You can't keep stringing us both along."

"That's not what I'm doing," I said. "Not intentionally."

"That's what it feels like."

"I have a lot of feelings to work through, and you know I'm not good with that."

Drew used a blank tile and played the word MINE.

———

We spent the next hour sipping wine, playing Scrabble, and discussing Markham's employees and customers. He didn't push me again on my decision, but he was right. It wasn't fair to anyone, including me, to keep both of them on the hook. I had kind of hoped one of them would take himself out of the running and make my decision a slam dunk.

At 4:00 PM, I received a phone call from the furniture store that my couch would be delivered within the hour, so when I heard the doorbell ring a few minutes later, I totaled my triple word score for AMITY, gave Drew a victory kiss, then opened the front door.

Not only were there not two brawny delivery giants standing on the porch, but the garden gnome that is John Without wanted one of the most cliché neighborhood favors ever. "Can I borrow a cup of sugar?" he asked.

"White or brown?"

"I don't know," he said. "White, I think."

"Granulated or powdered?"

"I don't…"

"What's it for?" I asked.

"John's making cookies for the HOA meeting tonight."

"Then why isn't he over here asking me?"

"Like I said, he's making cookies."

"Without sugar?"

John let out a hard exhale. "Do you have any or not?"

"Hang on," I said. I left the front door open while I went to the kitchen, then returned with three bottles, one each of agave nectar, maple syrup, and honey. "I don't have any sugar, but you can usually substitute one of these depending on the recipe."

John Without stepped off the porch and turned toward his house.

"Uh, John, aren't you forgetting something?" I said.

He looked down at the bottles cradled in his arms. "I don't think so."

"Thank you?"

"For what?"

I shut the door on my neighborhood nemesis, only to receive a phone call from my work nemesis. "Bovina!" I said. "How udderly wonderful to hear from moo."

Drew snorted wine out of his nose and jumped up to get a paper towel.

"I'm done with that one," she said. "Sounds like something the CDC issued a bulletin for last week. Causes facial tics."

I thought that sounded like Olive herself, but said, "How can I help you on my day off?"

"Where are we on Colonel Chow's?"

"I left you a message."

"You left a message for someone named Viv, so I deleted it."

I repeated the message I had left and told her I would return to General Chow's later. If she assumed that I meant today, that would be her mistake. "What should I call you when I report in?" I asked.

"Amber."

"You know that's a color, right?"

"Wrong, Markham. It's Russian jewelry."

"That flies get trapped in."

Twenty minutes later, the doorbell rang. To my ten-point word score, I added my fifty-point bonus for using all my letters, gave Drew another victory kiss, then opened the front door.

Again, no delivery giants, but I welcomed this John on my doorstep. John With wore long brown shorts, a pale pink shirt that set off his dark curls and skin, and a vintage red apron with a black silhouette of W.C. Fields and the words "Who put pineapple juice in my pineapple juice?" He held the bottles I had given to John Without.

I stepped aside to let him in, then reached up and thumbed a smear of flour from his chin. "Those won't work?" I asked.

"I'm making sugar cookies and need a little more to sprinkle on top. John went to the store."

John With followed me into the kitchen and placed the bottles on the counter. He shook hands with Drew, then tapped the score sheet. "When are you going to learn, my friend?"

"I like a challenge," Drew said.

"You would have to," John said, then to me, "Are you coming to the meeting tonight?"

"Drew and I have plans to sit on my new couch and watch *The Big Lebowski*," I said.

"You'll miss my cookies," John said.

"I'll also miss a bunch of petty complaints about unscooped dog poop and neighbors taking their recycling to the curb a day early."

"It can't be that bad," John said.

"You'll see," I said. "Why does John want to be president, anyway?"

"He wants parking passes for the neighborhood."

In the past decade, Austin's population has grown much faster than its infrastructure, which is a problem in neighborhoods like ours that were built in the forties and fifties to support bread-winning dads who kissed their wife and kids goodbye before driving the family car to work. Most houses have a single-car carport and a short driveway that will accommodate one other car, which means that visitors usually park on the street.

It works for most people, but when you have a tribe of frat boys down the street that throws weekend parties for friends who think the term "carpool" means filling up an old Karmann Ghia with water, the street clogs up fast. This is a problem for people like the Johns who like to throw their own parties for friends who think the term "carpool" means pooling their cars at a central location. So the city came up with a voluntary program for neighborhoods that can require non-residents to dangle a temporary parking permit from their rearview mirror when they park on the street. Violators are to be hanged from the playground swings or something.

"We have that in my neighborhood," Drew said. "He has to get a majority of signatures from homeowners, then get permission from the city."

John nodded. "That's the platform he's running on."

A nicer person would have told John With that they could skip the cookie bribe, that his boyfriend could campaign on a platform of free air and sunshine for all residents and he would win the election. But John With likes to bake cookies, and I thought that John Without would make a superb parking Nazi. "I wish him luck," I said.

"Can Liza stay with you while we're at the meeting?" John asked.

Liza is a Maltese puppy John Without gave to John With a few months ago. She was part anniversary present and part replacement for their first Maltese, Judy, who had been squashed in their driveway a couple of years ago by the moving company they hired to move them from one side of me to the other. When they're gone, they usually leave her in a small cage in the guest bedroom—a well-appointed canine condo with a pink-and-white monogrammed bed, squeaky toys, and a radio—but they prefer she has company.

I looked at Drew, who said, "Sure."

I walked John to the door. "Don't bring her over until the delivery guys leave, okay?"

Thirty minutes later, the shadow of five o'clock had started to sprout when the doorbell rang again. Drew was already standing to pour more wine into our glasses and said, "I'll get it."

He opened the door not to giants or Johns, but to Jamie.

TWENTY-SIX

I HEARD, "WHAT ARE you doing here?" and "What are *you* doing here?" and knew *I* didn't want to be there, so I took the highest road available in that situation—I escaped out the kitchen door and ran to the Johns' house.

It was one thing to be forced into a decision early, but if they expected me to decide between them in front of them, and without a couch to lay on afterward, they were wrong.

"Hi, Poppy Markham," John With said when I entered through the back door without knocking. "Did you come for Liza?" He held her in one hand and a full cookie sheet in the other.

"Relationship asylum," I said.

He handed Liza to me who licked a smile onto my face. "Did Drew finally beat you at Scrabble?"

"Hey," John Without said as he entered the kitchen from the dining room, "that crazy girl has *both* of her boyfriends—" He stopped when he saw me. "Do you know Jamie Sherwood is at your house?"

John With looked at me. "Oh, I see," he said. "Well, no I don't. What exactly is going on with you three?"

John Without dropped a one-pound bag of sugar on the countertop, then began to put away the other groceries he bought, which were mostly protein bars, black canisters of protein drink powders with "Monster," "Mega," and "Power" in the name, and a bottle of grenadine. John With used scissors to cut open the sugar, poured some into a measuring cup, then began to sprinkle the tops of the cookies.

I sat at the table, settled Liza onto my lap, and briefly described the situation with Jamie being unfaithful to me, which they already knew about, and me seeing Drew while Jamie was away, which they also knew about, and how Jamie returned six weeks early, which was a new development. "And now I have to decide between them," I said.

John Without *ghrfed*. "It's not exactly Sophie's choice."

"No, but it's not an easy one," John With said. He handed me a small blue plate with two oven-warm cookies. "Without butter," he said, then sprinkled more sugar onto more cookies. "If you had to choose right now, who would it be?" he asked.

"If I knew that, I wouldn't be sitting here," I said.

"If only," John Without said as he began packing the sweet bribes into a round, red tin lined with foil.

John With said, "Which one do you love?"

"Both."

"Which one makes you happy?"

"Both."

"Okay, let's review the issues that broke you up."

"Yes!" I said, glad to have a map to push pins into.

John Without mewled his disapproval, then snatched up the packed tin and his car keys and walked into the living room. His actions were on the short side of rude, but only because he thought my help would make him King of the HOA. A non-campaigning John would have queued up the latest Longhorn's game he Tivoed and blasted me back to my house with inane football babble.

John With sat down across from me. "Jamie got drunk one night and cheated on you," he said.

"Right," I said. "Just the one time, but I'm still having a hard time trusting him."

"And Drew had a serious health situation in Colorado and didn't call you for three years."

I bit into a cookie. "Yeah. He lost his leg from the knee down and said he didn't call because he was depressed for a long time. He went through tons of rehab and counseling, but I feel like he abandoned me, so it's hard to trust him, too."

"Your new couch is here," John Without announced louder than he needed to.

"The guys can handle it," I said, then to John With, "Both of them were crummy to do what they did."

"Not necessarily," John With said.

"Oh, right. Should I date the one who cheated on me or the one who left me hanging for years?"

"The question is *why* did they do what they did? Why did Jamie cheat? Why did Drew leave you hanging?"

"Oh, for Pete's sake!" John Without called from the living room. "Choose the one who gives you peace!" He flew into the kitchen. "We *have* to go, John. Now."

John With apologized with his endearing crooked smile, then leaned over and gave me a hug and Liza a kiss. "Stay as long as you like, Poppy Markham."

"Thanks," I said. "Good luck tonight."

After they left, I peeked out the front window. Jamie and the delivery van were gone, thank goodness, so I washed the cookie sheet, spatula, and blue plate, then collected Liza and walked back to my house.

I came through the back door into the kitchen, but Drew wasn't at the table. I stupidly wondered if Jamie had given him a ride to his car. Then I heard, "Hey, man, I'm not trying to scam anybody here."

In the living room, Drew was reclined on my new sage green couch, the DVD remote in his hand. Liza squirmed and yipped when she saw him.

"Do you want me to back up to the beginning?" Drew asked.

"I've seen this movie a hundred and thirty-eight times. The big Lebowski just asked the Dude if he's expected to pay for every rug that gets micturated upon in their fair city." I sat next to him. "Sorry about earlier."

He nodded, then smiled when Liza jumped onto his lap and deluged him with kisses. "Sherwood didn't believe me that you took off, but after he poked his nose into all the rooms and closets, he finally left."

"I went to the Johns."

"I figured."

"I'm *really* sorry I left you to deal with that. Are you okay?"

"Yeah, you?"

"For now."

———

Drew was quiet during the movie and on the drive to Markham's to pick up his truck. He drove my Jeep around to the back, then cut the ignition and stared out the windshield. The cars from earlier were gone, which left only Drew and me, sitting in a car together behind a closed restaurant, like so many other times in our lives.

"You know I love you," he said finally.

"Drew—"

"This isn't what you think," he said. "Please, let me finish."

I nodded.

"Things were going great for us, for you ... until Sherwood showed up last night."

So far, it was what I thought: an indictment of my relationship with Jamie.

"It hurts me to see you hurting," he said. "So ... I'm taking myself out of it."

What! "What?"

"You don't have to choose between us."

"Just like that? Did something happen between you and Jamie earlier that you're not telling me?"

"Besides him acting like he owns you? No."

"What about what *I* want?"

He shrugged, then heaved himself out of the Jeep, and I saw his sad smile in the greenish glow of the street light. "That's what you need to figure you, Sugar Pop," he said before getting into his truck.

I was too stunned to feel either relief or aggravation that Drew had broken up with me. Sure, a decision was going to have to be made between him and Jamie, but it was *my* decision to make. Or so I had thought. I should have talked to Daisy earlier. She would have reminded me not to be so selfish, that there were two other people besides me with feelings and desires.

And now I had an unfettered shot to Jamie. I wasn't sure how to feel about that, either, but I knew I needed to sleep on it. Then do the smart thing and talk this over with Daisy.

I had left Liza in her condo at the Johns' house while Drew and I went to Markham's because I didn't trust her not to tinkle or teethe on my new couch. The Johns were back by the time I returned, so I washed mine and Drew's wine glasses and popcorn bowls, then went to bed.

As usual, I woke up at 5:00 the next morning. For all of the strife in my life at that moment, I felt strangely peaceful. Someone not living my life would probably attribute it to my relaxing day off, but I just knew that today I would see Dana's murderer in handcuffs.

The farmers were already up, of course, but the harvest would keep them busy for most of the morning, and their attention would be scattered if I tried to talk to them. Better to wait until later for maximum return on investment.

I dressed in my black uniform, put on a red lightweight jacket against an October chill that had reluctantly shown its face, dropped my cell phone and a couple of Red Delicious apples into my backpack, and drove north to surprise a few sleepy breakfast cooks.

At my first restaurant, a diner famous for its black olive and artichoke heart quiche, I observed several flats of eggs stacked on a prep table. According to my infrared thermometer, the temperature of the ambient air surrounding the egg was 55 degrees, which is ten degrees higher than the proper storage temperature of 45 degrees for eggs, which meant that either their cooler wasn't working properly, or more likely the cooks had ignored the health code and removed more flats from the cooler than they could work with in fifteen minutes or less.

I also witnessed them open cans of black olives, artichoke hearts, jalapeños, and peaches without washing the tops to prevent contamination from the dirty lid dropping into the can and into the food. A visual examination of the lid won't reveal the sweat from the guy who made the delivery or the urine and feces of the rodents that used the can as a latrine at the storage warehouse.

If the food had been spoiled due to a vendor's or manufacturer's error, I would have put a detained sticker on the items to keep them out of service until the manager could return them and get a refund.

However, it was their own fault that the ingredients were unsafe, so I asked the manager to throw the eggs and can contents into the trash. Then I poured bleach over everything in case they had ideas about salvaging those ingredients. Oh, yes, it happens. All the time.

And that was only one breakfast shift at one diner. Imagine the thousands of cooks doing similar mindless things during hundreds of shifts in hundreds of food establishments all over the city.

I got in two more inspections before the smell of burnt bacon made me queasy, and I knocked off at 9:30 AM.

A little after 10:00 AM, I swung my Jeep into the gravel parking lot of Good Earth Preserves. So intent was I on resuming my investigation, I was momentarily confused by all the BMWs, Lexuses (or is it Lexi?), FJ Cruisers, and Outbacks that belonged to the farm's subscribers. They had driven out, I realized, to pick up their CSA boxes.

I gathered my backpack and crocheted hemp bags into which I would transfer my box contents, then approached the buildings. Megan and Tanya stood by the washing shed, chatting with subscribers as they transferred generous bunches of leafy chard, onions, and broccoli into their own reusable canvas bags, placing items they didn't want in the community box for other subscribers to take and taking extra of ones they did.

Subscribers know what to do, so it seemed odd that the women were socializing after all that had happened in the past thirty-six hours. But like Perry says, a farmer's work is never done. Both of them looked tense and tired with overwrought smiles that couldn't distract from their red eyes and noses.

I wanted to ask Megan what she remembered about Dana during the party, so after greeting them and expressing my condolences at all the recent unpleasantness, I asked Megan to check the expiration date of my CSA subscription.

"I'm glad to see Tanya feeling better," I said as I followed Megan from the washing shed to the office.

"Our little T-bag is such a help on pick-up days," she said unkindly.

I stood in the doorway while she sat at the desk and paged through a drawer of manila folders until she came to the M's. "Markham comma Mitch, Markham comma Nina," Megan said. "And, here, Markham comma Poppy."

Yet another place Nina came between me and my father.

Megan wagged her head. "Kevin put all of this information into the computer, but it beeps at me whenever I try to find something."

As she shuffled through the paperwork, I said, "How is Cory?"

"Perry got him freed on bail early this morning. They're both still sleeping."

"You heard about Dana, I assume?"

Megan squeezed her eyes shut and nodded. "The police arrived yesterday before the roosters woke up to start confiscating Cory's plants, then detectives came out after lunch and asked us questions about Dana."

Her eyes moistened with emotion, and since I'm as good at comfort and tenderness as I am at maintaining my lawn, I said, "What did the police want to know?" Their specific queries would let me know if they suspected something sinister.

Megan sat back in the chair and wiped her eyes. "They said it was routine. They wanted to know if we noticed Dana acting strangely before she passed out or if she seemed ill."

"Did she?"

Megan flipped her braid over her shoulder. "We all said she was fine as far as we could tell. Busy, excited about her Friends win, worried that she didn't bring enough meat for the skewers."

"I suppose she was also excited to open Herbivore out here."

"She was thrilled!" Megan said. If she thought it strange that I knew about the restaurant, she didn't let on.

"Was everyone else thrilled?"

"Yes, of course. We've discussed opening a restaurant for a number months."

"But I understand you took a family vote."

"We do that for all major decisions," she said. "That way, we can express our dissent without rocking the boat."

I would believe John Without had a sensitive emotional core before I believed that. The thing that would qualify something as a major decision would be an issue that divided the farmers in the first place. "Did you vote for her?" I asked.

"We keep them confidential," she said, then held my eyes and nodded.

"I guess all had been forgiven."

"I'm sorry?"

"Mitch told me that Dana and Perry started the farm with Ian and Tanya. I thought Dana might still have had some sort of resentment that she'd been kicked off the farm."

Megan laughed. "She left on her own, and that is seriously ancient history. Dana and Herb have been good customers for years."

"What happens to the restaurant now? Are you still going to open?" She gave me a strange look and I realized that I no longer sounded merely curious. "Does it say when my subscription expires?" I asked.

"You're good until March of next year," she said, confirming what I already knew.

I looked around the office at the old photographs of the farmers with sun-smooched skin and long hair, years away from being diluted with gray. They were all in the frames—Tanya and Megan holding baby boys, Perry and Ian holding heads of cabbage. Young, idealistic back-to-the-landers.

"I can't believe Ian cut his hair," I said.

"Ian's doing a lot of things that are hard to believe." She put the manila folders into the file drawer. "You like radishes? We've got bunches of them."

"I'd love extra," I said. "And if you don't mind, I'd like to go into the kitchen and eliminate the possibility that Dana died from food poisoning."

She swung wide brown eyes up to me. "Food poisoning? Are we in danger?"

"Whatever it is has a short incubation period, so if you didn't get sick during the party, you're safe. I think it's an isolated incident." *Of murder.*

"Bjorn's still cleaning up from this morning."

"I won't get in his way."

TWENTY-SEVEN

BEFORE I RODE SHANK's mare into Bjorn's lair, I stopped outside the office and took in the serenity of the farm. It looked much like it had the last time I had seen it two days before. The roosters and chickens pecked and scratched at the ground, and the Cornhusker's staircase stood in the same place close to the barn. Even the subscribers talking and laughing gave off the essence of a festal atmosphere. Everything appeared to be the same, but nothing was the same.

Brandon drove up to the washing shed on a shiny green four-wheeler loaded with radishes. The farm begins to harvest produce at first light, but a couple of years ago, they were short-handed, which delayed the morning harvest. They hauled in the produce and made up boxes with help from subscribers. It created such a positive buzz about "fresh from the fields" that Perry and Ian decided to do it on purpose every once in a while on pick-up days. On request, they'll also take subscribers into the fields to harvest their own produce.

Brandon stepped out of the vehicle and hugged me. "Thanks for everything the other night, Pop," he said.

"How is everyone? How's Core?"

"Haven't talked to him," he said. "Been a one-man show all morning."

"Isn't Kevi helping?"

He snorted. "Around here, MBA stands for Moist Brow Aversion."

"He's always been more of an idea man," I said. "He told me at the party that he had a lot of plans for this place."

"Most of them unworkable."

"Was Herbivore one of his ideas?" I asked. To Brandon's obvious surprise, I said, "Your mom told me about the vote. Did you want Dana's restaurant?"

"Did you hear?" he said. "Dana didn't make it."

"That's why I'm here. It might be an isolated case of food poisoning. You were in and out of the kitchen serving food. Did you notice her acting strangely?"

"I couldn't really say," he said. "She'd come out to the farm a bunch lately to talk about the restaurant, but she mostly met with Dad and Uncle Ian, so I don't know how she usually was." He motioned to one of the interns to unload the radishes. "I told the police she was sweating and drinking a lot of water, but that's normal, I guess. It was like a furnace in there."

"Did you see anyone in the kitchen who didn't belong?"

"I don't know what you mean by not belonging. We own the place, and all of us went in there at some point. Me, Core, and Kevi serving food, but also Mom and Dad, and Aunt Tanya. And Bjorn, of course."

"Tanya? I thought she had a headache."

"She came down to get some aspirin from the first-aid kit." The intern called for him. "Gotta get," he said.

I started up the walkway, realizing that Brandon hadn't told me whether he voted for Dana, so I still didn't know whether families or individuals had squared off over Herbivore.

I entered the kitchen and saw Bjorn in his usual black chef's coat and checks. He stood at the small prep table drinking coffee and reading the *Statesman*. He looked like he had slept upside down in a cave. He frowned when he saw me, so I held up both hands. "I come in peace," I said. Unless he was a murderer.

"Coffee?" he asked.

"Thanks." I filled a cup from the full carafe. "I'm sure you've heard about Dana by now."

He flicked the paper with his index finger. "Still front-page news."

I waited for him to say more, that he was sorry it happened or how Austin had lost a talented chef, but apparently he thought it was my turn to talk. It wasn't. When you're talking, the other person isn't, which means you're not getting information. I nodded and sipped coffee. I had poured it myself and felt confident that Bjorn hadn't poisoned it. Plus, he didn't know I was coming.

"I knew you'd be here this morning," he said.

I set the cup on the counter. "Oh?"

"It wasn't our food, though," he said. "It was something Dana brought."

"But everything at the dinner is from the farm," I said.

"Not everything."

I don't like when people drop a provocative statement like that, then smile like they've eaten a Michelin chef's meal, basking in their secret knowledge, waiting for you to ask them to elaborate. Why can't they just continue with the explanation? But I wasn't there to give anyone a lesson in civility, so I said, "What do you mean?"

Bjorn smiled bigger, widening the divide between what he knew and what I wanted to know. I displayed my inspector's badge. "Are you confessing to a county health inspector that you brought in produce from an unapproved source?"

That erased his smug smile. "No! Goodness, no," he spluttered. "Perry would feed me to the pigs. No, the onion crop was light because of the drought, so Dana sent one of her cooks to Whole Foods for some."

"So you *are* confessing."

"I said *Dana* did it. And it was a private party."

"What's your impression of the restaurant Dana planned to open at the farm?"

His blue eyes flashed with barely contained furor.

"Was the farm going to let you go?" I pressed. "Is that why you asked Dana for a job?"

I expected him to deny it, but he set his mouth and nodded.

Another good reason for Bjorn to poison Dana. He knew the dangers of food-grade hydrogen peroxide. His intent may not have been to kill her, but he may have wanted to get even with her for upheaving his life and then for denying him a job, or make her sick enough to stop her from opening the restaurant. When you act out of emotion, plans and consequences rarely make it onto the drawing board.

"When did they decide to bring in a restaurant?" I asked.

"A few months ago," he said. "All of a sudden, one day that's all everyone's talking about."

"Were they arguing?"

"Look, it doesn't matter now. Dana is dead and so is the restaurant."

"Don't you think they'll bring in another chef?" I asked. "Those are a lot of plans to throw onto the compost heap."

"They didn't want just any chef," Bjorn said, clearly angry that they didn't want him. "They wanted the great Dana White."

Right then, my phone rang in my backpack. I extracted it and looked at the display. Olive. "I have to take this," I said to Bjorn.

I went out to the washing shed, which, except for the muddy floor, looked orderly after the morning's boxing, and found a quiet place away from the activity. "What's the buzz, Amber?"

"Kelly," Olive said.

"Like Kelly green?"

"Doggone it," she said, then hung up.

I waited for her to call back with either her new identity or the reason she called in the first place, but after a couple of minutes of silence I returned my phone to my backpack and returned myself to the kitchen, resolved to lock Bjorn in the walk-in if I had to and squeeze every drop of Dana-related information out of him.

But he was gone, replaced by someone better.

Tanya McDougal stood in front of the walk-in door, fanning her tan, lined face and neck with a large, round plastic lid, even though the cool morning had warmed up to the low seventies outside and it felt like the mid-eighties in the kitchen. She wore plaid shorts and a faded red T-shirt under a white apron, her cotton-candy hair pulled back into a messy ponytail. She also wore blue rubber gloves, which could have accounted for her overheating. Those things don't breath.

"Hey, Tanya," I said.

She turned with a jolt, then fanned down her shirt with the lid. "Oh, hi, Poppy. I didn't know you were still here."

"I'm investigating a possible food poisoning incident," I said. "You heard what happened to Dana?"

She nodded and I noticed sweat on her forehead, running down from her hairline. "The police were here yesterday." She closed the walk-in door and resumed fanning herself. "We're all just sick about it."

Not everyone. "I spoke with Bjorn a few minutes ago, and I understand that y'all took a vote on whether to bring Dana's restaurant to the farm." I made it sound like Bjorn had given me the information to see how Tanya reacted to it.

"Bjorn," she said through tight lips. "That's family business."

I assumed she had no intention of discussing family matters with me either, so I headed her toward something only she could tell me, which is when she had come into the kitchen to get aspirin. "We missed you at the party. Megan said you had a headache."

"I still do," she said, "but I had to make the preserves this morning." She wiped her face on her sleeve. "I wish Perry had never made us start selling that blasted stuff."

"The night of the party, you were seen getting aspirin from the first-aid kit," I said. "Did you talk to Dana while you were here?"

Tanya blinked wide blue eyes at me. "I don't ... I feel ... "

Faint, apparently, because that's what she did.

"Here we go again," I said as I rushed to her.

She had reached for the walk-in's door handle to steady herself and pulled open the door when she went down. I left it open to give us some cool air, then knelt next to her. She was breathing and I saw her neck pulsing, so she didn't need resuscitation. Just a simple faint from the heat.

For some reason, I pictured the revival skills I had seen in the movies. That part of the story typically involved a drunk either being rousted by the police with shouting and taps against his foot with a billy club, or his friends dousing him with cold water and slapping him into consciousness. I took a kinder approach.

I went to the sink and wetted a grill towel, then placed it on Tanya's forehead, then I lifted up her apron to get air circulating around her legs. I struggled to peel off one of her rubber gloves, because her hand was sweaty inside and it didn't come off easily. But when I finally got it off, her fingernails were painted bright pink!

I leaned in and lightly stroked her cheek. "Tanya, honey, wake up. Get up." That close, I got a good whiff of gin on her breath.

She opened her eyes, then closed them and removed the wet towel. She didn't ask what happened, so I imagined that her fainting wasn't an uncommon occurrence, if not a regular one. I helped her sit up and propped her against the prep table, then filled a coffee cup with cold water and she guzzled it.

"Feeling better?" I asked.

She dropped her eyes. "I'm so embarrassed," she said. "This never happens."

"Tanya?" Bjorn called from the doorway. We were on the other side of the prep table, so he couldn't see us. "Kevin and Ian just drove up."

Tanya grabbed my arm and mouthed, "*Please don't tell.*"

I popped up. "We're here, Bjorn."

He came around and scowled at Tanya. "Why are you on the floor?" he barked.

Tanya's eyes pleaded with me not to tell him the truth, so I said, "I dropped my badge and we bent down at the same time to pick it up and bonked heads."

Tanya rubbed her forehead for realism, and I did the same.

Bjorn closed the walk-in door, saying, "Those preserves done?"

"I have enough pecans for another small batch, so I need more brandy," Tanya said.

Bjorn left us in reproachful silence, and Tanya heaved herself up to standing. "Thanks for not saying anything," she said as she peeled off the other glove.

"Why didn't you want Bjorn to know you fainted?"

"It's ... a private matter."

"Because of your drinking?"

"What?" she said with a faltering laugh.

"The night of the party, I found an AA newcomer's medallion in the washing shed. Is it yours?"

"We had a lot of people at the farm that night. Why do you think it's *mine*?" She picked up a marker and wrote the date and "Pecan" on a Good Earth Preserves label, then affixed it to one of the jars cooling on the table.

"Because it had bright pink nail polish on it," I said.

She made both hands into fists to hide her fingernails. "That doesn't mean I'm an alcoholic." Then her body shook and her face flushed and she sniffled.

I turned her away from the table so she didn't contaminate the prep area with her tears and snot. "Was that your gin in the Oxy-Growth bottle in the walk-in?" I asked.

She nodded. "I'm trying to quit, but it's sooooo hard." She gulped air then bent down and wiped her face with the skirt of her apron. "Bjorn's an alcoholic, a recovering alcoholic, and he's trying to help, but he's making things worse."

"Is he your sponsor?"

"No. You're not supposed to . . . he quit cold turkey and he thinks I should do the same. He doesn't understand why I'm having a hard time."

I didn't know what to say to encourage her: "Good luck." "You'll do better next time." "Keep your chin up." "Take it one day at a time." Are you allowed to say that if you're not an alcoholic?

Tanya said, "I'm getting yanked six ways from Sunday right now, and I'm having a hard time dealing, you know?"

She seemed like she wanted to confide in someone about her hard times, and if I was going to play the role of her confessor, she was going to confess what I wanted her to. "Does it have anything to do with bringing Dana and Herbivore to the farm?"

"That's part of it," she mumbled.

"Did you vote against her?"

"Are you kidding? No!"

"You *wanted* her here?"

Before Tanya answered, Bjorn erupted into the room. "*You* voted for that Nazi!"

Tanya hid behind me, which I didn't appreciate, but she found her voice. "You were *spying* on us? I can't believe you, Bjorn!"

He stepped toward us and we both skittered back. "What do you expect?" he said. "Every day you come in late and hung over or you don't show up at all because of one of your humidity headaches. You say we'll talk later, but you leave early." He slammed a half-full bottle of brandy on the prep table. "I can't hunt you down at your house, now *can* I?"

"Because you do this!" Tanya said. "You go crazy when you hear something you don't like."

"How long have I covered for you, Tanya? How long? *Years*." His face suddenly lost its hard edge and so did his tone. "You're supposed to be getting help."

"I don't want help!" she cried, punctuating her declaration with her fist against my back. "I *like* to drink." *Punch*. "I *want* to drink." *Punch*. "All day, every day. But I can't because of these stupid preserves, this stupid kitchen!"

She moved past me and lunged for the brandy, but Bjorn stepped between her and the table, and I held her arm. And then she fell into Bjorn and blubbered incoherent syllables into his chest.

He hugged her and kissed her hair and said, "It's okay, baby. One day at a time, okay? Just take it one day at a time."

TWENTY-EIGHT

BABY? WELL, I SUPPOSE it was inevitable with them working so closely together and having the common interests of cooking and alcoholism. But if they were having an affair, why would Tanya vote for Herbivore when it would put Bjorn's future at the farm in jeopardy?

"Sorry to interrupt y'all," I said, "but who voted against Herbivore?" They could rehearse this soap opera on their own time.

Tanya drew back from Bjorn and looked away from him. "I don't know," she said. Bjorn grunted his dissenting opinion, and she said, "Really. We did it anonymous. Nobody knows."

"Surely y'all had some discussion," I said.

"Oh, there was plenty of discussion," Bjorn said, the comfort gone from his voice, "but *some* people lied about what they wanted."

"Don't start, Bjorn," Tanya said tightly. "Pour the brandy and let me finish the preserves."

He picked up the bottle of brandy and a plastic measuring cup and held them up in front of Tanya's face while he poured, taunting her. I saw tears in her eyes as she went back to printing on the labels.

A more considerate person would have left them alone to cool off, but they were both high on the emotions of anger and disappointment, which are often a potent truth serum, and I wouldn't have another chance like this. They were also invested in our conversation and wouldn't stop to wonder why I was poking my nose into the farm's business instead of poking a thermometer into the preserves.

Bjorn began to stir the brandy into a large stock pot on the stove, so I walked over to Tanya. "Before we bonked heads earlier, I asked about you coming into the kitchen to get aspirin." She stopped writing, but otherwise didn't move. "Do you remember what time you were here?" I asked.

She shrugged. "They were really busy, though."

"Was Dana around?"

"I don't know," she said. "I didn't feel good."

"You were *drunk*," Bjorn said.

Tanya dropped her shoulders and closed her eyes briefly. "I got the aspirin then went home."

"Did you come down again during the party?" I asked.

"No," she said, then sniffled.

I felt bad for her—married to Ian the jerk, having an affair with a worse jerk, and drinking day and night to get away from something emotionally that she couldn't get away from physically.

"Are you sure?" I asked. "I heard you arguing with a man in the office after Dana left in the ambulance." I didn't know for sure if it was Tanya, but since she had voted for Dana, and it had enraged Bjorn, it might have enraged someone else.

Tanya glanced at Bjorn, then went to the pot on the stove. "Yeah, I remember now," she said. "I went in there to get a bottle I hid—"

"You what!" Bjorn yelled.

I shot a hard look at him. "Leave that for later." I turned to Tanya. "Who came in?"

"Kevin," she said.

Her own son had talked to her like that? "I thought the votes were confidential," I said.

"They are, but everyone kept arguing and changing their minds."

"*Et tu*," Bjorn said.

Tanya ignored that Shakespearean reference to being a traitor and continued, "Bjorn told me Cory was voting against her, so I . . . evened things out."

"She wasn't supposed to be voted in!" Bjorn yelled. "Dana didn't belong here!"

"It's not up to you!" Tanya shot back. "*This* is how we do things. This is how we've *always* done things. Perry won this time."

Reading between the lines of Tanya's reason, it sounded to me like she really did want the restaurant. She probably saw it as the only way to get rid of beastly Bjorn. Whatever soft feelings she ever had for him were obviously used up. If she had made sure Dana was in, she wouldn't have killed her.

I decided to strike a match against Bjorn. "How did you know that Cory was going to vote against Dana? Because you forced him to?"

"You need medication," he said.

"I heard y'all arguing in the Field, remember? Did you threaten to expose his pot crop?"

Tanya gaped at him. "*You* called the police on Cory?"

Bjorn put his hand up in a stop-right-there gesture. "No, I did not."

"You didn't threaten him or you didn't call the police?" I said.

He gave me what I will now refer to as his signature hateful glare. "I used his illegal activities to sway his vote, but—"

"You what!" Tanya cried.

"But I did not call the police," Bjorn said. "I had no reason to."

I said, "Unless you thought he lied to you when he said he voted against her, and you were getting even with him."

"I did think that, actually, but I already told you, I didn't call the police."

I didn't want to defend Bjorn to Tanya, but I couldn't let them continue down this bunny trail. "They wouldn't have arrested Cory after one phone call from Bjorn," I said. "They already had evidence against him, so I bet they've been undercover out here for a while."

"Not with my help," Bjorn said, ever interested in covering his own butt.

"Getting back to that night," I said to Tanya. "How did Kevin know you voted for Dana? Did you tell him?"

"He came into the office a few minutes after I did, saying he knew it was me and I messed everything up."

"What did you mess up?"

Tanya shrugged.

I looked at Bjorn. "Did Kevin know that Cory planned to scuttle Herbivore?"

He scoffed. "How would I know what those kids know?"

I couldn't think of anything else to ask them—other than the obvious question about whether either of them had killed Dana—but that would tip a hand I wasn't sure I held, so I left them to marinate in their man-made mess.

I walked out of the kitchen and my eyes landed on Brandon rolling toward the fields on the four-wheeler. I took off after him, shouting, "Brandon! Wait up!"

He idled near the hedge of the Field until I caught up to him. "Be right back," he said. "I have to tell the guys they can knock off for now."

"Can I come?" I asked.

"Hop in," he said. He hit the gas pedal and we took off. Well, not gas because it was all electric.

We hummed past plots of dirt that had been rowed out with sticks and string to be planted soon, and fields of lettuces and corn, the co-operative product of nature and farmer. I can grow gobs of mold in my refrigerator, but I have a necrotic thumb when it comes to growing anything with roots. I certainly don't know all the ins and outs, all the what-have-yous about organic farming, but I know it's harder than I want to work for a salad.

From what I remember of Perry's talk during the tour and others I've heard him give in years past, their farm lives revolve around such things as sustainable soil fertility and nutrient levels, crop rotation to confuse and disrupt harmful insects, host plants to bring in beneficial birds and bugs, and weed control—all with minimal environmental disturbance. And then there's the USDA certification paperwork.

This is part of the reason Brandon, Cory, and Kevin are still living at home as it were, well past the age of marriage and family. The farm depends on the boys for its survival.

I wouldn't want to be Dana's killer, but I especially wouldn't want to be the one who put the family business at risk.

"That's a pretty good idea y'all had to pre-wash the vegetables for lazy subscribers," I said. The ride was so quiet, I didn't have to raise my voice.

"Not lazy, *busy*," Brandon said as we turned onto a dirt road that led to the back of the farm. "It was Kevin's idea. To bring in more money."

"Bjorn told me you weren't using food-grade peroxide at the farm anymore, but didn't you use some for the demo?"

"We switched over to iodine, but Dad wanted us to use peroxide the other night because it looks nicer." He parked and stood up in the passenger side, then whistled at a group of interns and waved them in.

"What did you do with the bottle when you were done?" I asked after he sat down again. "You usually store it in the kitchen freezer, right?"

"Dad didn't want Dana or her cooks to accidentally use it, so he said to take it back to the house. That's some wicked stuff if you don't handle it right."

"Did you take it home right after the demo?"

"Cory said he'd do it." Brandon did a K-turn to get us going back where we came from.

"It's like a mini Jeep, this thing," I said.

"Uncle Ian's working on getting us two more." He gunned it and we shot up the road, shaken and stirred all the way to the buildings. He slowed down when we had to maneuver around the staircase that had, in our absence, been moved in front of the dirt road leading out of the fields, then rolled to a stop by the chicken coop. "We're running low on juice," he said. "I need to get this in the barn before it dies."

"Really?" I asked, not believing my luck at not having to finagle a reason to see inside the barn. "I mean, can I see how it works? Daisy and Erik are saving up to buy one."

"Giddyup!" he said.

He rolled up to the closed barn doors and put the gear in Park, but I stepped out before he did. "I'll get it."

"It's heavy," he said.

"I do power yoga," I said, displaying a bicep. "I'm strong like bull."

I unhooked the latch, then tried to slide the right side of the door open. Brandon smiled and put his feet up on the steering wheel, settling in for a long wait. I used both hands and gave the door a hard jerk. It scraped and squeaked and moved only a couple of inches. I did that a few more times until I had enough room to wedge my body between the two doors. I put my legs and back into it, but couldn't push it open. I hated to do it, but I looked to Brandon for help.

He swung out of the four-wheeler and slid open the left side, chuckling to himself as he returned to the vehicle.

"You could have told me," I said as he passed me and parked under the stairs that led up to the loft.

He cut the engine then switched on the overhead lights. The barn looked and smelled as it had in my youth, its looming bigness giving me the same mixture of excitement and dread. In the center of the dirt floor was a pyramid of hay bales stacked about eight feet high, with wide dirt corridors between it and a series of livestock stalls in the wings. Instead of milk cows, the stalls on the left held more hay bales, the ones on the right, underneath the hay loft, held SUVs. Three of them. The same model, all painted charcoal gray, and all parked nose in.

I whistled. "Fan-cy."

Brandon pointed quickly at each one as he said, "Ian's, Tanya's, Kevin's."

"What are they doing in here?"

"Dad wants them out of sight when subscribers are around."

I thought I knew the reason, but asked Brandon anyway. "Why?"

"He wants everyone to believe that we're but humble hippie farmers."

"Where's yours?" I asked.

"My Honda from college still has a few miles left in her." He uncoiled a thick orange electrical cord from the wall and plugged it into the front of the four wheeler.

"How long does it take to charge?" I asked.

"Full charge? About eight hours. If Ian left it alone long enough."

"Where is Ian, anyway? He's usually here on pick-up days."

"We slid the pick-up day to today because of Dana, and it messed up our other deliveries. Him and Kevin took some boxes to our drop

231

at Zilker Park. Dad makes them take the Veedub on official farm business." He thumped the gauges on the four-wheeler's dash and seemed satisfied that everything was charging properly. "They should be back by now."

"I suppose they don't much like the bus after driving one of these," I said as an excuse to move closer to the three vehicles. I couldn't tell which one I had seen sneak away from the barn the night before. But then I had an idea. "Are they automatic or standard?" I asked, opening the driver's side door of the one closest to the barn doors. The interior light came on. Dang.

"I don't know," Brandon said. "They just got them. I haven't seen inside yet." He opened the middle one and that light came on, too.

I pinned all my hopes on getting that third car door open. If the light came on, I would have to figure out another way to know who left so secretly, but if it didn't come on, I would have another angle to work while I was at the farm. I had run out of excuses to open doors, but Brandon was occupied with admiring the interior of the car he opened, so I slipped over to the third car and opened the door. No light! "They're all sticks," I said. "Even Tanya's."

"That one's Kevin's," Brandon said as he shut his door.

"How can you tell them apart?" I said as I surveyed the front seat, passenger seat, dash, and console. I saw mud on the driver's side carpet, but that was nowhere close to suspicious.

"They always park in the same stall."

The police required more than that to point the finger at Kevin, but I didn't. I hadn't seen Kevin in the Field shooing people off the farm after the party, so he may have been the one driving off. And according to Tanya, he was in the "no Dana" camp, which automatically clicked him up a notch on the suspect list.

I wanted to search the barn for whatever evidence Kevin may have left inside, so I had to think of a way to keep Brandon in the barn with me. I headed for the back and tried for a nostalgic tone when I said, "Do you remember when y'all used to have that cow?"

Brandon closed the car door and came out of the stall to lean against a post. "Yeah, Mrs. Hoofster. She was mean."

I inspected the wooden countertops, but saw only rusty cans of bolts and screws, empty egg crates, old hand tools, and undisturbed dust. "You tried to show me and Daisy how to milk her that one time and—"

"She kicked Kevin in the jewels," Brandon finished with a snicker.

I opened one of the lower cabinets. "Can you believe he used to fit in here when we played hide-and-seek?" I squatted down, pretending to assess the cabinet's size. "Hard to believe he was that little." Nothing but a bunch of crumbly rubber belts and an old horseshoe.

"He's still mad about that time we locked him inside on his birthday."

"He's mad about a lot of things," I said. "I think he needs a girl-friend."

"He says he's working on building a nest egg first. Ever since that MBA, it's nothing but money, money, money." He started for the open barn door. "I've got to get back to work, okay?"

I couldn't come up with a good reason to keep us inside, so I followed him, taking my time as I looked up, down, and around. I saw an open cardboard box on the dirt floor by the door and—holy fortuitous serendipity!—soldiered inside were several slender white necks wearing little red hats!

TWENTY-NINE

I FIGURED THERE WAS no need for stealth, so I picked up a bottle and said, "Does this OxyGrowth stuff work? Daisy and Erik would love it at their nursery if it does."

"I don't know," Brandon said. "Dad's still not convinced we should use it. Take a bottle and let them try it."

"Are you sure?"

"We have tons of the stuff," he said. "Kevin got us a deal."

"Thanks," I said as I inserted the bottle into the outside pocket of my backpack. "And thanks for the tour."

"Any time, Pop." He turned off the lights before he slid the doors closed, then we walked over to the buildings. He waved to one of the subscribers beckoning to him. "Excuse me," he said.

"Of course."

I stood outside the barn and processed what I had learned. First and most relevant, Perry insisted that Brandon and Cory use peroxide for the demo. Was it really because he thought it looked better or did he want the peroxide out of the kitchen where he could get to it easily? No, that didn't make sense for two reasons: one, the farm is his domain and he could have gotten the peroxide at any time, and two, why direct the boys to take the bottle to the house afterward?

I assumed that with Ian's opposition to an all-organic restaurant, Perry had advocated bringing Dana and Herbivore to the farm, so he wanted Dana there as far as that went. Unless something went sideways between them at the last minute, like Dana insisted on a higher percentage of the partnership, or she changed her mind about the menu and wanted to serve pork sandwiches and bowls of chili.

And all those brand-new McDougal SUVs were strange. The money, the impact on the environment, the reliance on oil—the opposite of green and sustainable, the opposite of the farm's values. What had Megan said in the office earlier when I mentioned Ian cutting his hair? That he was doing a lot of things that were hard to believe. It had all the hallmarks of a run-of-the-mill midlife crisis, but why buy new cars for his wife and son, too? Guilt perhaps? That he had raised such a smarmy kid and had driven Tanya to drink and into another man's tongs.

At least I knew that food-grade peroxide was still on the premises, and now I had a bottle of OxyGrowth to test. It mattered which one the killer had used because it would either cull my suspects or swell the herd. The peroxide was known to and accessible by only a few of the farmers, whereas OxyGrowth was available to anyone at the party—especially those who had interrupted my phone call to Mitch in the storage pantry under one pretense or another.

I bent down and plucked a couple of blades of grass, then went to the bathroom and hung my backpack on the coat hook on the back of the door. I pulled out the bottle of OxyGrowth, jammed my finger through the foil seal, and, as I had done with the gin the night of the party, poured a small amount into the lid. I laid the bottle and lid on the edge of the sink, then pinched off a small piece of grass and dropped it into the OxyGrowth. And then…nothing…more nothing…still nothing.

Had I thought to sniff the bottle's contents, all of that would have been unnecessary. It gave off a distinct chemical smell, and the liquid was pale yellow. OxyGrowth had the color and stench of urine, but the remains in Dana's cup were clear and odorless, so she had definitely gulped food-grade hydrogen peroxide, which definitely pointed to Bjorn or one of the farmers as the murderer, which meant that I was definitely in the right place.

My best assumption was that Dana's killer had voted against her and Herbivore, so I needed to find more farmers and ask more questions. However, I had no authority outside the kitchen, so I would have to try to get information based on personal relationship. And that meant I had to court the company of persons.

I walked up to the washing shed and found my name on the list of subscribers attached to a clipboard next to the sink. I initialed my entry then heaved up a box of vegetables from the now-shortened stack and placed it on the table. As I transferred my haul into my crocheted bags, I caught sight of Perry on the plywood walkway between the shed and the office talking to Jesse Muñoz, the owner of a local equipment supply company. Megan had told me earlier that Perry slept late, but he didn't look well-rested.

Perry and Jesse shook hands, and I stowed my bags under the table and hurried over to speak with Perry before something else captured his attention. His face remained solemn as he watched me approach, and I wasn't sure if it was due to my presence or to the dope-dealing son and dead ex-girlfriend situations.

"Hello, Poppy."

"Hey, Perry. How are you? Megan told me you were able to get Cory out on bail."

"That was step one. We have another hundred to go."

"I'm really sorry you're having to deal with all that mess," I said. "Dana, too. Mitch tells me you started the farm with her."

He dropped his eyes and said softly, "That was a lifetime ago."

"What's the status of Herbivore now?"

He looked up at me. "What's with all the questions?"

I had already come up with an excuse in case someone thought to ask me that. I was just surprised that it hadn't been asked sooner. "Jamie Sherwood wants me to gather some facts for him while I'm here."

"Facts for what?"

"A story he's doing on Dana."

"What kind of story?"

That, I didn't have a ready-made answer for. The mention of Jamie's name usually induces logorrhea in people. "One on Herbivore. That was the announcement she going to make after dinner, right?"

He nodded.

"Did you vote to bring it to the farm?"

"Look, Jamie'll have to get his facts some other way," Perry said. "My attorney doesn't want anyone talking to anyone for a while."

"Not even to say who won the recipe contest?"

He finally smiled. "I guess we never got to announce it, did we? Daisy's daughter, Logan. Her sweet potato pie." He pressed his lips together. "That was the last thing Dana and I discussed. She said she was impressed with its complexity."

Perry struck me as truly heartbroken by Dana's death—not that a killer can't feel pain or remorse—and I didn't think he did it, and since I felt my investigation slipping into a coma, I decided to take a chance and come clean with him. If he kicked me off the farm, the police would have to solve it themselves. "I wish it weren't true, Perry, but I think Dana was murdered."

He frowned at me. "She had another heart attack."

"Induced by drinking food-grade hydrogen peroxide."

"It didn't come from here," he said. "We use iodine."

"Brandon told me they used some for the washing demo. He said you gave it to him."

Perry put his hands on his hips and gazed up at the sky. "I forgot about that." He turned to me, finally grasping what had happened to Dana. "She *drank* that stuff?"

"One of you put it in the measuring cup she was drinking from that night."

"One of… You have no proof of that."

"It didn't get into her cup accidentally."

He massaged the back of his neck. "Who would do that?"

"Someone who hated Dana and had access to the peroxide. Someone who didn't want Herbivore at the farm."

Perry whistled sharply at one of the interns on a golf cart. When he looked up, Perry waved him away from the foot-tall rosemary bush he had almost crushed. "Watch where you're going, son," Perry said to the intern, then to me, "Is that why you're here? To accuse one of us of killing Dana White?"

I had to be careful with my answer. Depending on whether Perry's loyalties lay more with protecting the farm or with doing the right thing, he might either banish me from Good Earth or give me the name of the killer. "We both owe it to Dana to learn the truth," I said.

"What if I did it?" he asked.

"It's possible," I said, "but I'd be surprised if you did something to hurt the farm." I pointed to his T-shirt and read the tagline. "Honest food from honest folks. Do you still believe that? Will you help me?"

He shook his head and I slumped my shoulders. "I won't stop you, though," he said.

That may have been the best thing to happen! If my intuition had fed me faulty vibes about Perry, he would run straight to any evidence still on the farm and destroy it. If he knew who killed Dana, he would run straight to that person and raise the alarm. And if he wasn't sure who did it, he would run straight to the person he himself suspected. I tracked his movements toward the Field, but he stopped a few yards away and pulled his cell phone from his pocket.

"Dang," I said, then heard a faint ringing behind me.

My heart dialed all the way up to eleven as I whirled around, prepared to tackle someone if I had to. But as I scanned the crowd for a killer answering a call, I realized a timer had gone off in the kitchen.

Naturally, Perry wasn't there when I turned back, but Cory had appeared in the vicinity of the perfect place to hide evidence—the chicken coop. Coincidence or father-son collusion? I would soon find out. "Core!" I called, jogging up to him.

He waited outside the door to the coop, his body language mumbling nothing but shame—head down, shoulders rounded, a face that could be measured in cubits. He looked up briefly. "Hey, Pop."

"How was jail?" I asked. "Ursula told me they serve a lot of bologna."

He sniffed out a laugh. "Jail sucks."

"As it should. Have you talked to your dad recently?"

"Not since we got home," he said. "I just woke up."

I wanted to box his ears and ask what he was thinking growing marijuana on his family's farm! Didn't he know that the farm was everything to them? How could he do something so reckless? How could he jeopardize their relationships and their livelihood by bringing something like that into their midst? But he had probably already heard it or would hear it from people who mattered to him more than I did. So I said, "You're an idiot, Core."

He rubbed his face with both hands. "I know."

"Bjorn knew about your farm within a farm, didn't he?"

He toed some dirt over a squirt of chicken droppings.

"And he threatened to expose you if you voted for Dana White and Herbivore."

He nodded, still not making eye contact with me.

"Did you vote against her?"

He nodded.

"Did you know that Tanya voted for her?"

His eyebrows lifted an inch. "She did?"

"She said it's how things should have gone."

"I bet Uncle Ian's ticked."

"Ian didn't want Dana here?"

"Yes and no," Cory said. "He wanted a restaurant, but he didn't want it all organic."

"Why not?"

"He wants the farm to go conventional. He says it's too expensive to keep our organic certification and we can grow more and make more money."

"After all these years?"

Cory shrugged. "Mister MBA put it into his brain. They're all worried about costs, as usual."

"Which is why y'all switched to iodine to clean the vegetables," I said. "Except for the party. What did you do with the peroxide after the demo?"

He finally looked up at me. "The what?" Yes, he answered a question with a question, but he seemed truly confused rather than cannily evasive.

"At the party, you and Brandon washed the vegetables with food-grade—"

"Yeah, okay, that. I took it up to the house."

I sighed.

"What?"

"I'm having trouble with the timeline, Core. You said you stayed to make up more CSA boxes and then Ian called you to help him with the fence."

"Uh-huh."

"But Jerry Potter told me he was in the barn with you after the demo."

Cory covered more chicken droppings with dirt.

"So what exactly happened to the bottle of peroxide?"

"I don't know," he said. "I guess I left it by the sink."

"Did you ever go help Ian with the fence that night?"

He shook his head.

I sighed again. Whether it's a surprise inspection or a murder investigation, getting to the truth of something is so much more difficult when people lie.

"I need to clean the coop," Cory said.

"And I need to talk to Mister MBA. Have you seen him?"

"Not if I can help it. You might be able to spot him from up there." He pointed to the staircase. "You can see the whole farm."

With my first step toward the staircase, my stomach began to white-knuckle. "Forget it," I said to the hedge and changed course. Maybe Megan was still in the office and knew where Kevin was. Or Ian.

When I passed the kitchen, I heard my name and turned to see the very Moist Brow Averter I had set out to find.

Kevin stepped out of the doorway and said, "Mom says you've been snooping around our private family business." His tone was smirky and combative. My favorite. It takes the uncertainty out of things.

"Dana White is dead and I'm looking into the possibility of food poisoning."

"What does that have to do with Herbivore?" He took a step toward me, which forced me back.

"Well, if your current health practices can't keep deadly bacteria from contaminating a few simple ingredients, the health department has concerns about issuing a food permit for any future new restaurants." Even as I spoke those words, I knew that Kevin would be quick enough to figure out that my answer didn't exactly jive, so I followed it up with, "Did you know that Bjorn blackmailed Cory into voting against the restaurant?"

He smiled smugly. "I know *everything* that goes on in this place."

He kept advancing on me, so I kept moving back, but I can retreat and entreat at the same time. "It was you arguing with Perry in the storage pantry after the washing demo the other night, wasn't it? You said you didn't want Dana here."

"I don't. Didn't."

"Your mom voted for Herbivore. What did she mess up for you?"

"I think it's time for you to leave," he said. He took my elbow and escorted me down the walkway.

"Dana was murdered, Kevi. She drank peroxide."

Kevin stopped and rocked back on his heels. "What?"

I couldn't tell if his surprise came from him not knowing that fact or realizing that I knew that fact. "Someone replaced the water in her drinking cup with food-grade hydrogen peroxide. I saw you sneaking out of the barn when the party was breaking up. What were you doing?"

"It wasn't me," he said, conducting me toward the parking lot again.

"It wasn't you who killed Dana or it wasn't you sneaking out of the barn?"

"Both … neither." Kevin let go of my arm when we reached the office. "I didn't do anything."

"Well someone drove your car out of the barn the night of the party. And yes, I'm sure it was yours."

"We leave the keys in them. It could have been anyone."

"Do you happen to know who?"

"Even if I did, I wouldn't tell you." He pointed at the parking lot. "Goodbye, Poppy."

"Tell me why you didn't want Dana White at the farm."

"*Goodbye*, Poppy."

I walked slowly in the direction of my car, trying to dredge up something to say to reach détente with Kevi and get me back onto the farm. I would have to come up with something really good, like offer to make a contribution to his IRA or tell him which rainbow pooled into a pot of gold. Or … I could give him enough time to get involved with some farm business, then sneak back on.

During this commercial break, I sat in my Jeep and went over the facts I had uncovered. Except for the vote switcheroo between Cory and Tanya, I was pretty sure the vote went along family lines. Perry, Megan, and Brandon voted for Dana, but Cory didn't because of Bjorn; Ian and Kevin voted against her, but Tanya didn't because she wanted to either maintain equilibrium or punt Bjorn off the farm and out of her life. So, from that slant, Ian, Kevin, Tanya, and Bjorn belonged high on the suspect list.

So, who drove Kevin's SUV out of the barn? I put myself on that staircase the night of the party and tried to remember who I had seen and where—Ian and Brandon shooing people out of the Field, Bjorn standing outside the storage shed, Perry and Kevin talking in front of the office. Any one of them could have made it to the barn in less than a minute.

I looked up but didn't see Kevin on the sidewalk. Only a couple of subscribers with full bags squeezing between the two painted VW buses. And then one of the seeds I had planted in my mind began to germinate, and I realized I had been thinking locally instead of globally.

Holy obviousness! I knew who killed Dana.

THIRTY

THE EXTRAVAGANT CARS, THE expensive four-wheelers, the push for conventional growing methods and using pesticide, putting costs ahead of values. Dana and her 100-percent organic fresh-from-this-particular-farm restaurant threatened to squash all of his plans, which meant reduced profits, which meant one very desperate Ian McDougal. Whether Ian was lured by his son Kevin, or he had found his own way to this consumerist aggression, Ian had changed his priorities and he needed operations at the farm to go in a new direction.

Of course, the killer could also be Kevin for all those same reasons, but since he had just tried to shut down my investigation, I would have a go at Ian first.

I shook my hair out of its ponytail, then slipped on my sunglasses and red jacket. It wasn't much of a disguise, but I could work it long enough to sneak onto the farm. If Kevin was smart, and he was, he had already told his family that I was *persona non grata*. And if Ian had talked to Perry, he already knew that I suspected one of them of murder.

But perhaps Ian hadn't seen the smoke signals, so perhaps I still had the element of surprise.

I got halfway across the parking lot before I realized that my backpack would give me away, doubled back to leave it in my Jeep, then circled to the left to come up from the other side of the parking lot. I kept my face down and affected a limp as I went down the sidewalk past the office to the washing shed. My veggie bags were where I had left them under the table, and if anybody asked, I would tell them that I came back for them.

I took off my sunglasses and matador-red jacket and bundled them with my bags, then looked for Ian. I hadn't seen him all morning, but, yeah, I expected him to materialize just because I wanted to talk to him.

I had about convinced myself that ascending the staircase wouldn't be that bad when I saw red hair riding in the four-wheeler coming from that direction, making straight for the barn. Ian. Finally!

I waited for him to pull inside, then entered a few minutes later. He had pushed open the left side door, which cast bright morning light into the interior of the left side of the barn. The four-wheeler sat parked between the pyramid of hay bales in the center and one of the hay-filled stalls on the left.

I heard movement at the back of the barn. "Ian?" I called. "It's Iris and Mitch's daughter, Poppy Markham." I knew he heard me, or rather, he couldn't have not heard me. I took a couple of steps into the barn, but not so far that I couldn't flee in case he came at me with a pointy farm implement. "Ian?"

He emerged from the shadows wearing heavy leather work gloves, a pitchfork in one hand and clippers in the other. Hell's gardener.

"Hi, Poppy," he said as if he had expected me. He leaned the pitchfork against the front of the four-wheeler and entered the stall. "You working for the USDA now?" he asked as he bent down out of sight.

"No," I said, my eye on the pitchfork. "I'm still a county employee."

"And a curious one," he said. He stood up and indicated that I should move to the right, then he tossed a tangle of baling wire past me. "Kevin said you've been asking about Dana's restaurant."

"Oh? When did you talk to him?"

Ian grabbed the pitchfork and started forking heaps of hay into the back of the four-wheeler. "Why are you so interested in the farm's business?" he asked. "And don't give me that line about food poisoning. Tanya told me you didn't check any of the food."

Ian seemed angry, but that's how he always comes across, so his tone didn't tell me whether he knew of my true suspicions. Still, if my decision to be alone with a killer in a barn full of spiked and serrated tools were weighed on the great scale of dumbness, I would be crowned the Grand Poobess of Dumb.

I wanted to solve this mystery, but I also wanted to live to see Ian get sentenced for it. I figured I had enough to take to the police. "You're right," I said. "I forgot to do that." I backed up. "Is Tanya still in the kitchen?"

I heard squeaking and became aware of darkness spreading through the barn, the shaft of light slowly condensing to a sliver. I saw a figure backlit in the doorway, but that person didn't matter as much as Ian, whom I had turned away from. When I faced him again, I saw three fat iron tines pointed at me.

Hadn't I just decided to leave psychos well enough alone? And now I was trapped in the barn with one, possibly two. I didn't know if the door-closer was friend or foe, but no one could be more foe than Ian. I backed into the right side of the barn to get a wide-angle view of both of them at the same time.

The newcomer flipped on the light switch. Megan!

Ian stabbed the pitchfork into hay. "This doesn't concern you, Meg."

She shut the door the rest of the way and came toward us.

"I'm handling this," Ian said more forcefully.

I looked at her and shook my head. *No! He's! Not!*

"You?" Megan said with a scornful laugh. "You don't know how to handle anything." Then she glared at me—the Grand Poobess of Dumb.

"Are y'all really debating who's going to get to kill me right in front of me?" I asked.

"No!" Ian said at the same time Megan said, "Yes."

According to my calculations, those answers should have been reversed. "Which one of you killed Dana?" I said.

"What are you talking about?" Ian asked.

He sounded genuinely mystified, and I regarded his sister, trying to recast the facts to accuse her—Perry's first love coming back to the farm as both Friends president and executive chef of Herbivore, back into Perry's life. Dana the wolf hunting Megan's sheep. The reason really was local—and universal. "You were jealous of Dana," I said to Megan. "She threatened your pastoral life out here."

"She threatened *all* of our lives!" Megan said, heat singeing her words.

"Meg, no," Ian said. He still had his fist around the handle of the pitchfork, so his obvious surprise and dismay didn't comfort me as much as it should have. He might either take his disappointment out on me or try to protect his sister. "Perry adores you," he said.

"And Dana hates me because of it!" Megan cried. "*She's* the one who messed everything up for y'all in the beginning! *She's* the one who came onto you, remember?"

"That was a long time ago, Meg," Ian said, his voice taking on a brotherly timbre. "Dana married Herb. We all moved on."

"And then she came back to steal Perry away and ruin our lives!" Megan looked up at Ian and took a breath. "I didn't mean to … I wanted to make her sick, keep her away from us."

While Megan made Ian an accessory after the fact, I crabwalked slowly toward the barn doors.

"Where are you going?" Megan demanded. "To the police? Or your boyfriend?"

"Why would I go … oh, you mean Jamie. No. I need to get to work, actually. Tuesday is Monday for a lot of restaurants."

Megan threw her braid over her shoulder. "You're not leaving, Poppy."

"Let her go, Meg," Ian said.

"She's going to wreck everything," Megan said. "Like Dana. What do you propose we do with her?"

We waited for Ian to work out an answer. I could only imagine that in a choice between his sister, the farm, and life as he knew it and a nosy health inspector, he would choose—

"Just let her go," Ian said. "We can ask Cory's lawyer for a family deal."

I don't know if he intended to be funny, but I laughed at his words as much as from relief that not all the fruit of their family tree had ripened on the crazy branch.

Laughing, however, was the exact wrong thing to do.

Megan flew at me and tackled me to the floor, my face a fraction away from cracking on an SUV's tow ball. I had only ever engaged in hand-to-hand combat with my brother, Luke, so I did what I always did and kneed her in the groin. She grunted and flipped me onto my back as if preparing to tenderize the other side of the brisket, then straddled my stomach and kneeled on my arms.

I'm strong, but I felt a physical authority and rage in her that I couldn't match. She gripped my shoulders and slammed the back of my skull against the ground. The dirt floor cushioned the whacks, but a dozen more of those would make me dizzy and feeble. Or the whiplash would snap my neck.

I used all of my strength to pin my head and shoulders to the ground, resisting her pull on them. Megan bent closer to me and strained to raise my shoulders, both of us sweating and panting. She smelled like pecan preserves. I rushed my head up and hit my forehead against her nose. She called me a bad word and listed to the right. I freed my right arm, then bucked and rolled her off of me. She kicked at me, connecting with my hip.

I threw dirt in her face, then jumped up and sprinted to the barn door. But I had lost my sense of direction and when I stopped, I was farther inside the barn, behind the pyramid of hay bales. At least I would be able to see her coming from either side.

And then the lights went out.

Gah! No backpack, no cell phone, no flashlight, no rubber gloves. I didn't know what I would do with that last item, but I could have MacGyvered a use for them. Maybe tied them together and made a slingshot.

If I called out to Megan, I would give away my location, so I had to wait for her to give hers away. I slowed my breath to help calm my entire system and muffle the sound of blood running Olympic sprints through my veins. Then I tried widening my eyes in the darkness to give my pupils more room to dilate, but they didn't take the hint.

I heard movement on the other side of the hay bales, but couldn't relate it to anything. Was she leaving? Climbing over the bales? Laying her hands on the bottle of food-grade peroxide she had hidden so she could blind me with it and make me dependent on seeing-eye dogs and Nina for the rest of my life? That got me moving.

I stepped onto a hay bale and then another. They're knee-high, so it was like hiking up a staircase custom made for Michael Jordan. Whether sensible or stupid, I didn't know, but my frantic mind didn't offer up anything else. Funny, given my fear of heights. But the barn was dark, and for us acrophobes, it's not the elevation, but the perception that's incapacitating, so in a way, it was a blessing that I couldn't see. Two more steps and I reached the top.

If I could crawl to the other side, the side by the barn door, I had a chance to make it to safety.

I heard what sounded like a match strike and, like anyone in a panic, assumed that Megan had calculated my coordinates and was fixing to light the hay on fire, damn the barn and damn the farm. I threw my body toward the far edge and my right leg wedged between two hay bales.

The sound wasn't a match striking, but the four-wheeler coming to electric life. What was Megan doing? She couldn't outrun me in that thing, much less run me down. And then the headlights came on.

Oh.

I watched the four-wheeler roll forward and start to turn the corner, the recharged lights painting Guernical shadows over the wooden beams and plank walls. I tried to free my leg, but the bales pushed apart and my leg sank farther down. I put my other leg between the bales to get enough leverage to heave it off the edge, which left me four bales high. I jumped off the side and came down on my ankle, which pitched me onto my back, landing me in the exact spot I had just escaped.

Megan exploded out of the four-wheeler and pounced on me, her hands around my neck. I tried to push her away, but she was used to wrangling cattle, and I ran out of air before she ran out of strength.

And then I did the only thing I could do in that situation. I let her win—or *think* she won. I closed my eyes and went into *savasana*, a yoga pose that has you relax every muscle, going completely limp. The English translation is corpse pose.

"Megan!" Ian cried.

Her grip slackened and I inhaled desperately.

"Shut up, Ian!" she said, and tightened her fingers.

Ian dragged her off me. "You're going to kill her!"

I let my head loll to the left, overselling the idea that I had passed out. The four-wheeler's headlights weren't directly on me, so I slitted open my right eye and saw Megan stand up and wipe sweat and blood from her face.

"That's the idea," she said. And then she kicked me in the thigh. Hard. Not to see if I would move, but to punish me, the way a redneck kicks a dog that gets into his TV dinner when he goes to the fridge for another Pabst.

"Not like this, Meg," Ian said. "They can figure out she was strangled."

Megan began to pace, fussing up dust, but not moving more than two or three feet away from me. I felt safe for the moment, and my eye was watering, so I closed it and listened.

"We could burn down the barn," Megan said. "Blame it on her."

Oh, come on! Why on earth would I burn down their barn? I don't smoke. It wasn't the dead of winter, so I didn't need to start a fire for warmth. I'm not an arsonist. Yes, I had earned my Fire Starter badge in Girl Scouts, but that was years ago.

"Burn her alive?" Ian said. I heard disgust in his voice, but whether it came from the idea of me being grilled like a T-bone or that his sister was serious, I didn't know.

"Smoke inhalation will get her first," Megan said seriously.

"We can't operate without the barn," Ian said. "And I'm not burning the cars."

"Then run her down with one of them."

I actually felt heartened. I had a slim chance of surviving that, depending on what parts of my body were hit and if they didn't park the car on top of me. How much did an SUV weigh, anyway?

"How are we going to explain that to the police?" Ian asked. "That I was driving too fast inside the barn and couldn't stop?"

"Where's the pitchfork?" Megan asked.

Pitchfork! I almost threw my arms across my belly, but I waited for Ian to talk her out of death by perforation.

"How's that going to work?" he said.

"She attacked you, and—"

"No, Meg. They can tell if she was already lying down."

Didn't they have farm chores to do? Where were all the interns? The sons? The alcoholics? Somebody to come into the barn and halt these grotesque plans of theirs.

I opened my left eye, the one turned away from them, and saw a tire, so I knew I was near an SUV. If they really did leave the keys in them as Kevin had said, and I could get inside of it, I would…be captured before I got the car door shut. If I crawled under it…they would pitchfork me out.

"The loft," Megan said. "Take her up and drop her. We'll say she fell."

"What was she doing up there?" Ian asked.

"Why does it matter?" Megan said, demonstrating what insanity sounds like. "She was chasing a cat."

I waited for Ian to ask why an on-duty health inspector, or anyone over the age of six, would ever chase a cat, but he said, "I can't lift her. Not with my back."

The four-wheeler's headlights flickered, and I realized that it was running out of juice! The effect was a sort of 1970s disco stroboscope thing that distracted them for the five seconds I needed to jump to my feet and run.

Two yards from the exit, from freedom, from survival, I was tripping and falling, caught up in a nest of baling wire. I landed hard on my stomach, and tried to kick off my wiry trap as I elbowed my body toward the door. If I could wedge it open a few inches, I would let loose a scream that had been building in me since I realized it was two against one. I was three inches from the door when I felt small, rough hands dragging me away. *Nooooo!*

I reached out my right arm and thrust my hand inside a cardboard box full of my last hope. I used my teeth to twist off the little red top then poked my finger through the foil. I flipped onto my back and squirted Megan's face with OxyGrowth. She shrieked and fell to her knees, and Ian rushed me. I sat up and aimed the bottle at him, but he vaulted past me, flung open the barn door, and tore outside.

I tugged the baling wire off my legs and pulled myself to standing.

"You ruined it *all*!" Megan screamed, crying through her hands covering her face.

"No, she didn't, Meg," Ian said. He had returned with a garden hose and squirted water on his sister's face. He looked at me. "Are you alright?"

I still didn't trust him, so I backed out of the barn and ran for my life.

THIRTY-ONE

APPARENTLY, GIRL FIGHTING TAKES a lot out of you, so I didn't wake up until 8:00 the next morning, and to a surprisingly clear decision about my two good men. After I washed my face and combed hay out of my hair, I called the one I knew I wanted and invited him over for breakfast.

I made coffee, swallowed a couple of ibuprofen tablets, then checked local news sites. Megan's arrest had used up a lot of bandwidth: "Farmer's Wife Kills Rival" and "Dana White Murdered" and "Organic Means to an End." That last one from Amooze-Boosh.

After I escaped the barn, I had run Chariots of Fire to my Jeep and called the police, telling them where to find me in the parking lot and to send an ambulance for Megan. Half an hour later, while I gave my statement to the police, the EMTs debrided my scrapes with, of all things, peroxide. They said I had a bruised windpipe, but I declined their offer of a ride to the emergency room. Sunshine is the best thing for a bruise, and there's none of that in a hospital. So I took the rest of the day off, went home and indulged in a bubble bath, then sat near a sunny window and read the dictionary until I felt sleepy.

As I pressed the button to power down my monitor, my phone rang. "Morning, boss," I said. I didn't know Olive's latest alias, and boss was as unfitting as the other names she had tried on.

"We got another tip," she said. "A customer saw a busboy pick his nose at the Alright Flashlight."

"It's All-Night Flashlight," I said. "Do you ever eat anywhere besides a vending machine?"

"I get takeout from General Chew's a lot. Why?"

"It's General ... never mind. I'm getting a slow start this morning, but I'll be ready to go this afternoon."

"Good. Bennett quit, so you and Kowsaki are covering for her. He said to give you booger boy."

I laughed because I was sure that's what Gavin had called him, and I was also sure that Olive repeated it without thinking. "Speaking of names," I said, "did you settle on a new one for yourself?"

"Violet," she said.

"Violent," I repeated. "It's unusual, but, yeah, okay."

"*Let.* Like let sleeping dogs lay down. Vio*let.*"

"That's a color and a flower," I said. "And it's Olive rearranged with a T on the end."

"That's the poetry of it, Markham," she said, then hung up.

Poetry? More like she cheated an anagram. But I didn't have time to dwell on that because I had to answer my ringing doorbell. John With stood on my porch cuddling Liza. He handed her to me, but rather than lick me with glee, she sniffed the interesting smells in my hair.

"Are you okay?" he asked as I let him into the living room and we sat on the couch. "We read the paper. That farmer's wife killed the chef?"

"This whole thing is heartbreaking," I said, then told him about Dana White being a founding member of the farm in the seventies, but she left after Perry found out she hit on Ian one night. A few months later, Megan came to the farm and a few months after that, she married Perry. I told him that Megan admitted everything to the police.

She realized that voting Dana and Herbivore onto the farm was a mistake, so she had the idea to pour peroxide into Dana's cup when she delivered the tour eggs to the walk-in while Dana was in the Field yelling at Randy. Then she used the confusion at the end of the party to sneak off the farm in Kevin's SUV and throw the evidence in the nearest Dumpster.

"Dana died from a heart attack," I said, "but it's going to be hard to prove that Megan caused it." Liza started to fidget, so I placed her on the floor and she dashed down the hallway to my bedroom, which held my fresh-from-the-farm clothes. "Megan didn't intend to kill Dana," I said, "she just wanted to warn her to stay away."

"But she intended to kill *you*," he said, pointing to the violent violet poetry Megan had written around my neck.

I nodded. "That got her a charge of attempted murder, so she'll be serving time for that at least."

He covered my hand with his. "Do you need anything? I can make you breakfast."

"I'm fine," I said, "but thank you."

He stood and called for Liza, then said, "I'm a holler away."

"How is John doing in the election?" I asked.

His face brightened. "No one wanted to run against him, so he's the new president of the HOA!"

"Is that so."

John With called again for Liza, and she came tearing into the living room as if being chased by all the bulls in Pamplona. He scooped her up, waved her paw at me and said, "Ciao, ciao, Poppy Markham." He opened the front door, then called over his shoulder, "You have a visitor."

I went to the door and saw the one who gives me peace coming up the front walk, Drew Cooper, smiling like he knew all along I would choose him.

THE END

Acknowledgments

Heaps of love and thanks for my friends and helpers, Tina Neesvig Pfeiffer, Letty Valdes Medina, Paul Allen, and Hannah Matthes, who support me in unquantifiable ways; for my writing accountability partners, Melinda Freeland and Melody Valadez, who keep my butt in a chair and my fingers on a keyboard; for my first readers, Lorie Shaw and especially Melody Valadez for her eleventh-hour read-through and insightful suggestions that made this book better; for the Austin WriterGrrls and my talented brainstorming partners Wendy Wheeler, Jennifer Evans, and Kimber Cockrill, who know how to help when I don't even know what to ask; and for my yogis, who keep me humble.

Special thanks to my patient subject matter experts: Detective Brian Miller with the Austin Police Department, who always makes time to answer my questions about fake murders; former Austin/Travis County senior health inspector Susan Speyer, RS, owner of Safe Food 4 U in Austin, Texas, who makes Poppy credible; and Salem, Massachusetts, public health inspector Liz Gagakis, who told me the chicken story.

About the Author

Robin Allen lives and writes in the great state of Texas.